THE EYES
STILL
HAVE IT

· Robert J. Randisi, Editor ·

THE EYES STILL HAVE IT

THE SHAMUS AWARD–WINNING STORIES

A DUTTON BOOK

DUTTON
Published by the Penguin Group
Penguin Books USA Inc., 375 Hudson Street, New York, New York 10014, U.S.A.
Penguin Books Ltd, 27 Wrights Lane, London W8 5TZ, England
Penguin Books Australia Ltd, Ringwood, Victoria, Australia
Penguin Books Canada Ltd, 10 Alcorn Avenue, Toronto, Ontario, Canada M4V 3B2
Penguin Books (N.Z.) Ltd, 182–190 Wairau Road, Auckland 10, New Zealand

Penguin Books Ltd, Registered Offices:
Harmondsworth, Middlesex, England

First published by Dutton,
an imprint of Dutton Signet,
a division of Penguin Books USA Inc.
Distributed in Canada by McClelland & Stewart Inc.

First Printing, November, 1995

1 3 5 7 9 10 8 6 4 2

 REGISTERED TRADEMARK—MARCA REGISTRADA

LIBRARY OF CONGRESS CATALOGING-IN-PUBLICATION DATA
The eyes still have it : the Shamus award-winning stories / Robert J.
Randisi, editor.
p.   cm.
Contents: What you don't know can't hurt you / by John Lutz—
Cat's paw / by Bill Pronzini—By the dawn's early light / by
Lawrence Block—Eight mile and Dequindre / by Loren D. Estleman—
Fly away home / by Rob Kantner—Turn away / by Ed Gorman—The
crooked way / by Loren D. Estleman—The killing man / by Mickey
Spillane—Final resting place / by Marcia Muller—Dust devil /
by Nancy Pickard—Mary, Mary, shut the door / by Benjamin M.
Schutz—The merciful angel of death / by Lawrence Block.
ISBN 0-525-93988-1 (acid-free paper)
1. Detective and mystery stories, American.   I. Randisi, Robert J.
PS648.D4E943   1995
813'.087208—dc20   95–15521
                                                        CIP

Printed in the United States of America
Set in Weiss
Designed by Steven N. Stathakis

Contents

Contents

Introduction

THE FIRST YEAR THAT THE PRIVATE EYE WRITERS OF AMERICA WAS in existence was 1982. Proudly I claim the idea as my own. I was corresponding with a lot of private eye writers at the time, and I thought the time was ripe for an organization. If history is any judge, I was right.

I also created the Shamus Award that year. We gave out awards to the best PI novels for the year 1981. We did not, however, give out a short story award. That was not instituted until the year 1983, when the best story of 1982 was honored. That first year Bill Pronzini was president and I was vice-president. That was a long time ago. I don't remember why we didn't give out a short story award. I suspect there were not enough published to support the category. That has not been the case since.

The twelve stories that appear in this collection are very representative of the PI genre. In twelve years, ten different writers have won the short story award. The repeat authors are Loren D. Estleman and Lawrence Block, each having won twice. They would be standouts in any genre.

Repeating for the Shamus is very difficult. In thirteen years there have been only three repeaters for best novel: Max Allan Collins, Sue Grafton, and the aforementioned Lawrence Block. Block, with his four Shamus Awards, has tied for the most honors with Rob Kantner, who has won once in the short story category and three times in the best paperback category.

These twelve stories are the best the genre has had to offer over the past dozen years. They are here for you to discover, or to enjoy again, whichever the case may be.

—BOB RANDISI
St. Louis, Missouri
November 1994

· JOHN LUTZ ·

What You Don't Know Can Hurt You

John Lutz has run the gamut of awards and honors in the PWA. He is a past president of the organization (1987–88), and has won the best novel award with his Carver novel Kiss *(1988). This Nudger story was the very first story ever honored with a Shamus Award. It appeared in 1982 in* Alfred Hitchcock's Mystery Magazine. *John has also won a Mystery Writers of America Edgar Award in the same category.*

"YOU ARE NUDGER?"

"I am Nudger."

The bulky woman who had leaned over Nudger and confirmed his identity had a halo of dark frizzy hair, a round face, round cheeks, round rimless spectacles, and a small round pursed mouth. She reminded Nudger of one of those dolls made with dried whole apples, whose faces eerily resemble those of aged humans. But the apple dolls' usually are benign; the face looming over Nudger came equipped with tiny dark eyes that danced with malice.

Behind the round-faced woman had stood two silent male companions. She and the two men hadn't spoken when they'd entered Nudger's office without having sounded the buzzer and in workmanlike fashion had begun beating him up.

"Who? What? Why?" a frightened Nudger had asked, wrapping his arms around his head and trying to think of who other than his former wife would want to do this to him. He couldn't divine an answer. "I don't need this!" he'd implored. "Stop it, please!"

And they had stopped. Extent of damage: sore ribs, cut forehead, but no damaged pride. Nudger was still alive; that was the object of his game.

But there was more to it. He'd felt his shirtsleeve being unbuttoned, shoved roughly up his forearm. And the abrupt bite of a dull hypodermic needle as it was inserted just below his elbow.

Sodium Pentothal, he deduced, before floating away on a private, agreeable cloud. His mouth seemed to become completely disassociated from his brain. He was vaguely aware that he was answering questions posed by the round-faced woman, that he was rambling uncontrollably. Yet he couldn't remember the questions or his answers a few seconds after they were uttered.

Then an emptiness, a breathtaking slippage of light and time.

Nudger opened his eyes and wondered where he'd been dropped. It didn't seem proper that he should be slowly revolving. Then the sensation of motion ceased, and with relief he realized he was lying on his back on his office floor. He felt remarkably heavy and comfortable.

Moving only his eyes, he gazed around and took in the open desk drawers and file cabinets, the papers and yellow file folders strewn about the floor. He remembered the hulking round-faced woman and her greedy pig's eyes and her two silent masculine helpers. He tried to recall the round-faced woman's questions but he couldn't.

Nudger struggled to a sitting position and a headache fell on him like a slab from the ceiling. When he'd become somewhat accustomed to the idea of enduring throbbing pain for the rest of his life, he stood, dizzily staggered to his desk, and sat down. The squeal of his swivel chair penetrated his brain like a hot stiletto.

What was it all about? What could he know that the round-faced woman wanted to know? All he was working on now was a divorce case, like dozens of other divorce cases he'd handled as a private investigator. The husband was sleeping with his secretary, the wife had a compensatory affair going with her hairdresser, the husband had hired Nudger to get the goods on the wife. That would be easy; she was flaunting the affair. All of these people were suburbanites who wouldn't know a round-faced woman who shot up people with sodium Pentothal; they were mostly concerned about who was going to come away with the TV and the blender.

Nudger made his way over to where the coffeepot sat on the floor by the plug in the corner. He tried to pour a cupful but found that the round-faced woman and friends had emptied the pot and spread the grounds around on the floor. Maybe it was diamonds they were looking for.

Sloshing through a shallow sea of papers and file folders, Nudger got his tan overcoat from its brass hook, wriggled into it, put on his crushproof hat, and went out, not locking the door behind him. He took the steep steps down the narrow stairwell to the door to the street, feeling the temperature drop as he descended. He shoved open the outer door and braced himself as the winter air stiffened the hairs in his nostrils. The sudden rush of cold made his headache go away. He almost smiled as he stepped out onto the treacherous pavement and walked quickly but gingerly in a neat loop through the door of Danny's Donuts, directly above which his office was located.

Nobody was in the place but Danny. That was the usual state of the business. Nudger breathed in deeply the sudden warmth and cloying sweetness of the doughnuts and unbuttoned his coat. He sat on a stool at the end of the stainless steel counter. Without being asked, Danny set a large plastic-coated paper cup of steaming black coffee before him. Danny was Danny Evers, a fortyish guy like Nudger, and, some might say, a loser like Nudger. Even Danny might say that, aware as he was that he made doughnuts like sash weights.

But what he said was, "You cut yourself shaving?" as he pointed at the cut on Nudger's forehead.

Nudger had forgotten about the injury. He raised tentative fingers, felt ridges of blood coagulated by the cold. "I had a visit from some friends," he said.

"Some friends!" Danny said, changing the emphasis. He put some iced cake doughnuts and a couple of glazed into a grease-spotted carryout box. He was a sad-featured man who seemed to do everything with apprehensive intensity, a concerned basset hound.

"Actually I never met them before this morning," Nudger said, sipping the coffee and burning his tongue. "So naturally we were curious about each other, but they asked all the questions."

"Yeah? What kinda questions?"

"That's the odd thing," Nudger said. "I can't remember."

Danny laughed, then cocked his head of thick graying hair and squinted again at the cut on Nudger's forehead. "You serious about not remembering?"

"It's not the knock on the head," Nudger assured him. "They shot me up with a drug that made me a regular mindless talking machine. It's called truth serum. It works even better than cheap scotch."

"Maybe you oughta see a doctor, Nudge."

"Find me one that doesn't charge twenty dollars a stitch."

"I mean about the memory."

"That kind of a doctor charges twenty dollars a question."

Both men were silent while a blond secretary from the office building across the street came in, paid for the carryout order, and left. Nudger smiled at her but she ignored him. It took a while for the doughnut shop to warm up again.

"I could drive you," Danny offered. "Emil is coming in to take over here in about fifteen minutes." Emil was Danny's hired help, a

sometime college student working odd jobs. He made better doughnuts than his boss's.

"I've got my car here," Nudger said.

"But maybe you shouldn't drive."

"I won't drive anywhere for a while," Nudger said. "What I'll
do is go back upstairs and straighten up my office. If you'll give me
another cup of coffee and a jelly doughnut, and put them on my
tab."

"Straighten up why?" Danny asked, reaching into the display
case.

"It's always a mess after friends drop by unexpectedly," Nudger
told him.

"Some friends, those boys and girls," Danny reiterated, dropping the doughnut into a small white bag. It hit bottom with a solid
smack.

As he trudged back up the unheated stairwell to his office, Nudger
tried again, with each painful step, to surmise some reason for his
interrogation. He could think of none. Business had been slow ever
since summer, and he had been a good boy. Danny's horrendous
coffee had started his stomach roiling. He'd take a few antacid tablets before drinking a second cup.

He stopped at his office door and stood holding the sack. It was
a morning for surprises. In the chair by the desk sat a slender man
wearing a camel hair topcoat with a fur collar. On his lap were expensive brown suede gloves. On his gloves rested pale, still, well-
manicured hands. The man's bony face was as calm as his hands were.

"There's no need to introduce myself, Mr. Nudger," he said in
a smoothly modulated voice. "On your desk is a sealed envelope.
In the envelope is five thousand dollars. You've proved yourself a
clever man, so you can't be bought cheap." A thin smile did nothing
for him. "But, like all men, you can be bought. I know your present
financial status, so five thousand should suffice."

The man stood up, unfolding in sections until he was at least
four inches taller than Nudger's six feet. But he was thin, very thin,

not a big man. He gazed down his narrow nose at Nudger with the remote interest of a scientist observing familiar bacteria.

"The problem is," Nudger told him, "I don't know who you are or what you're buying."

"I'll make myself clear, Mr. Nudger: stay away from Chaser Heights, or next time you'll be paid a visit of an altogether more unpleasant nature."

He turned and left the office with wolflike loping strides.

Nudger stood stupefied, listening to the man's descending footfalls on the wooden stairs to the street. He heard the street door open and close. The papers on the floor stirred.

Nudger went to the office door and shoved it closed. He walked to his desk, and sure enough there was an envelope, sealed. He opened it and counted out five thousand dollars in bills of various denominations. Earning this money would be a cinch, since he'd never been near any place or anyone named Chaser Heights. Then he reconsidered.

There was little doubt of a connection between the round-faced woman and the tall man. What bothered Nudger was that if these unsettling characters thought he'd been around Chaser Heights at least once when he hadn't, what was going to keep them from thinking he'd been there again? And acting forcefully on their misconception?

Now the five thousand didn't look so good to Nudger. This occupation of his had gotten him into trouble again. He put the money back into its envelope and tucked in the flap. He opened a desk drawer and got out a fresh roll of antacid tablets. He wished he knew how to paint a house.

After his stomach had calmed down, Nudger set about putting his office back together. Small as the place was, the task took the rest of the morning. Most of the time was spent matching the footprinted papers on the floor with the correct file folders. When he was finished he looked around with satisfaction, straightened the shade on his desk lamp, then went out for some lunch.

At a place he knew on Grand Avenue, Nudger drank a glass of milk, picked at the Gardener's Delight lettuce omelette special, and studied the phone directory he'd borrowed from the proprietor. Within a few minutes he found what he was looking for: Chaser Heights Alcoholic Rehabilitation Center, with an Addington Road address way out in the county.

Nudger knew what he had to do, even if it cost him five thousand dollars.

He finished his milk but pushed his omelette away, jotted down the Chaser Heights address on a paper napkin, and put it into his pocket.

Outside, he slammed his Volkswagen's door on the tail of his topcoat, as he invariably did, reopened the door and tried again, and twisted the key in the ignition switch. When the tiny motor was clattering rhythmically, he pulled the dented VW out into traffic.

It had been a large and palatial country home in better days, with sentry-box cupolas, tall colonial pillars, and ivy-covered brick. Now it was called Chaser Heights, which Nudger gathered was a sort of clinic where alcoholics went to tilt the odds in their battle with booze. It was isolated, set well back from the narrow road on a gentle rise, and mostly surrounded by woods that in their present leafless state conveyed a depressing reminder of mortality.

Nudger parked halfway up the long gravel drive to study the house. He realized that the longer he sat there in the cozy warm car, the more difficult it would be to do what he intended. He put the VW in gear and listened to the tires crunch on the gravel as he drove the rest of the way to the house.

He entered a huge foyer with a gleaming tiled floor that smelled of pine disinfectant. There were brown vinyl easy chairs scattered about, and behind a high, horseshoe-shaped desk stood a tall elderly woman wearing a stiff white uniform. The starch seemed to have affected her face.

"May I help you?" she asked without real enthusiasm, as if she risked ripping her lips by parting them to speak.

"I'd like to see whoever's in charge," Nudger told her, removing his hat. He leaned with his elbow on the desk as if it were a bar and he was about to order a drink.

"Do you have an appointment with Dr. Wedgewick?" the woman asked.

"No, but I believe he'll want to see me. Tell Dr. Wedgewell that a Mr. Nudger is here and needs to talk with him."

"Dr. Wedge*wick*," his mannequin corrected him. She was so lifelike you expected her eyes to move. She picked up a beige telephone and conveyed Nudger's message, then without change of expression directed him down a hall and to the last door on his left.

He entered an anteroom and was told by an efficient-looking young brunet on her way out that he should go right in, Dr. Wedgewick was expecting him.

And Nudger was expecting Dr. Wedgewick to be exactly who he turned out to be: the tall, camel-coated unfriendly who had delivered the five thousand dollars. He was wearing a dark blue suit and maroon tie and was seated behind a slate-topped desk a bit smaller than a Ping-Pong table. There wasn't so much as a paper clip to break its smooth gray surface. Behind him was a floor-to-ceiling window that overlooked bare-limbed trees and brown grass sloping away toward the distant road. Probably in the summer it was an impressive view. He didn't get up.

"I am surprised to see you here," he said flatly.

"You'll be more surprised by why I came," Nudger told him.

Dr. Wedgewick arched an inquisitive eyebrow impossibly high. Obviously he'd practiced the expression, had it down pat, and knew there was no need for words to accompany it.

"I'm here to return this," Nudger said, and tossed the envelope with the five thousand dollars onto the desk. It looked as lonely as a center fielder there. "Its return should prove to you that you've made a mistake. I can't be who you think; I can't sell you whatever

it is you want to buy, because I don't have it and don't know what
it is."

"That is nonsense, Mr. Nudger. You've been followed from
here several times by Dr. Olander, observed going to your office
by the back entrance, observed emerging at times and coming here,
snooping around here. Where you hid the pertinent information
regarding your client, and how you managed to fool Dr. Olander
when she administered her drugs, I can't say, nor do I care."

"I didn't fool her," Nudger said. "I have no client and I didn't
know the answers to her questions. But I understand somewhat
more of what's going on. Dr. Olander and her two silent helpers
couldn't make any progress with me their way, so you came around
and tried to buy me."

"We live in a mercantile society."

"The thing is, there was no reason for Dr. Olander to hassle
me, and there was nothing I could tell her. I wish there were some
way to get you to believe that."

"Oh, I'll bet you do."

"And I wish you'd tell me why a doctor would want to follow
me to begin with, me without medical insurance."

Dr. Wedgewick smiled with large, stained, but even teeth. "Dr.
Olander is not a medical doctor. You might say hers is an honorary
title. She is chief of security here at Chaser Heights."

"Then I needn't expect a bill." He felt in his pocket for his
tablets.

"What you should expect, Mr. Nudger, is to suffer the consequences of being stubborn."

Nudger saw Dr. Wedgewick's gaze shift to something over his
left shoulder. He turned and saw the round, malicious features of
Dr. Olander. She had taken a few silent steps into the office. Now
she stood very still, staring through her gleaming spectacles at the
bulge of the hand concealed in Nudger's coat.

He realized that she thought he had a gun.

"What's this wimp doing here?" Dr. Olander asked. "I thought
he'd been taken care of."

Nudger, still with his hand inside his coat, perspiring fingers wrapped tightly around his roll of antacid tablets, backed to the door, keeping as far as possible from her. His stomach was fluttering a few feet beyond him, beckoning him on.

Dr. Wedgewick said, "He brought back the five thousand dollars." He looked somewhat curiously at Nudger. "Someone must be paying you a great deal of money," he said. His slow, discolored smile wasn't a nice thing to see. "You'll find that it isn't enough to make it worth your while, Mr. Nudger. You can't put a price on your health."

But Nudger was out into the hall and half running to the lobby. There were a few patients in the vinyl armchairs now. One of them, a ruddy old man wearing a pale blue robe and pajamas, glanced up from where he sat reading *People* and smiled at Nudger. The waxwork behind the counter didn't.

Nudger shoved open the outside door and broke into a run. He piled into his car fast, started the engine, and heard the tires fling gravel against the insides of the fenders as he drove toward the twin stone pillars that marked the exit to the road and safety.

All the way down Addington Road to the alternative highway he kept checking his rearview mirror, expecting to be followed by troops from Chaser Heights. But as he turned onto the cloverleaf he realized they didn't have to follow; they knew where to find him.

When he got back to the office he parked in front, out on the busy street, instead of in his slot behind the building. As he climbed out of the car he noticed that the tail of his topcoat was crushed and grease-stained where he'd shut the door on it again. The coattail had flapped in the wind like a flag all the way back from Chaser Heights. For once Nudger didn't care. He went up to his office, locked the door behind him, and sat for a while chomping antacid tablets.

When his stomach had untied itself, he picked up the phone

and dialed the number of the Third Precinct and asked for Lieutenant Jack Hammersmith.

Hammersmith had been Nudger's partner a decade ago in a two-man patrol car, before Nudger's jittery nerves had forced him to retire from the police force. Now Hammersmith had rank and authority, and he always had time for Nudger, but not much time.

"What sort of quicksand have you got yourself into this time, Nudge?" Hammersmith asked.

"The sort that might be bottomless. What do you know about a place called Chaser Heights, out on Addington Road?"

"That clinic where drunks dry out?"

Nudger said that was the one.

"It's a second-rate operation, maybe even a front, but it's out of my jurisdiction, Nudge. I got plenty to worry about here in the city limits."

"What about the director out there? Guy named Dr. Wedgewick?"

"He's new in the area. From the East Coast, I been told." Nudger heard the rhythmic wheezing of Hammersmith laboriously firing up one of his foul-smelling cigars and was glad this conversation was by phone. "Anything else, Nudger?" The words were slightly distorted by the cigar.

"How about Wedgewick's assistant and chief of security, a two-hundred-pound chunk of feminine wiles named Dr. Olander?"

"Hah! That would be Millicent Olaphant, and she's no doctor, she's a part-time bone crusher for some of the local loan sharks."

"Isn't that kind of unusual work for a woman?"

"Yes, I would say it is unusual," Hammersmith said dryly, "and I meet all sorts of people in my job. You be careful of that crew, Nudge. The law out there is the Mayfair County sheriff, Dale Caster."

"What kind of help could I expect from Caster if I did get in the soup?"

"He'd drop crackers on you. Let's just say it would be difficult for a place like Chaser Heights to stay in business if they didn't grease the proper palms."

"And they grease palms liberally," Nudger said. He expected Hammersmith to ask him to elaborate, but the very busy lieutenant repeated his suggestion that Nudger be careful and then hung up.

Nudger sat for a long time, leaning back in the swivel chair, gazing at the ceiling's network of cracks that looked like a rough map of Illinois including major highways. He thought. Not about Illinois.

He thought until the telephone rang, then he picked up the receiver and identified himself.

"This is Danny, downstairs, Nudge," came the answering voice. "Your ex, Eileen, was by here about an hour ago looking for you. She was frowning. You behind with your alimony payments?"

"No further than with the rent," Nudger said. "Thanks for the warning, Danny."

"No trouble, Nudge. She bought half a dozen cream horns."

"Then she's doing better than I am."

When Nudger had replaced the receiver in its cradle he sat staring at it instead of Illinois, and he remembered something Danny had said this morning. "Some friends, those boys and girls," he had said. But Nudger hadn't mentioned Dr. Olander-Olaphant's gender.

Nudger put on his coat and tromped downstairs, gaining more understanding as he descended. He went outside, but instead of taking a few steps to the right and entering Danny's Donuts, he cut through the gangway and entered the building through the rear door, then opened another unlocked door and was in the aromatic back room of the doughnut shop. On a coat tree he saw Danny's topcoat, similar to the rumpled tan coat he, Nudger, was wearing and Danny's sold-by-the-thousands brown crushproof hat that was identical with Nudger's. Nudger and Danny were about the same height, and seen from a distance and wearing bulky coats they were of a similar build. Things were making sense at last.

Nudger walked into the greater warmth of the doughnut shop

proper, nodded to the surprised Danny, and sat on a stool on the customers' side of the counter. He and Danny were alone in the shop; Emil got off work at two, after the almost nonexistent lunch trade.

"I shoulda said something to you earlier, Nudge," Danny said, no longer looking surprised, nervously wiping the already gleaming counter. "I seen them people from Chaser Heights go up to your place this morning, but I couldn't figure out why until you came down here and told me you'd been roughed up."

"You've been sniffing around there, haven't you?" Nudger said.

Danny nodded. He poured a large cup of his terrible coffee and placed it in front of Nudger like an odious peace offering.

"You were spotted at Chaser Heights," Nudger went on, "and they followed you to find out who you were. You're close to my size, you were wearing a coat and hat like mine, and you came and went the back way. They checked to see who occupied the building and naturally figured it was the private investigator on the second floor. Whoever did the following probably staked out the front of the building and verified the identification when I left my office."

"It was a mistake, Nudge, honest! I didn't mean for you to come to any harm. Absolutely. I wouldn't want that."

Nudger sipped at the coffee, wondering why, if what Danny had said was true, he would serve him a cup of this. "I believe you, Danny," he said, "but what *were* you doing reconnoitering at Chaser Heights?"

Danny wiped at his forehead with the towel he'd been using on the counter. "My uncle's in there," he said.

"Is he there for the cure?"

Danny looked disgusted. "He's an alcoholic, all right, Nudge. That's how he got conned into admitting himself into Chaser Heights. But what they really specialize in at that place is getting the patients drugged up and having them sign over damn near everything they own in payment for treatment, or as a 'donation' that actually goes into somebody's pocket."

Nudger tried another sip of his formidable coffee. It was easier to get down now that it was cooler. "Does your uncle have much to donate?"

"Plenty. Now don't think small of me, Nudge, but it's no secret he plans to leave most of it to me, his only living relative. And he's not a well man; on top of his alcoholism he's got a weak heart."

"And Chaser Heights is about to get your inheritance before you do. Have you tried talking to your uncle?"

"Sure. They always tell me he's in special care, under detoxification quarantine—whatever that is. So I went back there a few times in secret and hung around thinking I might get a glimpse of old Benj and get to talk to him, at least see what they're doing to him. But they've got him doped up in a locked room with wire mesh on the windows. Some quarantine. I'm worried about him."

"And his money."

"I don't deny it. But that ain't the only consideration."

Danny rinsed his towel, wrung it out, and started wiping the counter again. Nudger sat slowly sipping his coffee. *Growl*, went his stomach.

"You help me, Nudge, and I'll pay you a couple of thousand —when the inheritance comes."

Nudger eased the coffee cup off to the side. He looked at Danny. "I think it's time your Uncle Benj checked out of Chaser Heights," he said.

"You know a way to manage it?"

Nudger always figured there was a way. That was a two-edged attitude, though, because he always had to figure there was a way for the other guy, too. All of which didn't help Nudger's nervous stomach. Nor did the knowledge that he had to go back out to Chaser Heights that night and case the joint.

The next evening, Nudger and Danny parked Nudger's Volkswagen on a narrow dirt access road that ran through the woods behind Chaser Heights. Nudger was glad to see that Danny was only slightly nervous; the fool had complete faith in him. Both men put on the long black vinyl raincoats with matching hooded caps that

Nudger had rented. They pinned badges on the coats and on the fronts of the caps. The sun was down and it was almost totally dark as they made their way through the trees and across the clearing to the rear of Chaser Heights.

They huddled against a brick back wall. Nudger checked the tops of the leafless trees, where the moon seemed to be nibbling at the thin upper branches, to verify which way the breeze was blowing. From a huge pocket of his raincoat he drew a plastic bag stuffed with oil-soaked rags. Danny drew a similar bag from his pocket. They laid the bags near the rear of the building, in tall dry grass that would catch well and produce a maximum amount of smoke. Danny was smiling confidently in the fearlessness born of incomprehension, a kid playing a game.

Nudger used a cigarette lighter to ignite the two bags and their contents. While Danny crept around to the side of the building to set fire to a third bag, Nudger forced open a basement window and lowered himself inside. He had noticed the sprinkler system in the halls on his first visit. Following the yellowish beam of a penlight, he made his way to the system's pressure controls in the basement and turned the lever that built the water pressure all the way to high, hearing an electric pump hum to life and the hiss of rushing water.

With a hatchet strapped inside his coat, Nudger broke the lever from the spigot with one sharp blow and then headed for the stairs to the upper floor. He opened the door to the back first-floor hall and then the rear door to admit Danny. Already he could hear movement, voices. And as Danny stepped inside and both men put on their respirator masks, Nudger saw that the burning bags and weeds were creating plenty of smoke, all of it drifting away from Chaser Heights.

Just then the pressure built up enough to activate the sprinkler system in the halls throughout the building, raining a cold spray on anyone caught outside a room. There were several startled shouts, a few curses.

Each carrying a hatchet, Nudger and Danny bustled down the

halls in their badge-adorned black slickers and hoods, the respirators snug over their faces. They pulled the respirators away just enough to yell, "Fire department! Everyone remain calm! Everyone out of the building!" They began kicking doors open and ushering patients through the watery halls toward the exits. Nudger was beginning to enjoy this. Not for nothing did small boys want to be firemen when they grew up.

In the distance they could hear wails of sirens. The genuine fire department had been called and was on the way. A white-uniformed attendant, one of the thugs who had been in Nudger's office, jogged past them with only a worried glance.

"Where do you suppose Wedgewick and Olander are?" Danny asked.

"You can bet they were among the first out," Nudger said. "Go get Uncle Benj and head for the car."

Dr. Wedgewick's office was empty, as he'd thought it would be. Through the wide window behind the slate-topped desk, Nudger could see more than a dozen people gathered on the front grounds. Beyond them flashing red lights were approaching, casting wavering, distorted shadows; the sirens had built to a deafening warble. The Mayfair County fire engine even had a loud bell that jangled with a frantic kind of gaiety, as if fires were fun.

The door of a wall safe was hanging open. Nudger went to it and found that the safe was empty. After glancing again out the front window, he left the office.

Everyone in front of Chaser Heights seemed to be shouting. Volunteer firemen were paying out hose and advancing on the building like an invading army. Patients and staff were milling about, asking questions. Nudger joined them. At the edge of the crowd stood Dr. Wedgewick, holding a large brown briefcase.

"Are you in charge, sir?" Nudger inquired from beneath his respirator.

Dr. Wedgewick hesitated. "Yes, I'm Dr. Wedgewick, chief administrator here."

"Could you come with me, sir?" Nudger asked. "There's something you should see." He wheeled and began walking briskly toward the side of the building. All very official.

Dr. Wedgewick followed.

When they had turned the corner, Nudger removed his respirator. "The briefcase, please," he said, not meaning the please.

"Why, you can't! . . ." Then Dr. Wedgewick's eyes darted to the hatchet Nudger had raised, and remained fixed there. He handed the briefcase to Nudger. His hand was trembling.

"Millicent!" Dr. Wedgewick suddenly whirled and ran back the way they had come, all the time pointing to Nudger.

Nudger saw the unmistakably bulky figure of Millicent Olander-Olaphant. He took off for the woods behind the building. He didn't have to look back to know Millicent and the good doctor were following.

Running desperately through the woods, Nudger shed his cumbersome coat, hood, and respirator. He kept the axe and briefcase, using both to smash through the branches that whipped at his face and arms. Behind him someone was crashing through the dry winter leaves.

Nudger had the advantage. He knew where the car was parked. He put on as much speed as he could. The pounding of his heart was almost as loud as his rasping breath.

As he broke onto the road, Nudger saw a dark form in the VW's rear seat. Still wearing raincoat and hood, Danny stood leaning against the left front fender with his arms crossed.

"Quick, get in!" Nudger shouted as he yanked open the driver's side door. He tossed the briefcase and hatchet onto the backseat next to Uncle Benj. His chest ached; his heart was trying to escape from his body.

Danny was barely into the passenger's seat when the engine caught and began its anxious clatter. As Nudger hit first gear and pulled away, he saw the fleeting shadows of pursuing figures in the rearview mirror.

"Who was chasing you?" Danny asked, straining to peer behind them into the darkness.

"My quarrelsome friends from that morning in my office."

"You think they'll get the cops, Nudge?" Danny sounded apprehensive.

Nudger snorted. "I think it's going to be the other way around." He jerked the VW into a two-wheeled turn, bounced over some ruts, and was back on the main road, picking up speed.

From behind him came a chuckle and Uncle Benj said, "Hey, young fella, where's the fire?"

Nudger thought it wise to stay in the presence of witnesses while he had the briefcase he'd taken from Dr. Wedgewick. He'd known that Dr. Wedgewick wouldn't have paid off the county sheriff, Caster, without keeping some sort of receipts. And when fire supposedly broke out at Chaser Heights and Dr. Wedgewick hurriedly cleaned out the safe, it figured that the doctor would number those receipts among his most valuable possessions.

In Danny's Donuts, Nudger examined the briefcase's contents. There was a great deal of money inside. Also some stock certificates. And among other various papers a notebook containing the dates, times, and amounts of the payoffs to Sheriff Caster. There also were several videocassettes, which the notebook referred to as documentation of the payoffs. Nudger had to admit that Dr. Wedgewick was thorough, but then wasn't the doctor the type?

Nudger went to the phone and called Jack Hammersmith at the Third Precinct. Hammersmith said he'd be around in ten minutes. "I don't understand how you manage to emerge from these misadventures relatively unscathed," he said. He was quite serious.

"Pureness of heart very probably is a factor," Nudger told him. Hammersmith broke the connection without saying good-bye.

"I forgot to give this to you earlier, Nudge," Danny said, holding out a small lavender envelope. "It's from Eileen. She said she could never find you and I was to deliver it."

Nudger grunted and crammed the envelope into his shirt pocket. "Ain't you gonna open it?" Uncle Benj asked, from where he sat near the end of the counter.

"I know what it is," Nudger told him. "It's from my former spouse and makes more than passing reference to neglected alimony payments."

Uncle Benj chortled. "Women can do that to you—drive you to drink if you let 'em." He sat up straighter and drew a deep breath. "You know, Danny boy," he said heartily, "despite the drugs and all the arm-twisting out at that place, I ain't had a drop of the sauce for weeks and I think my stay there did help me. I feel great, like I'll live to be a hundred!"

Danny bit his lower lip glumly, then he smiled and ducked behind the counter.

"Have a doughnut, Uncle Benj," he said.

Nudger thought about Danny's inheritance, about the rent due upstairs, about the envelope from Eileen.

"Don't forget to give him some of your coffee," he said to Danny with a meaningful nod.

If Uncle Benj was going to escape the bottle, maybe he'd fall prey to the cup.

· BILL PRONZINI ·

Cat's-Paw
A Nameless Detective Story

Perhaps one of the longest stories ever to win the award, Bill Pronzini's Nameless story "Cat's-Paw" was published in limited edition by Waves Press of Richmond, Virginia, in 1983. Bill, the PWA's first president (1982–83), also won the Shamus for best PI novel the very first year it was awarded with his Nameless novel Hoodwink, *and was subsequently named a winner of The Eye, the life achievement award, the youngest such winner. President John Lutz, in presenting the award, made mention of Bill's youth, and then stated that the board had "no medical knowledge" that the recipient was not aware of. Bill Pronzini's body of work speaks for itself. This is just a small—well, not so small—sample.*

THERE ARE TWO PLACES THAT ARE ORDINARY ENOUGH DURING the daylight hours but that become downright eerie after dark, particularly if you go wandering around in them by yourself. One is a graveyard; the other is a public zoo. And that goes double for San Francisco's Fleishhacker Zoological Gardens on a blustery winter night when the fog comes swirling in and makes everything look like capering phantoms or two-dimensional cutouts.

Fleishhacker Zoo was where I was on this foggy winter night

—alone, for the most part—and I wished I was somewhere else instead. *Anywhere* else, as long as it had a heater or a log fire and offered something hot to drink.

I was on my third tour of the grounds, headed past the sea lion tank to make another check of the aviary, when I paused to squint at the luminous dial of my watch. Eleven forty-five. Less than three hours down and better than six left to go. I was already half-frozen, even though I was wearing long johns, two sweaters, two pairs of socks, heavy gloves, a woolen cap, and a long fur-lined overcoat. The ocean was only a thousand yards away, and the icy wind that blew in off of it sliced through you to the marrow. If I got through this job without contracting pneumonia, I would consider myself lucky.

Somewhere in the fog, one of the animals made a sudden roaring noise; I couldn't tell what kind of animal or where the noise came from. The first time that sort of thing had happened, two nights ago, I'd jumped a little. Now I was used to it, or as used to it as I would ever get. How guys like Dettlinger and Hammond could work here night after night, month after month, was beyond my comprehension.

I went ahead toward the aviary. The big wind-sculpted cypress trees that grew on my left made looming, swaying shadows, like giant black dancers with rustling headdresses wreathed in mist. Back beyond them, fuzzy yellow blobs of light marked the location of the zoo's café. More nightlights burned on the aviary, although the massive fenced-in wing on the near side was dark.

Most of the birds were asleep or nesting or whatever the hell it is birds do at night. But you could hear some of them stirring around, making noise. There were a couple of dozen different varieties in there, including such esoteric types as the crested screamer, the purple gallinule, and the black crake. One esoteric type that used to be in there but wasn't any longer was something called a bunting, a brilliantly colored migratory bird. Three of them had been swiped four days ago, the latest in a rash of thefts the zoological gardens had suffered.

The thief or thieves had also got two South American Harris hawks, a bird of prey similar to a falcon; three crab-eating macaques, whatever they were; and half a dozen rare Chiricahua rattlesnakes known as *Crotalus pricei*. He or they had picked the locks on buildings and cages, and got away clean each time. Sam Dettlinger, one of the two regular watchmen, had spotted somebody running the night the rattlers were stolen, and given chase, but he hadn't got close enough for much of a description, or even to tell for sure if it was a man or a woman.

The police had been notified, of course, but there was not much they could do. There wasn't much the Zoo Commission could do either, beyond beefing up security—and all that had amounted to was adding one extra night watchman, Al Kirby, on a temporary basis; he was all they could afford. The problem was, Fleishhacker Zoo covers some seventy acres. Long sections of its perimeter fencing are secluded; you couldn't stop somebody determined to climb the fence and sneak in at night if you surrounded the place with a hundred men. Nor could you effectively police the grounds with any less than a hundred men; much of those seventy acres is heavily wooded, and there are dozens of grottoes, brushy fields and slopes, rush-rimmed ponds, and other areas simulating natural habitats for some of the zoo's fourteen hundred animals and birds. Kids, and an occasional grown-up, have gotten lost in there in broad daylight. A thief who knew his way around could hide out on the grounds for weeks without being spotted.

I got involved in the case because I was acquainted with one of the commission members, a guy named Lawrence Factor. He was an attorney, and I had done some investigating for him in the past, and he thought I was the cat's nuts when it came to detective work. So he'd come to see me, not as an official emissary of the commission but on his own; the commission had no money left in its small budget for such as the hiring of a private detective. But Factor had made a million bucks or so in the practice of criminal law, and as a passionate animal lover, he was willing to foot the bill himself. What he wanted me to do was sign on as another night watchman, plus nose around among my contacts to find out if there was any word on the street about the thefts.

It seemed like an odd sort of case, and I told him so. "Why would anybody steal hawks and small animals and rattlesnakes?" I asked. "Doesn't make much sense to me."

"It would if you understood how valuable those creatures are to some people."

"What people?"

"Private collectors, for one," he said. "Unscrupulous individuals who run small independent zoos, for another. They've been known to pay exorbitantly high prices for rare specimens they can't obtain through normal channels—usually because of the state or federal laws protecting endangered species."

"You mean there's a thriving black market in animals?"

"You bet there is. Animals, reptiles, birds—you name it. Take the *pricei*, the southwestern rattler, for instance. Several years ago, the Arizona Game and Fish Department placed it on a special permit list; people who want the snake first have to obtain a permit from the Game and Fish authority before they can go out into the Chiricahua Mountains and hunt one. Legitimate researchers have no trouble getting a permit, but hobbyists and private collectors are turned down. Before the permit list, you could get a *pricei* for twenty-five dollars; now, some snake collectors will pay two hundred and fifty dollars and up for one."

"The same high prices apply on the other stolen specimens?"

"Yes," Factor said. "Much higher, in the case of the Harris hawk."

"How much higher?"

"From three to five thousand dollars, after it has been trained for falconry."

I let out a soft whistle. "You have any idea who might be pulling the thefts?"

"Not specifically, no. It could be anybody with a working knowledge of zoology and the right—or wrong—contracts for disposal of the specimens."

"Someone connected with Fleishhacker, maybe?"

"That's possible. But I damned well hope not."

"So your best guess is what?"

"A professional at this sort of thing," Factor said. "They don't usually rob large zoos like ours—there's too much risk and too much publicity; mostly they hit small zoos or private collectors, and do some poaching on the side. But it *has* been known to happen when they hook up with buyers who are willing to pay premium prices."

"What makes you think it's a pro in this case? Why not an amateur? Or even kids out on some kind of crazy lark?"

"Well, for one thing, the thief seemed to know exactly what he was after each time. Only expensive and endangered specimens were taken. For another thing, the locks on the building and cage doors were picked by an expert—and that's not my theory, it's the police's."

"You figure he'll try it again?"

"Well, he's four-for-four so far, with no hassle except for the minor scare Sam Dettlinger gave him; that has to make him feel pretty secure. And there are dozens more valuable, prohibited specimens in the gardens. I like the odds that he'll push his luck and go for five straight."

But so far the thief hadn't pushed his luck. This was the third night I'd been on the job and nothing had happened. Nothing had happened during my daylight investigation either; I had put out feelers all over the city, but nobody admitted to knowing anything about the zoo thefts. Nor had I been able to find out anything from any of the Fleishhacker employees I'd talked to. All the information I had on the case, in fact, had been furnished by Lawrence Factor in my office three days ago.

If the thief was going to make another hit, I wished he would do it pretty soon and get it over with. Prowling around here in the dark and the fog and that damned icy wind, waiting for something to happen, was starting to get on my nerves. Even if I was being well paid, there were better ways to spend long, cold winter nights.

Like curled up in bed with a copy of *Black Mask* or *Detective Tales* or one of the other pulps in my collection. Like curled up in bed with Kerry Wade. . . .

I moved ahead to the near doors of the aviary and tried them to make sure they were still locked. They were. But I shone my flash on them anyway, just to be certain that they hadn't been tampered with since the last time one of us had been by. No problem there, either.

There were four of us on the grounds—Dettlinger, Hammond, Kirby, and me—and the way we'd been working it was to spread out to four corners and then start moving counterclockwise in a set but irregular pattern; that way, we could cover the grounds thoroughly without all of us congregating in one area, and without more than fifteen minutes going by from one building check to another. We each had a walkie-talkie clipped to our belts so one could summon the others if anything went down. We also used the things to radio our positions periodically, so we'd be sure to stay spread out from each other.

I went around the other side of the aviary, to the entrance that faced the long, shallow pond where the bigger tropical birds had their sanctuary. The doors there were also secure. The wind gusted over the pond as I was checking the doors, like a williwaw off the frozen Arctic tundra; it made the cypress trees genuflect, shredded the fog for an instant so that I could see all the way across to the construction site of the new Primate Discovery Center, and clacked my teeth together with a sound like rattling bones. I flexed the cramped fingers of my left hand, the one that had suffered some severe nerve damage in a shooting scrape a few months back; extreme cold aggravated the chronic stiffness. I thought longingly of the hot coffee in my thermos. But the thermos was over at the zoo office behind the carousel, along with my brown-bag supper, and I was not due for a break until one o'clock.

The path that led to Monkey Island was on my left; I took it, hunching forward against the wind. Ahead, I could make out the high dark mass of man-made rocks that comprised the island home of sixty or seventy spider monkeys. But the mist was closing in again, like wind-driven skeins of shiny gray cloth being woven together magically; the building that housed the elephants and pachyderms, only a short distance away, was invisible.

One of the male peacocks that roam the grounds let loose with its weird cry somewhere behind me. The damned things were always doing that, showing off even in the middle of the night. I had never cared for peacocks much, and I liked them even less now. I wondered how one of them would taste roasted with garlic and anchovies. The thought warmed me a little as I moved along the path between the hippo pen and the brown bear grottoes, turned onto the wide concourse that led past the front of the Lion House.

In the middle of the concourse was an extended oblong pond, with a little center island overgrown with yucca trees and pampas grass. The vegetation had an eerie look in the fog, like fantastic creatures waving their appendages in a low-budget science fiction film. I veered away from them, over toward the glass-and-wire cages that had been built onto the Lion House's stucco facade. The cages were for show: inside was the Zoological Society's current pride and joy, a year-old white tiger named Prince Charles, one of only fifty known white tigers in the world. Young Charley was the zoo's rarest and most valuable possession, but the thief hadn't attempted to steal *him*. Nobody in his right mind would try to make off with a frisky, five-hundred-pound tiger in the middle of the night.

Charley was asleep; so was his sister, a normally marked Bengal tiger named Whiskers. I looked at them for a few seconds, decided I wouldn't like to have to pay their food bill, and started to turn away.

Somebody was hurrying toward me, from over where the otter pool was located.

I could barely see him in the mist; he was just a moving black shape. I tensed a little, taking the flashlight out of my pocket, putting my cramped left hand on the walkie-talkie so I could use the thing if it looked like trouble. But it wasn't trouble. The figure called my name in a familiar voice, and when I put my flash on for a couple of seconds I saw that it was Sam Dettlinger.

"What's up?" I said when he got to me. "You're supposed to be over by the gorillas about now."

"Yeah," he said, "but I thought I saw something about fifteen minutes ago, out back by the cat grottoes."

"Saw what?"

"Somebody moving around in the bushes," he said. He tipped back his uniform cap, ran a gloved hand over his face to wipe away the thin film of moisture the fog had put there. He was in his forties, heavyset, owl-eyed, with carrot-colored hair and a mustache that looked like a dead caterpillar draped across his upper lip.

"Why didn't you put out a call?"

"I couldn't be sure I actually saw somebody and I didn't want to sound a false alarm; this damn fog distorts everything, makes you see things that aren't there. Wasn't anybody in the bushes when I went to check. It might have been a squirrel or something. Or just the fog. But I figured I'd better search the area to make sure."

"Anything?"

"No. Zip."

"Well, I'll make another check just in case."

"You want me to come with you?"

"No need. It's about time for your break, isn't it?"

He shot the sleeve of his coat and peered at his watch. "You're right, it's almost midnight—"

Something exploded inside the Lion House—a flat cracking noise that sounded like a gunshot.

Both Dettlinger and I jumped. He said, "What the hell was that?"

"I don't know. Come on!"

We ran the twenty yards or so to the front entrance. The noise had awakened Prince Charles and his sister; they were up and starting to prowl their cage as we rushed past. I caught hold of the door handle and tugged on it, but the lock was secure.

I snapped at Dettlinger, "Have you got a key?"

"Yeah, to all the buildings. . . ."

He fumbled his key ring out, and I switched on my flash to help him find the right key. From inside, there was cold dead silence; I couldn't hear anything anywhere else in the vicinity except for faint animal sounds lost in the mist. Dettlinger got the door unlocked, dragged it open. I crowded in ahead of him, across a short foyer and through another door that wasn't locked, into the building's cavernous main room.

A couple of the ceiling lights were on; we hadn't been able to tell from outside because the Lion House had no windows. The interior was a long rectangle with a terra-cotta tile floor, now-empty feeding cages along the entire facing wall and the near side wall, another set of entrance doors in the far side wall, and a kind of indoor garden full of tropical plants flanking the main entrance to the left. You could see all of the enclosure from two steps inside, and there wasn't anybody in it. Except—

"Jesus!" Dettlinger said. "Look!"

I was looking, all right. And having trouble accepting what I saw. A man lay sprawled on his back inside one of the cages diagonally to our right; there was a small glistening stain of blood on the front of his heavy coat and a revolver of some kind in one of his outflung hands. The small access door at the front of the cage was shut, and so was the sliding panel at the rear that let the big cats in and out at feeding time. In the pale light, I could see the man's face clearly: his teeth were bared in the rictus of death.

"It's Kirby," Dettlinger said in a hushed voice. "Sweet Christ, what—?"

I brushed past him and ran over and climbed the brass railing that fronted all the cages. The access door, a four-by-two-foot barred inset, was locked tight. I poked my nose between two of the bars, peering in at the dead man. Kirby, Al Kirby. The temporary night watchman the Zoo Commission had hired a couple of weeks ago. It looked as though he had been shot in the chest at close range; I could see where the upper middle of his coat had been scorched by the powder discharge.

My stomach jumped a little, the way it always does when I come face-to-face with violent death. The faint, gamy, big-cat smell that hung in the air didn't help it any. I turned toward Dettlinger, who had come up beside me.

"You have a key to this access door?" I asked him.

"No. There's never been a reason to carry one. Only the cat handlers have them." He shook his head in an awed way. "How'd Kirby get in there? What *happened*?"

"I wish I knew. Stay put for a minute."

I left him and ran down to the doors in the far side wall. They were locked. Could somebody have had time to shoot Kirby, get out through these doors, then relock them before Dettlinger and I busted in? It didn't seem likely. We'd been inside less than thirty seconds after we'd heard the shot.

I hustled back to the cage where Kirby's body lay. Dettlinger had backed away from it, around in front of the side-wall cages; he looked a little queasy now himself, as if the implications of violent death had finally registered on him. He had a pack of cigarettes in one hand, getting ready to soothe his nerves with some nicotine. But this wasn't the time or the place for a smoke; I yelled at him to put the things away, and he complied.

When I reached him I said, "What's behind these cages? Some sort of rooms back there, aren't there?"

"Yeah. Where the handlers store equipment and meat for the cats. Chutes, too, that lead out to the grottoes."

"How do you get to them?"

He pointed over at the rear side wall. "That door next to the last cage."

"Any other way in or out of those rooms?"

"No. Except through the grottoes, but the cats are out there."

I went around to the interior door he'd indicated. Like all the others, it was locked. I said to Dettlinger, "You do have a key to this door?"

He nodded, got it out, and unlocked the door. I told him to keep watch out here, switched on my flashlight, and went on through. The flash beam showed me where the light switches were; I flicked them on and began a quick, cautious search. The door to one of the meat lockers was open, but nobody was hiding inside. Or anywhere else back there.

When I came out I shook my head in answer to Dettlinger's silent question. Then I asked him, "Where's the nearest phone?"

"Out past the grottoes, by the popcorn stand."

"Hustle out there and call the police. And while you're at it, radio Hammond to get over here on the double—"

"No need for that," a new voice said from the main entrance. "I'm already here."

I glanced in that direction and saw Gene Hammond, the other regular night watchman. You couldn't miss him; he was six-five, weighed in at a good two-fifty, and had a face like the back end of a bus. Disbelief was written on it now as he stared across at Kirby's body.

"Go," I told Dettlinger. "I'll watch things here."

"Right."

He hurried out past Hammond, who was on his way toward where I stood in front of the cage. Hammond said as he came up, "God—what happened?"

"We don't know yet."

"How'd Kirby get in there?"

"We don't know that either." I told him what we did know, which was not much. "When did you last see Kirby?"

"Not since the shift started at nine."

"Any idea why he'd have come in here?"

"No. Unless he heard something and came in to investigate. But he shouldn't have been in this area, should he?"

"Not for another half hour, no."

"Christ, you don't think that he—"

"What?"

"Killed himself," Hammond said.

"It's possible. Was he despondent for some reason?"

"Not that I know about. But it sure looks like suicide. I mean, he's got that gun in his hand, he's all alone in the building, all the doors are locked. What else could it be?"

"Murder," I said.

"How? Where's the person who killed him, then?"

"Got out through one of the grottoes, maybe."

"No way," Hammond said. "Those cats would maul anybody who went out among 'em—and I mean anybody; not even any of the handlers would try a stunt like that. Besides, even if somebody made it down into the moat, how would he scale that twenty-foot back wall to get out of it?"

I didn't say anything.

Hammond said, "And another thing: why would Kirby be locked in this cage if it was murder?"

"Why would he lock himself in to commit suicide?"

He made a bewildered gesture with one of his big hands.

"Crazy," he said. "The whole thing's crazy."

He was right. None of it seemed to make any sense at all.

I knew one of the homicide inspectors who responded to Dettlinger's call. His name was Branislaus and he was a pretty decent guy, so the preliminary questions-and-answers went fast and hassle-free. After which he packed Dettlinger and Hammond and me off to the zoo office while he and the lab crew went to work inside the Lion House.

I poured some hot coffee from my thermos, to help me thaw out a little, and then used one of the phones to get Lawrence Factor out of bed. He was paying my fee and I figured he had a right to know what had happened as soon as possible. He made shocked noises when I told him, asked a couple of pertinent questions, said he'd get out to Fleishhacker right away, and rang off.

An hour crept away. Dettlinger sat at one of the desks with a pad of paper and a pencil and challenged himself in a string of tick-tacktoe games. Hammond chain-smoked cigarettes until the air in

there was blue with smoke. I paced around for the most part, now
and then stepping out into the chill night to get some fresh air: all
that cigarette smoke was playing merry hell with my lungs. None
of us had much to say. We were all waiting to see what Branislaus
and the rest of the cops turned up.

Factor arrived at one-thirty, looking harried and upset. It was
the first time I had ever seen him without a tie and with his usually
immaculate Robert Redford hairdo in some disarray. A patrolman
accompanied him into the office, and judging from the way Factor
glared at him, he had had some difficulty getting past the front
gate. When the patrolman left I gave Factor a detailed account of
what had taken place as far as I knew it, with embellishments from
Dettlinger. I was just finishing when Branislaus came in.

Branny spent a couple of minutes discussing matters with Factor. Then he said he wanted to talk to the rest of us one at a time,
picked me to go first, and herded me into another room.

The first thing he said was, "This is the screwiest shooting case
I've come up against in twenty years on the force. What in bloody
hell is going on here?"

"I was hoping maybe you could tell me."

"Well, I can't—yet. So far it looks like a suicide, but if that's
it, it's a candidate for Ripley. Whoever heard of anybody blowing
himself away in a lion cage at the zoo?"

"Any indication he locked himself in there?"

"We found a key next to his body that fits the access door in
front."

"Just one loose key?"

"That's right."

"So it could have been dropped in there by somebody else
after Kirby was dead and after the door was locked. Or thrown in
through the bars from outside."

"Granted."

"And suicides don't usually shoot themselves in the chest," I
said.

"Also granted, although it's been known to happen."

"What kind of weapon was he shot with? I couldn't see it too well from outside the cage, the way he was lying."

"Thirty-two Iver Johnson."

"Too soon to tell yet it if was his, I guess."

"Uh-huh. Did he come on the job armed?"

"Not that I know about. The rest of us weren't, or weren't supposed to be."

"Well, we'll know more when we finish running a check on the serial number," Branislaus said. "It was intact, so the thirty-two doesn't figure to be a Saturday night special."

"Was there anything in Kirby's pockets?"

"The usual stuff. And no sign of a suicide note. But you don't think it was suicide anyway, right?"

"No, I don't."

"Why not?"

"No specific reason. It's just that a suicide under those circumstances rings false. And so does a suicide on the heels of the thefts the zoo's been having lately."

"So you figure there's a connection between Kirby's death and the thefts?"

"Don't you?"

"The thought crossed my mind," Branislaus said dryly. "Could be the thief slipped back onto the grounds tonight, something happened before he had a chance to steal something, and he did for Kirby—I'll admit the possibility. But what were the two of them doing in the Lion House? Doesn't add up that Kirby caught the guy in there. Why would the thief enter it in the first place? Not because he was trying to steal a lion or a tiger, that's for sure."

"Maybe Kirby stumbled on him somewhere else, somewhere nearby. Maybe there was a struggle; the thief got the drop on Kirby, then forced him to let both of them into the Lion House with his key."

"Why?"

"To get rid of him where it was private."

"I don't buy it," Branny said. "Why wouldn't he just knock Kirby over the head and run for it?"

"Well, it could be he's somebody Kirby knew."

"Okay. But the Lion House angle is still too much trouble for him to go through. It would've been much easier to shove the gun into Kirby's belly and shoot him on the spot. Kirby's clothing would have muffled the sound of the shot; it wouldn't have been audible more than fifty feet away."

"I guess you're right," I said.

"But even supposing it happened the way you suggest, it *still* doesn't add up. You and Dettlinger were inside the Lion House thirty seconds after the shot, by your own testimony. You checked the side entrance doors almost immediately and they were locked; you looked around behind the cages and nobody was there. So how did the alleged killer get out of the building?"

"The only way he could have got out was through one of the grottoes in back."

"Only he *couldn't* have, according to what both Dettlinger and Hammond say."

I paced over to one of the windows—nervous energy—and looked out at the fog-wrapped construction site for the new monkey exhibit. Then I turned and said, "I don't suppose your men found anything in the way of evidence inside the Lion House?"

"Not so you could tell it with the naked eye."

"Or anywhere else in the vicinity?"

"No."

"Any sign of tampering on any of the doors?"

"None. Kirby used his key to get in, evidently."

I came back to where Branislaus was leaning hipshot against somebody's desk. "Listen, Branny," I said, "this whole thing is *too* screwball. Somebody's playing games here, trying to muddle our thinking—and that means murder."

"Maybe," he said. "Hell, probably. But how was it done? I can't come up with an answer, not even one that's believably far-fetched. Can you?"

"Not yet."

"Does that mean you've got an idea?"

"Not an idea; just a bunch of little pieces looking for a pattern."

He sighed. "Well, if they find it, let me know."

When I went back into the other room I told Dettlinger that he was next on the grill. Factor wanted to talk some more, but I put him off. Hammond was still polluting the air with his damned cigarettes, and I needed another shot of fresh air; I also needed to be alone for a while.

I put my overcoat on and went out and wandered past the cages where the smaller cats were kept, past the big open fields that the giraffes and rhinos called home. The wind was stronger and colder than it had been earlier; heavy gusts swept dust and twigs along the ground, broke the fog up into scudding wisps. I pulled my cap down over my ears to keep them from numbing.

The path led along to the concourse at the rear of the Lion House, where the open cat-grottoes were. Big, portable electric lights had been set up there and around the front so the police could search the area. A couple of patrolmen glanced at me as I approached, but they must have recognized me because neither of them came over to ask what I was doing there.

I went to the low, shrubberied wall that edged the middle cat-grotto. Whatever was in there, lions or tigers, had no doubt been aroused by all the activity; but they were hidden inside the dens at the rear. These grottoes had been newly renovated—lawns, jungly vegetation, small trees, everything to give the cats the illusion of their native habitat. The side walls separating this grotto from the other two were man-made rocks, high and unscalable. The moat below was fifty feet wide, too far for either a big cat or a man to jump; and the near moat wall was sheer and also unscalable from below, just as Hammond and Dettlinger had said.

No way anybody could have got out of the Lion House through the grottoes, I thought. Just no way.

No way it could have been murder then. Unless—

I stood there for a couple of minutes, with my mind beginning, finally, to open up. Then I hurried around to the front of the Lion House and looked at the main entrance for a time, remembering things.

And then I knew.

Branislaus was in the zoo office, saying something to Factor, when I came back inside. He glanced over at me as I shut the door.

"Branny," I said, "those little pieces I told you about a while ago finally found their pattern."

He straightened. "Oh? Some of it or all of it?"

"All of it, I think."

Factor said, "What's this about?"

"I figured out what happened at the Lion House tonight," I said. "Al Kirby didn't commit suicide: he was murdered. And I can name the man who killed him."

I expected a reaction, but I didn't get one beyond some widened eyes and opened mouths. Nobody said anything and nobody moved much. But you could feel the sudden tension in the room, as thick in its own intangible way as the layers of smoke from Hammond's cigarettes.

"Name him," Branislaus said.

But I didn't, not just yet. A good portion of what I was going to say was guesswork—built on deduction and logic, but still guesswork—and I wanted to choose my words carefully. I took off my cap, unbuttoned my coat, and moved away from the door, over near where Branny was standing.

He said, "Well? Who do you say killed Kirby?"

"The same person who stole the birds and other specimens. And I don't mean a professional animal thief, as Mr. Factor suggested when he hired me. He isn't an outsider at all; and he didn't climb the fence to get onto the grounds."

"No?"

"No. He was *already* in here on those nights and on this one, because he works here as a night watchman. The man I'm talking about is Sam Dettlinger."

That got some reaction. Hammond said, "I don't believe it," and Factor said, "My God!" Branislaus looked at me, looked at Dettlinger, looked at me again—moving his head like a spectator at a tennis match.

The only one who didn't move was Dettlinger. He sat still at one of the desks, his hands resting easily on its blotter; his face betrayed nothing.

He said, "You're a liar," in a thin, hard voice.

"Am I? You've been working here for some time; you know the animals and which ones are endangered and valuable. It was easy for you to get into the buildings during your rounds: just use your key and walk right in. When you had the specimens you took them to some prearranged spot along the outside fence and passed them over to an accomplice."

"What accomplice?" Branislaus asked.

"I don't know. You'll get it out of him, Branny; or you'll find out some other way. But that's how he had to have worked it."

"What about the scratches on the locks?" Hammond asked. "The police told us the locks were picked—"

"Red herring," I said. "Just like Dettlinger's claim that he chased a stranger on the grounds the night the rattlers were stolen. Designed to cover up the fact that it was an inside job." I looked back at Branislaus. "Five'll get you ten Dettlinger's had some sort of locksmithing experience. It shouldn't take much digging to find out."

Dettlinger started to get out of his chair, thought better of it, and sat down again. We were all staring at him, but it did not seem to bother him much; his owl eyes were on my neck, and if they'd been hands I would have been dead of strangulation.

Without shifting his gaze, he said to Factor, "I'm going to sue this son of a bitch for slander. I can do that, can't I, Mr. Factor?"

"If what he says isn't true, you can," Factor said.

"Well, it isn't true. It's all a bunch of lies. I never stole anything. And I sure never killed Al Kirby. How the hell could I? I was with this guy, *outside* the Lion House, when Al died inside."

"No, you weren't," I said.

"What kind of crap is that? I was standing right next to you, we both heard the shot—"

"That's right, we both heard the shot. And that's the first thing that put me onto you, Sam. Because we damned well *shouldn't* have heard it."

"No? Why not?"

"Kirby was shot with a thirty-two-caliber revolver. A thirty-two is a small gun; it doesn't make much of a bang. Branny, you remember saying to me a little while ago that if somebody had shoved that thirty-two into Kirby's middle, you wouldn't have been able to hear the pop more than fifty feet away? Well, that's right. But Dettlinger and I were a lot more than fifty feet from the cage where we found Kirby—twenty yards from the front entrance, thick stucco walls, a ten-foot foyer, and another forty feet or so of floor space to the cage. Yet we not only heard a shot, we heard it loud and clear."

Branislaus said, "So how is that possible?"

I didn't answer him. Instead I looked at Dettlinger and I said, "Do you smoke?"

That got a reaction out of him. The one I wanted: confusion. "What?"

"Do you smoke?"

"What kind of question is that?"

"Gene must have smoked half a pack since we've been in here, but I haven't seen you light up once. In fact, I haven't seen you light up the whole time I've been working here. So answer me, Sam—do you smoke or not?"

"No, I don't smoke. You satisfied?"

"I'm satisfied," I said. "Now suppose you tell me what it was you had in your hand in the Lion House, when I came back from checking the side doors?"

He got it, then—the way I'd trapped him. But he clamped his lips together and sat still.

"What are you getting at?" Branislaus asked me. "What *did* he have in his hand?"

"At the time I thought it was a pack of cigarettes; that's what it looked like from a distance. I took him to be a little queasy, a delayed reaction to finding the body, and I figured he wanted some nicotine to calm his nerves. But that wasn't it at all; he wasn't queasy, he was scared—because I'd seen what he had in his hand before he could hide it in his pocket."

"So what was it?"

"A tape recorder," I said. "One of those small battery-operated jobs they make nowadays, a white one that fits in the palm of the hand. He'd just picked it up from wherever he'd stashed it earlier—behind the bars in one of the other cages, probably. I didn't notice it there because it was so small and because my attention was on Kirby's body."

"You're saying the shot you heard was on tape?"

"Yes. My guess is, he recorded it right after he shot Kirby. Fifteen minutes or so earlier."

"Why did he shoot Kirby? And why in the Lion House?"

"Well, he and Kirby could have been in on the thefts together; they could have had some kind of falling-out, and Dettlinger decided to get rid of him. But I don't like that much. As a premeditated murder, it's too elaborate. No, I think the recorder was a spur-of-the-moment idea; I doubt if it belonged to Dettlinger, in fact. Ditto the thirty-two. He's clever, but he's not a planner, he's an improviser."

"If the recorder and the gun weren't his, whose were they? Kirby's?"

I nodded. "The way I see it, Kirby found out about Dettlinger pulling the thefts; saw him do the last one, maybe. Instead of reporting it, he did some brooding and then decided tonight to try a little shakedown. But Dettlinger's bigger and tougher than he was, so he brought the thirty-two along for protection. He also brought the recorder, the idea probably being to tape his conversation with Dettlinger, without Dettlinger's knowledge, for further blackmail leverage.

"He buttonholed Dettlinger in the vicinity of the Lion House, and the two of them went inside to talk it over in private. Then something happened. Dettlinger tumbled to the recorder, got rough, Kirby pulled the gun, they struggled for it, Kirby got shot dead—that sort of scenario.

"So then Dettlinger had a corpse on his hands. What was he going to do? He could drag it outside, leave it somewhere, make it look like the mythical fence-climbing thief killed him; but if he did that he'd be running the risk of me or Hammond appearing suddenly and spotting him. Instead he got what he thought was a bright idea: he'd create a big mystery and confuse hell out of everybody, plus give himself a dandy alibi for the apparent time of Kirby's death.

"He took the gun and the recorder to the storage area behind the cages. Erased what was on the tape, used the fast-forward and the timer to run off fifteen minutes of tape, then switched to record and fired a second shot to get the sound of it on tape. I don't know for sure what he fired the bullet into; but I found one of the meat locker doors open when I searched back there, so maybe he used a slab of meat for a target. And then piled a bunch of other slabs on top to hide it until he could get rid of it later on. The police wouldn't be looking for a second bullet, he thought, so there wasn't any reason for them to rummage around in the meat.

"His next moves were to rewind the tape, go back out front, and stash the recorder—turned on, with the volume all the way up. That gave him fifteen minutes. He picked up Kirby's body . . . most of the blood from the wound had been absorbed by the heavy coat Kirby was wearing, which was why there wasn't any blood on the floor and why Dettlinger didn't get any on him. And why I didn't notice, fifteen minutes later, that it was starting to coagulate. He carried the body to the cage, put it inside with the thirty-two in Kirby's hand, relocked the access door—he told me he didn't have a key, but that was a lie—and then threw the key in with the body. But putting Kirby in the cage was his big mistake. By doing that he made the whole thing too bizarre. If he'd left the body where it was, he'd have had a better chance of getting away with it.

"Anyhow, he slipped out of the building without being seen and hid over by the otter pool. He knew I was due there at midnight, because of the schedule we'd set up; and he wanted to be with me when that recorded gunshot went off. Make me the cat's-paw, if you don't mind a little grim humor, for what he figured would be his perfect alibi.

"Later on, when I sent him to report Kirby's death, he disposed of the recorder. He couldn't have gone far from the Lion House to get rid of it; he made the call, and he was back within fifteen minutes. With any luck, his fingerprints will be on the recorder when your men turn it up.

"And if you want any more proof I'll swear in court I didn't smell cordite when we entered the Lion House; all I smelled was the gamy odor of jungle cats. I should have smelled cordite if that thirty-two had just been discharged. But it hadn't, and the cordite smell from the earlier discharges had already faded."

That was a pretty long speech and it left me dry-mouthed. But it had made its impression on the others in the room, Branislaus in particular.

He asked Dettlinger, "Well? You have anything to say for yourself?"

"I never did any of those things he said—none of 'em, you hear."

"I hear."

"And that's all I'm saying until I see a lawyer."

"You've got one of the best sitting next to you. How about it, Mr. Factor? You want to represent Dettlinger?"

"Pass," Factor said thinly. "This is one case where I'll be glad to plead bias."

Dettlinger was still strangling me with his eyes. I wondered if he would keep on proclaiming his innocence even in the face of stronger evidence than what I'd just presented. Or if he'd crack under pressure, as most amateurs do.

I decided he was the kind who'd crack eventually, and I quit looking at him and at the death in his eyes.

"Well, I was wrong about that much," I said to Kerry the following night. We were sitting in front of a log fire in her Diamond Heights apartment, me with a beer and her with a glass of wine, and I had just finished telling her all about it. "Dettlinger hasn't cracked and it doesn't look as if he's going to. The DA'll have to work for his conviction."

"But you *were* right about most of it?"

"Pretty much. I probably missed a few details; with Kirby dead, and unless Dettlinger talks, we may never know some of them for sure. But for the most part I think I got it straight."

"My hero," she said, and gave me an adoring look.

She does that sometimes—puts me on like that. I don't understand women, so I don't know why. But it doesn't matter. She has auburn hair and green eyes and a fine body; she's also smarter than I am—she works as an advertising copywriter—and she is stimulating to be around. I love her to pieces, as the boys in the back room used to say.

"The police found the tape recorder," I said. "Took them until late this morning, because Dettlinger was clever about hiding it. He'd buried it in some rushes inside the hippo pen, probably with the idea of digging it up again later on and getting rid of it permanently. There was one clear print on the fast-forward button—Dettlinger's."

"Did they also find the second bullet he fired?"

"Yep. Where I guessed it was: in one of the slabs of fresh meat in the open storage locker."

"And did Dettlinger have locksmithing experience?"

"Uh-huh. He worked for a locksmith for a year in his mid-twenties. The case against him, even without a confession, is pretty solid."

"What about his accomplice?"

"Branislaus thinks he's got a line on the guy," I said. "From some things he found in Dettlinger's apartment. Man named Gerber—got a record of animal poaching and theft. I talked to Larry Factor this afternoon and he's heard of Gerber. The way he figures it, Dettlinger and Gerber had a deal for the specimens they stole with some collectors in Florida. That seems to be Gerber's usual pattern of operation anyway."

"I hope they get him too," Kerry said. "I don't like the idea of stealing birds and animals out of the zoo. It's . . . obscene, somehow."

"So is murder."

We didn't say anything for a time, looking into the fire, working on our drinks.

"You know," I said finally, "I have a lot of sympathy for animals myself. Take gorillas, for instance."

"Why gorillas?"

"Because of their mating habits."

"What *are* their mating habits?"

I had no idea, but I made up something interesting. Then I gave her a practical demonstration.

No gorilla ever had it so good.

· LAWRENCE BLOCK ·

By the Dawn's Early Light

"By the Dawn's Early Light" brought Lawrence Block his first Shamus Award, and inspired the fine Matthew Scudder novel When the Sacred Ginmill Closes. *In 1982 Block won the Shamus for best novel with his Scudder novel* Eight Million Ways to Die. *He also served as the PWA president in 1984. He has won a total of four Shamus Awards . . . and counting. He wrote this story at a time when he thought he had written all he could about Matthew Scudder. Luckily, this story seemed to give new life to the character, and the rest is history. Lawrence Block also won the MWA Shamus Edgar with this story, and has been presented with that organization's Grand Master Award.*

ALL THIS HAPPENED A LONG TIME AGO.

Abe Beame was living in Gracie Mansion, though even he seemed to have trouble believing he was really the mayor of the city of New York. Ali was in his prime, and the Knicks still had a year or so left in Bradley and DeBusschere. I was still drinking in those days, of course, and at the time it seemed to be doing more for me than it was doing to me.

I had already left my wife and kids, my home in Syosset and

the NYPD. I was living in the hotel on West Fifty-seventh Street where I still live, and I was doing most of my drinking around the corner in Jimmy Armstrong's saloon. Billie was the nighttime bartender. A Filipino youth named Dennis was behind the stick most days.

And Tommy Tillary was one of the regulars.

He was big, probably six-two, full in the chest, big in the belly, too. He rarely showed up in a suit but always wore a jacket and tie, usually a navy or burgundy blazer with gray flannel slacks or white duck pants in warmer weather. He had a loud voice that boomed from his barrel chest and a big, clean-shaven face that was innocent around the pouting mouth and knowing around the eyes. He was somewhere in his late forties and he drank a lot of top-shelf scotch. Chivas, as I remember it, but it could have been Johnnie Black. Whatever it was, his face was beginning to show it, with patches of permanent flush at the cheekbones and a tracery of broken capillaries across the bridge of the nose.

We were saloon friends. We didn't speak every time we ran into each other, but at the least we always acknowledged each other with a nod or a wave. He told a lot of dialect jokes and told them reasonably well, and I laughed at my share of them. Sometimes I was in a mood to reminisce about my days on the force, and when my stories were funny, his laugh was as loud as anyone's.

Sometimes he showed up alone, sometimes with male friends. About a third of the time, he was in the company of a short and curvy blond named Carolyn. "Carolyn from the Caro-line" was the way he occasionally introduced her, and she did have a faint southern accent that became more pronounced as the drink got to her.

Then, one morning, I picked up the *Daily News* and read that burglars had broken into a house on Colonial Road, in the Bay Ridge section of Brooklyn. They had stabbed to death the only occupant present, one Margaret Tillary. Her husband, Thomas J. Tillary, a salesman, was not at home at the time.

I hadn't known Tommy was a salesman or that he'd had a wife. He did wear a wide yellow-gold band on the appropriate finger, and it was clear that he wasn't married to Carolyn from the Caroline, and it now looked as though he was a widower. I felt vaguely sorry for him, vaguely sorry for the wife I'd never even known of, but that was the extent of it. I drank enough back then to avoid feeling any emotion very strongly.

And then, two or three nights later, I walked into Armstrong's and there was Carolyn. She didn't appear to be waiting for him or anyone else, nor did she look as though she'd just breezed in a few minutes ago. She had a stool by herself at the bar and she was drinking something dark from a lowball glass.

I took a seat a few stools down from her. I ordered two double shots of bourbon, drank one and poured the other into the black coffee Billie brought me. I was sipping the coffee when a voice with a Piedmont softness said, "I forget your name."

I looked up.

"I believe we were introduced," she said, "but I don't recall your name."

"It's Matt," I said, "and you're right, Tommy introduced us. You're Carolyn."

"Carolyn Cheatham. Have you seen him?"

"Tommy? Not since it happened."

"Neither have I. Were you-all at the funeral?"

"No. When was it?"

"This afternoon. Neither was I. There. Whyn't you come sit next to me so's I don't have to shout. Please?"

She was drinking a sweet almond liqueur that she took on the rocks. It tastes like dessert, but it's as strong as whiskey.

"He told me not to come," she said. "To the funeral. He said it was a matter of respect for the dead." She picked up her glass and stared into it. I've never known what people hope to see there, though it's a gesture I've performed often enough myself.

"Respect," she said. "What's he care about respect? I would have just been part of the office crowd; we both work at Tannahill; far as anyone there knows, we're just friends. And all we ever were is friends, you know."

"Whatever you say."

"Oh, *shit*," she said. "I don't mean I wasn't fucking him, for the Lord's sake. I mean it was just laughs and good times. He was married and he went home to Momma every night and that was jes' fine, because who in her right mind'd want Tommy Tillary around by the dawn's early light? Christ in the foothills, did I spill this or drink it?"

We agreed she was drinking them a little too fast. It was this fancy New York sweet-drink shit, she maintained, not like the bourbon she'd grown up on. You knew where you stood with bourbon.

I told her I was a bourbon drinker myself, and it pleased her to learn this. Alliances have been forged on thinner bonds than that, and ours served to propel us out of Armstrong's, with a stop down the block for a fifth of Maker's Mark—her choice—and a four-block walk to her apartment. There were exposed brick walls, I remember, and candles stuck in straw-wrapped bottles, and several travel posters from Sabena, the Belgian airline.

We did what grown-ups do when they find themselves alone together. We drank our fair share of the Maker's Mark and went to bed. She made a lot of enthusiastic noises and more than a few skillful moves, and afterward she cried some.

A little later, she dropped off to sleep. I was tired myself, but I put on my clothes and sent myself home. Because who in her right mind'd want Matt Scudder around by the dawn's early light?

Over the next couple of days, I wondered every time I entered Armstrong's if I'd run into her, and each time I was more relieved than disappointed when I didn't. I didn't encounter Tommy, either, and that, too, was a relief and in no sense disappointing.

Then, one morning, I picked up the *News* and read that they'd arrested a pair of young Hispanics from Sunset Park for the Tillary burglary and homicide. The paper ran the usual photo—two skinny kids, their hair unruly, one of them trying to hide his face from the camera, the other smirking defiantly, and each of them handcuffed to a broad-shouldered, grim-faced Irishman in a suit. You didn't need the careful caption to tell the good guys from the bad guys.

Sometime in the middle of the afternoon, I went over to Armstrong's for a hamburger and drank a beer with it. The phone behind the bar rang and Dennis put down the glass he was wiping and answered it. "He was here a minute ago," he said. "I'll see if he stepped out." He covered the mouthpiece with his hand and looked quizzically at me. "Are you still here?" he asked. "Or did you slip away while my attention was diverted?"

"Who wants to know?"

"Tommy Tillary."

You never know what a woman will decide to tell a man or how a man will react to it. I didn't want to find out, but I was better off learning over the phone than face-to-face. I nodded and took the phone from Dennis.

I said, "Matt Scudder, Tommy. I was sorry to hear about your wife."

"Thanks, Matt. Jesus, it feels like it happened a year ago. It was what, a week?"

"At least they got the bastards."

There was a pause. Then he said, "Jesus. You haven't seen a paper, huh?"

"That's where I read about it. Two Spanish kids."

"You didn't happen to see this afternoon's *Post*."

"No. Why, what happened? They turn out to be clean?"

"The two spicks. Clean? Shit, they're about as clean as the men's room in the Times Square subway station. The cops hit their place and found stuff from my house everywhere they looked. Jewelry they had descriptions of, a stereo that I gave them the serial number, everything. Monogrammed shit. I mean, that's how clean they were, for Christ's sake."

"So?"

"They admitted the burglary but not the murder."

"That's common, Tommy."

"Lemme finish, huh? They admitted the burglary, but according to them it was a put-up job. According to them, I hired them to hit my place. They could keep whatever they got and I'd have everything out and arranged for them, and in return I got to clean up on the insurance by over-reporting the loss."

"What did the loss amount to?"

"Shit, I don't know. There were twice as many things turned up in their apartment as I ever listed when I made out a report. There's things I missed a few days after I filed the report and others I didn't know were gone until the cops found them. You don't notice everything right away, at least I didn't, and on top of it, how could I think straight with Peg dead? You know?"

"It hardly sounds like an insurance setup."

"No, of course it wasn't. How the hell could it be? All I had was a standard homeowner's policy. It covered maybe a third of what I lost. According to them, the place was empty when they hit it. Peg was out."

"And?"

"And I set them up. They hit the place, they carted everything away, and I came home with Peg and stabbed her six, eight times, whatever it was, and left her there so it'd look like it happened in a burglary."

"How could the burglars testify that you stabbed your wife?"

"They couldn't. All they said was they didn't and she wasn't home when they were there, and that I hired them to do the burglary. The cops pieced the rest of it together."

"What did they do, take you downtown?"

"No. They came over to the house, it was early, I don't know what time. It was the first I knew that the spicks were arrested, let alone that they were trying to do a job on me. They just wanted to talk, the cops, and at first I talked to them, and then I started to get the drift of what they were trying to put onto me. So I said I wasn't saying anything more without my lawyer present, and I called him, and he left half his breakfast on the table and came over in a hurry, and he wouldn't let me say a word."

"And the cops didn't take you in or book you?"

"No."

"Did they buy your story?"

"No way. I didn't really tell 'em a story, because Kaplan wouldn't let me say anything. They didn't drag me in, because they don't have a case yet, but Kaplan says they're gonna be building one if they can. They told me not to leave town. You believe it? My wife's dead, the *Post* headline says, 'QUIZ HUSBAND IN BURGLARY MURDER,' and what the hell do they think I'm gonna do? Am I going fishing for fucking trout in Montana? 'Don't leave town.' You see this shit on television, you think nobody in real life talks this way. Maybe television's where they get it from."

I waited for him to tell me what he wanted from me. I didn't have long to wait.

"Why I called," he said, "is Kaplan wants to hire a detective. He figured maybe these guys talked around the neighborhood, maybe they bragged to their friends, maybe there's a way to prove they did the killing. He says the cops won't concentrate on that end if they're too busy nailing the lid shut on me."

I explained that I didn't have any official standing, that I had no license and filed no reports.

"That's okay," he insisted. "I told Kaplan what I want is somebody I can trust, somebody who'll do the job for me. I don't think they're gonna have any kind of a case at all, Matt, but the longer this drags on, the worse it is for me. I want it cleared up, I want it in the papers that these Spanish assholes did it all and I had nothing to do with anything. You name a fair fee and I'll pay it, me to you, and it can be cash in your hand if you don't like checks. What do you say?"

He wanted somebody he could trust. Had Carolyn from the Caroline told him how trustworthy I was?

What did I say? I said yes.

I met Tommy Tillary and his lawyer in Drew Kaplan's office on Court Street, a few blocks from Brooklyn's Borough Hall. There was a Syrian restaurant next door and, at the corner, a grocery store specializing in Middle Eastern imports stood next to an antique shop overflowing with stripped-oak furniture and brass lamps and bedsteads. Kaplan's office ran to wood paneling and leather chairs and oak file cabinets. His name and the names of two partners were painted on the frosted-glass door in old-fashioned gold-and-black lettering. Kaplan himself looked conservatively up-to-date, with a three-piece striped suit that was better cut than mine. Tommy wore his burgundy blazer and gray flannel trousers and loafers. Strain showed at the corners of his blue eyes and around his mouth. His complexion was off, too.

"All we want you to do," Kaplan said, "is find a key in one of their pants pockets, Herrera's or Cruz's, and trace it to a locker in Penn Station, and in the locker there's a foot-long knife with their prints and her blood on it."

"Is that what it's going to take?"

He smiled. "It wouldn't hurt. No, actually, we're not in such bad shape. They got some shaky testimony from a pair of Latins who've been in and out of trouble since they got weaned to Tropicana. They got what looks to them like a good motive on Tommy's part."

"Which is?"

I was looking at Tommy when I asked. His eyes slipped away from mine. Kaplan said, "A marital triangle, a case of the shorts, and a strong money motive. Margaret Tillary inherited a little over a quarter of a million dollars six or eight months ago. An aunt left a million two and it got cut up four ways. What they don't bother to notice is he loved his wife, and how many husbands cheat? What is it they say—ninety percent cheat and ten percent lie?"

"That's good odds."

"One of the killers, Angel Herrera, did some odd jobs at the Tillary house last March or April. Spring cleaning; he hauled stuff out of the basement and attic, a little donkeywork. According to Herrera, that's how Tommy knew him to contact him about the burglary. According to common sense, that's how Herrera and his buddy Cruz knew the house and what was in it and how to gain access."

"The case against Tommy sounds pretty thin."

"It is," Kaplan said. "The thing is, you go to court with something like this and you lose even if you win. For the rest of your life, everybody remembers you stood trial for murdering your wife, never mind that you won an acquittal.

"Besides," he said, "you never know which way a jury's going to jump. Tommy's alibi is he was with another lady at the time of the burglary. The woman's a colleague; they could see it as completely aboveboard, but who says they're going to? What they sometimes do, they decide they don't believe the alibi because it's his girlfriend lying for him, and at the same time they label him a scumbag for screwing around while his wife's getting killed."

"You keep it up," Tommy said, "I'll find myself guilty, the way you make it sound."

"Plus he's hard to get a sympathetic jury for. He's a big handsome guy, a sharp dresser, and you'd love him in a gin joint, but how much do you love him in a courtroom? He's a securities salesman, he's beautiful on the phone, and that means every clown who ever lost a hundred dollars on a stock tip or bought magazines over the phone is going to walk into the courtroom with a hard-on for him. I'm telling you, I want to stay the hell *out* of court. I'll *win* in court, I know that, or the worst that'll happen is I'll win on appeal, but who needs it? This is a case that shouldn't be in the first place, and I'd love to clear it up before they even go so far as presenting a bill to the grand jury."

"So from me you want—"

"Whatever you can find, Matt. Whatever discredits Cruz and Herrera. I don't know what's there to be found, but you were a cop and now you're private, and you can get down in the streets and nose around."

I nodded. I could do that. "One thing," I said. "Wouldn't you be better off with a Spanish-speaking detective? I know enough to buy a beer in a bodega, but I'm a long way from fluent."

Kaplan shook his head. "A personal relationship's worth more than a dime's worth of 'Me llamo Matteo y ¿como está usted?' "

"That's the truth," Tommy Tillary said. "Matt, I know I can count on you."

I wanted to tell him all he could count on was his fingers. I didn't really see what I could expect to uncover that wouldn't turn up in a regular police investigation. But I'd spent enough time carrying a shield to know not to push away money when somebody wants to give it to you. I felt comfortable taking a fee. The man was inheriting a quarter of a million, plus whatever insurance his wife had carried. If he was willing to spread some of it around, I was willing to take it.

So I went to Sunset Park and spent some time in the streets and some more time in the bars. Sunset Park is in Brooklyn, of course, on the borough's western edge, above Bay Ridge and south and west of Green-Wood Cemetery. These days, there's a lot of brownstoning going on there, with young urban professionals renovating the old houses and gentrifying the neighborhood. Back then, the upwardly mobile young had not yet discovered Sunset Park, and the area was a mix of Latins and Scandinavians, most of the former Puerto Ricans, most of the latter Norwegians. The balance was gradually shifting from Europe to the islands, from light to dark, but this was a process that had been going on for ages and there was nothing hurried about it.

I talked to Herrera's landlord and Cruz's former employer and one of his recent girlfriends. I drank beer in bars and the back rooms of bodegas. I went to the local station house, I read the sheets on both of the burglars and drank coffee with the cops and picked up some of the stuff that doesn't get on the yellow sheets.

I found out that Miguelito Cruz had once killed a man in a tavern brawl over a woman. There were no charges pressed; a dozen witnesses reported that the dead man had gone after Cruz first with a broken bottle. Cruz had most likely been carrying the knife, but several witnesses insisted it had been tossed to him by an anonymous benefactor, and there hadn't been enough evidence to make a case of weapons possession, let alone homicide.

I learned that Herrera had three children living with their mother in Puerto Rico. He was divorced but wouldn't marry his current girlfriend because he regarded himself as still married to his ex-wife in the eyes of God. He sent money to his children when he had any to send.

I learned other things. They didn't seem terribly consequential then and they've faded from memory altogether by now, but I wrote them down in my pocket notebook as I learned them, and every day or so I duly reported my findings to Drew Kaplan. He always seemed pleased with what I told him.

I invariably managed a stop at Armstrong's before I called it a night. One night she was there, Carolyn Cheatham, drinking bourbon this time, her face frozen with stubborn old pain. It took her a blink or two to recognize me. Then tears started to form in the corners of her eyes, and she used the back of one hand to wipe them away.

I didn't approach her until she beckoned. She patted the stool beside hers and I eased myself onto it. I had coffee with bourbon in it and bought a refill for her. She was pretty drunk already, but that's never been enough reason to turn down a drink.

She talked about Tommy. He was being nice to her, he said. Calling up, sending flowers. But he wouldn't see her, because it wouldn't look right, not for a new widower, not for a man who'd been publicly accused of murder.

"He sends flowers with no card enclosed," she said. "He calls me from pay phones. The son of a bitch."

Billie called me aside. "I didn't want to put her out," he said, "a nice woman like that, shit-faced as she is. But I thought I was gonna have to. You'll see she gets home?"

I said I would.

I got her out of there and a cab came along and saved us the walk. At her place, I took the keys from her and unlocked the door. She half sat, half sprawled on the couch. I had to use the bathroom, and when I came back, her eyes were closed and she was snoring lightly.

I got her coat and shoes off, put her to bed, loosened her clothing and covered her with a blanket. I was tired from all that and sat down on the couch for a minute, and I almost dozed off myself. Then I snapped awake and let myself out.

I went back to Sunset Park the next day. I learned that Cruz had been in trouble as a youth. With a gang of neighborhood kids, he used to go into the city and cruise Greenwich Village, looking for homosexuals to beat up. He'd had a dread of homosexuality, probably flowing as it generally does out of a fear of a part of himself, and he stifled that dread by fag bashing.

"He still doan' like them," a woman told me. She had glossy black hair and opaque eyes, and she was letting me pay for her rum and orange juice. "He's pretty, you know, an' they come on to him, an' he doan' like it."

I called that item in, along with a few others equally earth-shaking. I bought myself a steak dinner at the Slate over on Tenth Avenue, then finished up at Armstrong's, not drinking very hard, just coasting along on bourbon and coffee.

Twice, the phone rang for me. Once, it was Tommy Tillary, telling me how much he appreciated what I was doing for him. It seemed to me that all I was doing was taking his money, but he had me believing that my loyalty and invaluable assistance were all he had to cling to.

The second call was from Carolyn. More praise. I was a gentleman, she assured me, and a hell of a fellow all around. And I should forget that she'd been bad-mouthing Tommy. Everything was going to be fine with them.

I took the next day off. I think I went to a movie, and it may have been *The Sting*, with Newman and Redford achieving vengeance through swindling.

The day after that, I did another tour of duty over in Brooklyn. And the day after that, I picked up the *News* first thing in the morning. The headline was nonspecific, something like "KILL SUS-

PECT HANGS SELF IN CELL," but I knew it was my case before I turned to the story on page three.

Miguelito Cruz had torn his clothing into strips, knotted the strips together, stood his iron bedstead on its side, climbed onto it, looped his homemade rope around an overhead pipe, and jumped off the upended bedstead and into the next world.

That evening's six o'clock TV news had the rest of the story. Informed of his friend's death, Angel Herrera had recanted his original story and admitted that he and Cruz had conceived and executed the Tillary burglary on their own. It had been Miguelito who had stabbed the Tillary woman when she walked in on them. He'd picked up a kitchen knife while Herrera watched in horror. Miguelito always had a short temper, Herrera said, but they were friends, even cousins, and they had hatched their story to protect Miguelito. But now that he was dead, Herrera could admit what had really happened.

I was in Armstrong's that night, which was not remarkable. I had it in mind to get drunk, though I could not have told you why, and that *was* remarkable, if not unheard of. I got drunk a lot those days, but I rarely set out with that intention. I just wanted to feel a little better, a little more mellow, and somewhere along the way I'd wind up waxed.

I wasn't drinking particularly hard or fast, but I was working at it, and then somewhere around ten or eleven the door opened and I knew who it was before I turned around. Tommy Tillary, well dressed and freshly barbered, making his first appearance in Jimmy's place since his wife was killed.

"Hey, look who's here!" he called out, and grinned that big grin. People rushed over to shake his hand. Billie was behind the stick, and he'd no sooner set one up on the house for our hero than Tommy insisted on buying a round for the bar. It was an expensive gesture—there must have been thirty or forty people in there—but I don't think he cared if there were three or four hundred.

I stayed where I was, letting the others mob him, but he

worked his way over to me and got an arm around my shoulders. "This is the man," he announced. "Best fucking detective ever wore out a pair of shoes. This man's money," he told Billie, "is no good at all tonight. He can't buy a drink; he can't buy a cup of coffee; if you went and put in pay toilets since I was last here, he can't use his own dime."

"The john's still free," Billie said, "but don't give the boss any ideas."

"Oh, don't tell me he didn't already think of it," Tommy said. "Matt, my boy, I love you. I was in a tight spot, I didn't want to walk out of my house, and you came through for me."

What the hell had I done? I hadn't hanged Miguelito Cruz or coaxed a confession out of Angel Herrera. I hadn't even set eyes on either man. But he was buying the drinks, and I had a thirst, so who was I to argue?

I don't know how long we stayed there. Curiously, my drinking slowed down even as Tommy's picked up speed. Carolyn, I noticed, was not present, nor did her name find its way into the conversation. I wondered if she would walk in—it was, after all, her neighborhood bar, and she was apt to drop in on her own. I wondered what would happen if she did.

I guess there were a lot of things I wondered about, and perhaps that's what put the brakes on my own drinking. I didn't want any gaps in my memory, any gray patches in my awareness.

After a while, Tommy was hustling me out of Armstrong's. "This is celebration time," he told me. "We don't want to sit in one place till we grow roots. We want to bop a little."

He had a car, and I just went along with him without paying too much attention to exactly where we were. We went to a noisy Greek club on the East Side, I think, where the waiters looked like Mob hit men. We went to a couple of trendy singles joints. We wound up somewhere in the Village, in a dark, beery cave.

It was quiet there, and conversation was possible, and I found myself asking him what I'd done that was so praiseworthy. One man had killed himself and another had confessed, and where was my role in either incident?

"The stuff you came up with," he said.

"What stuff? I should have brought back fingernail parings, you could have had someone work voodoo on them."

"About Cruz and the fairies."

"He was up for murder. He didn't kill himself because he was afraid they'd get him for fag bashing when he was a juvenile offender."

Tommy took a sip of scotch. He said, "Couple days ago, huge black guy comes up to Cruz in the chow line. 'Wait'll you get up to Green Haven,' he tells him. 'Every blood there's gonna have you for a girlfriend. Doctor gonna have to cut you a brand-new asshole, time you get outa there.' "

I didn't say anything.

"Kaplan," he said. "Drew talked to somebody who talked to somebody, and that did it. Cruz took a good look at the idea of playin' drop the soap for half the jigs in captivity, and the next thing you know, the murderous little bastard was dancing on air. And good riddance to him."

I couldn't seem to catch my breath. I worked on it while Tommy went to the bar for another round. I hadn't touched the drink in front of me, but I let him buy for both of us.

When he got back, I said, "Herrera."

"Changed his story. Made a full confession."

"And pinned the killing on Cruz."

"Why not? Cruz wasn't around to complain. Who knows which one of 'em did it, and for that matter, who cares? The thing is, you gave us the lever."

"For Cruz," I said. "To get him to kill himself."

"And for Herrera. Those kids of his in Santurce. Drew spoke to Herrera's lawyer and Herrera's lawyer spoke to Herrera, and the message was, 'Look, you're going up for burglary whatever you do, and probably for murder; but if you tell the right story, you'll draw shorter time, and on top of that, that nice Mr. Tillary's gonna let bygones be bygones and every month there's a nice check for your wife and kiddies back home in Puerto Rico.' "

At the bar, a couple of old men were reliving the Louis-Schmeling fight, the second one, where Louis punished the German champion. One of the old fellows was throwing roundhouse punches in the air, demonstrating.

I said, "Who killed your wife?"

"One or the other of them. If I had to bet, I'd say Cruz. He had those little beady eyes; you looked at him up close and you got that he was a killer."

"When did you look at him up close?"

"When they came and cleaned the house, the basement, and the attic. Not when they came and cleaned me out; that was the second time."

He smiled, but I kept looking at him until the smile lost its certainty. "That was Herrera who helped around the house," I said. "You never met Cruz."

"Cruz came along, gave him a hand."

"You never mentioned that before."

"Oh, sure I did, Matt. What difference does it make, anyway?"

"Who killed her, Tommy?"

"Hey, let it alone, huh?"

"Answer the question."

"I already answered it."

"You killed her, didn't you?"

"What are you, crazy? Cruz killed her and Herrera swore to it, isn't that enough for you?"

"Tell me you didn't kill her."

"I didn't kill her."

"Tell me again."

"I didn't fucking kill her. What's the matter with you?"

"I don't believe you."

"Oh, Jesus," he said. He closed his eyes, put his head in his hands. He sighed and looked up and said, "You know, it's a funny thing with me. Over the telephone, I'm the best salesman you could ever imagine. I swear I could sell sand to the Arabs, I could sell ice in the winter, but face-to-face I'm no good at all. Why do you figure that is?"

"You tell me."

"I don't know. I used to think it was my face, the eyes and the mouth; I don't know. It's easy over the phone. I'm talking to a stranger, I don't know who he is or what he looks like, and he's not lookin' at me, and it's a cinch. Face-to-face, especially with someone I know, it's a different story." He looked at me. "If we were doin' this over the phone, you'd buy the whole thing."

"It's possible."

"It's fucking certain. Word for word, you'd buy the package. Suppose I was to tell you I did kill her, Matt. You couldn't prove anything. Look, the both of us walked in there, the place was a mess from the burglary, we got in an argument, tempers flared, something happened."

"You set up the burglary. You planned the whole thing, just the way Cruz and Herrera accused you of doing. And now you wriggled out of it."

"And you helped me—don't forget that part of it."

"I won't."

"And I wouldn't have gone away for it anyway, Matt. Not a chance. I'da beat it in court, only this way I don't have to go to court. Look, this is just the booze talkin', and we can forget it in the morning, right? I didn't kill her, you didn't accuse me, we're still buddies, everything's fine. Right?"

Blackouts are never there when you want them. I woke up the next day and remembered all of it, and I found myself wishing I didn't. He'd killed his wife and he was getting away with it. And I'd helped him. I'd taken his money, and in return I'd shown him how to set one man up for suicide and pressure another into making a false confession.

And what was I going to do about it?

I couldn't think of a thing. Any story I carried to the police would be speedily denied by Tommy and his lawyer, and all I had was the thinnest of hearsay evidence, my own client's own words when he and I both had a skinful of booze. I went over it for a few days, looking for ways to shake something loose, and there was nothing. I could maybe interest a newspaper reporter, maybe get Tommy some press coverage that wouldn't make him happy, but why? And to what purpose?

It rankled. But I would just have a couple of drinks, and then it wouldn't rankle so much.

Angel Herrera pleaded guilty to burglary, and in return, the Brooklyn DA's office dropped all homicide charges. He went upstate to serve five to ten.

And then I got a call in the middle of the night. I'd been sleeping a couple of hours, but the phone woke me and I groped for it. It took me a minute to recognize the voice on the other end.

It was Carolyn Cheatham.

"I had to call you," she said, "on account of you're a bourbon man and a gentleman. I owed it to you to call you."

"What's the matter?"

"He ditched me," she said, "and he got me fired out of Tannahill and Company so he won't have to look at me around the office. Once he didn't need me to back up his story, he let go of me, and do you know he did it over the phone?"

"Carolyn—"

"It's all in the note," she said. "I'm leaving a note."

"Look, don't do anything yet," I said. I was out of bed, fumbling for my clothes. "I'll be right over. We'll talk about it."

"You can't stop me, Matt."

"I won't try to stop you. We'll talk first, and then you can do anything you want."

The phone clicked in my ear.

I threw my clothes on, rushed over there, hoping it would be pills, something that took its time. I broke a small pane of glass in the downstairs door and let myself in, then used an old credit card to slip the bolt of her spring lock.

The room smelled of cordite. She was on the couch she'd passed out on the last time I saw her. The gun was still in her hand, limp at her side, and there was a black-rimmed hole in her temple.

There was a note, too. An empty bottle of Maker's Mark stood on the coffee table, an empty glass beside it. The booze showed in her handwriting and in the sullen phrasing of the suicide note.

I read the note. I stood there for a few minutes, not for very long, and then I got a dish towel from the Pullman kitchen and wiped the bottle and the glass. I took another matching glass, rinsed it out and wiped it, and put it in the drainboard of the sink.

I stuffed the note in my pocket. I took the gun from her fingers, checked routinely for a pulse, then wrapped a sofa pillow around the gun to muffle its report. I fired one round into her chest, another into her open mouth.

I dropped the gun into a pocket and left.

They found the gun in Tommy Tillary's house, stuffed between the cushions of the living-room sofa, clean of prints inside and out. Ballistics got a perfect match. I'd aimed for soft tissue with the round shot into her chest, because bullets can fragment on impact with bone. That was one reason I'd fired the extra shots. The other was to rule out the possibility of suicide.

After the story made the papers, I picked up the phone and called Drew Kaplan. "I don't understand it," I said. "He was free and clear; why the hell did he kill the girl?"

"Ask him yourself," Kaplan said. He did not sound happy. "You want my opinion, he's a lunatic. I honestly didn't think he was. I figured maybe he killed his wife, maybe he didn't. Not my job to try him. But I didn't figure he was a homicidal maniac."

"It's certain he killed the girl?"

"Not much question. The gun's pretty strong evidence. Talk about finding somebody with the smoking pistol in his hand, here it was in Tommy's couch. The idiot."

"Funny he kept it."

"Maybe he had other people he wanted to shoot. Go figure a crazy man. No, the gun's evidence, and there was a phone tip—a man called in the shooting, reported a man running out of there and gave a description that fitted Tommy pretty well. Even had him wearing that red blazer he wears, tacky thing makes him look like an usher at the Paramount."

"It sounds tough to square."

"Well, somebody else'll have to try to do it," Kaplan said. "I told him I can't defend him this time. What it amounts to, I wash my hands of him."

I thought of that when I read that Angel Herrera got out just the other day. He served all ten years because he was as good at getting into trouble inside the walls as he'd been on the outside.

Somebody killed Tommy Tillary with a homemade knife after he'd served two years and three months of a manslaughter stretch. I wondered at the time if that was Herrera getting even, and I don't suppose I'll ever know. Maybe the checks stopped going to Santurce and Herrera took it the wrong way. Or maybe Tommy said the wrong thing to somebody else and said it face-to-face instead of over the phone.

I don't think I'd do it that way now. I don't drink anymore, and the impulse to play God seems to have evaporated with the booze.

But then, a lot of things have changed. Billie left Armstrong's not long after that, left New York, too; the last I heard, he was off drink himself, living in Sausalito and making candles. I ran into Dennis the other day in a bookstore on lower Fifth Avenue full of odd volumes on yoga and spiritualism and holistic healing. And Armstrong's is scheduled to close the end of next month. The lease is up for renewal, and I suppose the next you know, the old joint'll be another Korean fruit market.

I still light a candle now and then for Carolyn Cheatham and Miguelito Cruz. Not often. Just every once in a while.

· LOREN D. ESTLEMAN ·

Eight Mile and Dequindre

Loren D. Estleman has never been president of the PWA. We thought we'd get that out of the way as soon as possible, lest the reader think that serving that office was a prerequisite for receiving the award. In fact, he has never run for any office in the PWA. He is, however, a two-time winner of the short story award, and has also won the Shamus for best PI novel with his Amos Walker novel Sugartown *(1984).*

1

THE CLIENT WAS A NO-SHOW, AS FOUR OUT OF TEN OF THEM tend to be.

She had called me in the customary white heat, a woman with one of those voices you hear in supermarkets and then thank God you're not married, and arranged to meet me someplace not my office and not her home. The bastard had been paying her the same alimony for the past five years, she'd said, and she wanted a handle on his secret bank accounts to prove he was making twice as much as when they split. In the meantime she'd cooled down or the situation had changed or she'd found a private investigator who worked even cheaper than I did, leaving me to drink yellow coffee alone at a linoleum counter in a gray cinder-block building on Dequindre at Eight Mile Road. I was just as happy. Why I'd agreed to meet her at all had to do with a bank balance smaller than my IQ, and since talking to her I'd changed my mind and decided to refer her to another agency anyway. So I worked on my coffee and once again considered taking on a security job until things got better.

A portable radio behind the counter was tuned to a Pistons game, but the guy who'd poured my coffee, lean and young with butch-cut red hair and a white apron, didn't look to be listening to it, whistling while he chalked new prices on the blackboard menu on the wall next to the cash register. Well, it was March and the Pistons were where they usually were in the standings at that time and nobody in Detroit was listening. I asked him what the chicken on a roll was like.

"Better than across the street," he said, wiping chalk off his hands onto the apron.

Across the street was a Shell station. I ordered the chicken anyway; unless he skipped some lines it was too far down on the board for him to raise the price before I'd eaten it. He opened a stainless steel door over the sink and took the plastic off a breaded patty the color of fresh sawdust and slapped it hissing on the griddle.

We'd had the place to ourselves for a while, but then the pneumatic front door whooshed and sucked in a male customer in his thirties and a sport coat you could hear across the street, who cocked a hip onto a stool at the far end of the counter and asked for a glass of water.

"Anything to go with that?" asked Butch, setting an amber-tinted tumbler in front of him.

"No, I'm waiting for someone."

"Coffee, maybe."

"No, I want to keep my breath fresh."

"Oh. That kind of someone." He wiped his hands again. "It's

okay for now, but if the place starts to fill up you'll have to order something, a Coke or something. You don't have to drink it."

"Sounds fair."

"This ain't a bus station."

"I can see that."

Nodding, Butch turned away and picked up a spatula and flipped the chicken patty and broke a roll out of plastic. The guy in the sport coat asked how the game was going, but Butch either didn't hear him or didn't want to. The guy gave up on him and glanced down the counter at me.

"You waiting for someone too?"

"I was," I said. "Now I'm waiting for that bird."

"Stood you up, huh? That's tough."

"I'm used to it."

He hesitated, then got down and picked up his glass and carried it to my end and climbed onto the stool next to mine. Up close he was about thirty, freckled, with a double chin starting and dishwater hair going thin in front. A triangle of white shirt showed between his belt buckle and the one button he had fastened on the jacket. He had prominent front teeth and looked a little like Howdy Doody. "This girl I'm waiting for would never stand anyone up," he said. "She's got manners."

"Yeah?"

"No, really. Looks too. Here's her picture." He took a fat curved wallet out of his hip pocket and showed me the head and torso of a blond in a red bandanna top, winking and grinning at the camera. She stank professional model.

"Nice," I said. "What's she do?"

"Waitress at the Peacock's Roost. That'll change when we're married. I don't want my wife to work."

"The girls in steel-rimmed glasses and iron pants will burn their bras on your lawn."

"To hell with them. Rena won't have anything to do with that kind. That's her name, Rena."

"I think it's dead now," I told Butch.

He landed the chicken patty on one half of the roll and planted the other half on top and put it on a china saucer and set the works on the linoleum. Howdy Doody finished putting away his wallet and stuck his right hand across his body in front of me. "Dave Tillet."

"Amos Walker." I shook the hand and picked up the sandwich. As it turned out I couldn't have done any worse across the street at the Shell station.

Tillet sipped his water. "That clock right?"

Butch looked up to see which clock he meant. There was only one in the place, advertising Stroh's beer on the wall behind the counter. "Give or take a minute."

"She ought to be here now. She's usually early."

"Maybe she stood you up after all," I said.

"Not Rena."

I ate the chicken and Tillet drank his water and the guy behind the counter picked up his chalk and resumed changing prices and didn't listen to the basketball game. I wiped my mouth with a cheesy paper napkin and asked Butch what the tariff was. He said, "Buck ninety-five." I got out my wallet.

"Maybe I better call her," said Tillet. "That phone working?"

Butch said it was. Tillet drained his glass and went to the pay telephone on the wall just inside the door. I paid for the sandwich and coffee. "Well, good luck," I told Tillet on my way past him.

"What? Yeah, thanks. You too." He was listening to the purring in the earpiece. I pushed on the glass door.

Two guys were on their way in and I stepped aside and held the door for them. They were wearing dark windbreakers and colorful knit caps and when they saw me they reached up with one hand apiece and rolled the caps down over their faces and the caps turned into ski masks. Their other hands were coming out of the slash pockets of the windbreakers and when I saw that I jumped back and let go of the door, but the man closest to it caught it with his arm and stuck a long-barreled .22 target pistol in my face while his partner came in past him and lamped the place quickly and then put the .22's twin almost against Tillet's noisy sport coat. Three flat reports slapped the air. Tillet's mouth was open and he was leaning one shoulder against the wall and he hadn't had time to start falling or even know he was shot when the guy fired again into his face and then deliberately moved the gun and gave him another in the ear. The guy's buddy wasn't watching. He was looking at me through the eyeholes in his mask and his eyes were as flat and gray as nickels on a pad. They held no more expression than the empty blue hole also staring me in the face.

Then the pair left, Gray Eyes backing away with his gun still on me while his partner walked swiftly to a brown Plymouth Volare and around to the driver's side and got in and then Gray Eyes let himself in the passenger's side and they were rolling before he got the door closed.

Tillet fell then, crumpling in on himself like a gas bag deflating, and folded to the floor with no more noise than laundry makes skidding down a chute. Very bright red blood leaked out of his ear and slid into a puddle on the gray linoleum floor.

I ran out to the sidewalk in time to see the Plymouth take the corner. Forget about the license number. I wasn't wearing a gun. I hardly ever needed one to meet a woman in a diner.

When I went back in, the counterman was standing over Tillet's body, wiping his hands over and over on his apron. His face was as pale as the cloth. The telephone receiver swung from its cord and the metallic purring on the other end was loud in the silence following the shots. I bent and placed two fingers on Tillet's neck. Nothing was happening in the big artery. I straightened, picked up the receiver, worked the plunger, and dialed 911. Standing there waiting for someone to answer I was sorry I'd eaten the chicken.

2

They sent an Adam and Eve team, a white man and a black woman in uniform. You had to look twice at the woman to know she was a woman. They hadn't gotten around to cutting uniforms to fit them, and her tunic hung on her like a tarpaulin. Her partner had baby fat in his cheeks and a puppy mustache. His face went stiff when he saw the body. The woman might have been looking at a loose tile on the floor for all her expression gave up. Just to kill time I gave them the story, knowing I'd have to do it all over again for the plainclothes team. Butch was sitting on one of the customers' stools with his hands in his lap and whenever they looked at him he nodded in agreement with my details. The woman took it all down in shorthand.

The first string arrived ten minutes later. Among them was a black lieutenant, coarse-featured and heavy in the chest and shoulders, wearing a gray suit cut in heaven and a black tie with a silver diamond pattern. When he saw me he groaned.

"Hello, John," I said. "This is a hike north from headquarters."

John Alderdyce of Detroit homicide patted all his pockets and came up with an empty Lucky Strikes package. I gave him a Winston from my pack and took one for myself and lit them both. He squirted smoke and said, "I was eight blocks from here when I got the squeal. If I'd known you were back of it I'd have kept driving."

John and I had known each other a long time, a thing I admitted to a lot more often than he did. While I was recounting the last few minutes in the life of Dave Tillet, a police photographer came in and took pictures of the body from forty different angles and then a bearded black homicide sergeant I didn't know tugged on a pair of surgical gloves and knelt and started going through Tillet's clothes. Butch had recovered from his shock by this time and came over to watch. "Them gloves are to protect the fingerprints, right?" he asked.

"Wrong. Catch." The sergeant tossed him Tillet's wallet.

Butch caught it against his chest. "It's wet."

"That's why the gloves."

Butch thought about it, then dropped the wallet quickly and mopped his hands on his apron.

"Can the crap," barked Alderdyce. "What's inside?"

Still chuckling, the sergeant picked up the wallet and went through the contents. He whistled. "Christ, it's full of C-notes. Eight, ten, twelve—this guy was carrying fifteen hundred bucks on his hip."

"What else?"

The celluloid windows gave up a Social Security card and a temporary driver's license, both made out to David Edward Tillet, and the picture of the blond.

"That Rena?" Alderdyce asked.

I nodded. "She waits tables at the Peacock's Roost, Tillet said."

Alderdyce told the sergeant to bag the wallet and its contents. To me: "You saw these guys before they pulled down their ski masks?"

"Not enough before. They were just guys' faces. I didn't much look at them till they went for the guns. The trigger was my height, maybe ten pounds to the good. His partner gave up a couple of inches, same build, gray eyes." I described the getaway car.

"Stolen," guessed the sergeant. He stood and slid a glassine bag containing the wallet into the side pocket of his coat.

Alderdyce nodded. "It was a market job. The girl was the finger. She's smoke by now. Dope?"

"That or numbers," said the sergeant. "He's a little pale for either one in this town, but the rackets are nothing if not an equal opportunity employer. Nobody straight carries cash anymore."

"I still owe a thousand on this building." Butch's upper lip was folded over his chin. "I guess I'd be dumb to pay it off now."

"The place is made," the sergeant told him.

"Yeah?" The counterman looked hopefully at Alderdyce, who grunted.

"The Machus Red Fox is booked into next year and has been ever since Hoffa caught his last ride from in front of it."

"Yeah?"

The lieutenant was still looking at me. "When can you come down and sign a statement?"

"Whenever it's ready. I'm not exactly swamped."

"Five o'clock, then." He paused. "Your part in this is finished, right?"

"When I work I get paid," I said.

"How come that doesn't comfort me?"

I said I'd see him at five.

The morgue wagon was just creaking its brakes in front when I came out into the afternoon sunlight and walked around the blue and white and a couple of unmarked units and a green Fiat to my heap. I was about to get in behind the wheel when I stopped and looked again at the Fiat. The girl Dave Tillet had called Rena was sitting in the driver's seat, staring at the blank cinder-block wall in front of the windshield.

3

I opened the door on the passenger side and got in next to her. She jumped in the seat and looked at me quickly. Her honey-colored hair was caught in a clasp behind her neck, below which a kind of ponytail hung down her back, and she was wearing a tailored navy suit over a cream-colored blouse open at the neck and jet buttons in her ears, but I recognized her large smoky eyes and the just slightly too-wide mouth that was built for grinning, although she wasn't grinning. The interior of the little car smelled of car and sandalwood.

She snatched up a blue bag from the seat and her hand vanished inside. I caught her wrist. She struggled, but I applied pressure and her face went white and she stopped struggling. I relaxed the hold, but just a little.

"Dave's dead," I said. "You can't help him now."

She said nothing. On "dead," her head jerked as if I'd smacked her. I went on.

"You don't want to be here when the cops come out. They've got your picture and they think you fingered Dave."

"That's stupid." Her voice came from just in back of her tongue. I didn't know how it was normally.

"It's not stupid. He was expecting you and got five slugs from a twenty-two. The cops know where you work and pretty soon they'll know where you live and when they find you they'll book you as a material witness and change it to accessory to the fact later."

"You talk like you're not one of them."

"Get real, lady. If I were we wouldn't be sitting here talking. On the other hand, if you set up Dave deliberately you wouldn't be here at all. It could just be you're someone who could use some help."

Her lips twisted. "And it could just be you're someone who could give it."

"We're talking," I reminded her. "I'm not hollering cop."

"Who the hell are you?"

I told her. Her lips twisted some more.

"A cheap snooper. I should have guessed it would be something like that."

I said, "It's a buyer's market. I don't set the price."

"What's the price?"

"Some truth. Not right now, though. Not here. Let's go somewhere."

"You go," she said. "I've got a pistol in this purse and when I pull the trigger it won't much matter whether it's inside or outside."

I didn't move. "Guns, everybody's got 'em. After a killer's screwed one in your face the rest aren't so scary."

We sat like that for a while, she with her hand in the purse and turned a little in the seat so that one silken knee showed under the hem of her pleated skirt while a cramp crawled across the palm I had clenched on her wrist. The morgue crew came out the front door of the diner wheeling a stretcher with a zipped bag full of Dave Tillet on it and folded the works into the back of the wagon. Rena didn't look at them. Finally I let go of her and got out one of my cards and a pen. I moved slowly to avoid attracting bullets.

"I'll just put my home address and telephone number on the back," I said, writing. "Open twenty-four hours. Just ring and ask for Amos. But do it before the cops get you or I'm just another spent shell."

She said nothing. I tucked the card under the mirror she had clamped to the sun visor on the passenger side and got out and into my crate and started the motor and swung out into the street and took off with my cape flying behind me.

4

I made some calls from the office, but none of the security firms or larger investigation agencies in town had anything to farm out. I bought myself a drink from the file drawer in the desk and when that was finished I bought myself another, and by then it was time to go to police headquarters at 1300 Beaubien, or just plain 1300 as it's known in town. The lady detective who announced me to John Alderdyce was too much detective not to notice the scotch on my breath but too much lady to mention it. Little by little they are changing things down there, but it's a slow process.

In John's office I gave my story again to a stenographer while Alderdyce and the bearded sergeant listened for variations. When the steno left to type up my statement I asked John what he'd found out.

"Tillet kept the books for Great Lakes Importers. Ever hear of it?"

"Front for the Mob."

"So you say. It's worth a slander suit if you say it in public, they're that well screened with lawyers and holding corporations." He broke open a fresh pack of Luckies and fired one up with a Zippo. I already had a Winston going. "Tillet rented a house in Southfield. A grand a month."

"Any grand jury investigations in progress?" I asked. "They're hard on the bookkeeping population."

He shook his head. "We got a call in to the feds, but even if they get back to us we'll still have to go up to the mountain to get any information out of those tight-mouthed clones. We're pinning our hopes on the street trade and this woman Rena. Especially her."

"What'd you turn on her?"

"She works at the Peacock's Roost like you said, goes by Rena Murrow. She didn't show up for the four P.M. shift today. She's got an apartment on Michigan and we have men waiting for her there, but she's empty tracks by now. Tillet's landlady says he's been away someplace on vacation. Lying low. Whoever wanted him out in the open got to Rena. By all accounts she is a woman plenty of scared accountants would break cover to meet."

"Maybe someone used her."

He grinned that tight grin that was always bad news for someone. "Your license to hunt dulcineas still valid?"

"Everyone needs a hobby," I said. "Stamps are sissy."

"Safer, though. According to the computer, this damsel has two priors for soliciting, but that was before she started bumming around with one Peter Venito. 'Known former associate,' it says in the printout. Computers have no romance in their circuits."

I smoked and thought. Peter Venito, born Pietro, had come up through the Licavoli Mob during Prohibition and during the old Kefauver Committee hearings had been identified as one of the five dons on the board of governors of that fraternal organization the Italian Anti-Defamation League would have us believe no longer exists.

"Venito's been dead four or five years," I said.

"Six. But his son Paul's still around and a slice off the old pizza. His secretary at Great Lakes Importers says he's in Las Vegas. Importing."

"Anything on the street soldiers?"

"Computer got a hernia sorting through gray eyes and the heights and builds you gave us. I'd go to the mugs but you say you didn't get a long enough hinge at them without their masks, so why go into golden time? Just sign the statement and give my eyes a rest from your ugly pan."

The stenographer had just returned with three neatly typewritten sheets. I read my words and wrote my name at the bottom.

"I have it on good authority I'm a heartbreaker," I told Alderdyce, handing him the sheets.

"What's a dulcinea, anyway?" asked the sergeant.

5

The shooting at Eight Mile and Dequindre was on the radio. They got my name and occupation right, anyway. I switched to a music station and drove through coagulating dusk to my little three-room house west of Hamtramck, where I put my key in a door that was already unlocked. I'd locked it when I left that morning.

I went back for the Luger I keep in a special compartment under the dash, and when I had a round in the chamber I sneaked up on the door with my back to the wall and twisted the knob and pushed the door open at arm's length. When no bullets tore through the opening I eased the gun and my face past the door frame. Rena was sitting in my one easy chair in the living room with a .32 Remington automatic in her right hand and a bottle of scotch and a half-full glass standing on the end table on the other side.

"I thought it might be you," she said. "That's why I didn't shoot."

"Thanks for the vote of confidence."

"You ought to get yourself a dead-bolt lock. I've known how to slip latches since high school."

"All they taught me was algebra." I waved the Luger. "Can we put up the artillery? It's starting to get silly."

She laid the pistol in her lap. I snicked the safety into place on mine and put it on the table near the door and closed the door behind me. She picked up her glass and sipped from it. "You buy good whiskey. Keyhole peeping must pay pretty good."

"That's my Christmas bottle."

"Your friends must like you."

"I bought it for myself." I went into the kitchen and got a glass and filled it from the bottle.

She said, "The cops were waiting for me at my place. One of them was smoking a pipe. I smelled it the minute I hit my floor."

"The world's full of morons. Cops come in for their share." I drank.

"What's it going to cost me to get clear of this?"

"How much you got?"

She glanced down at the blue bag wedged between her left hip and the arm of the chair. It was a nice hip, long and slim with the pleated navy skirt stretched taut over it. "Five hundred."

I shrugged.

"All of it?"

"It'd run you that and more to put breathing space between you and Detroit," I said. "It wouldn't buy you a day in any of the safe houses in town."

"What will I eat on?"

"On the rest of it. You knew damn well I'd set my price at whatever you said you had, so I figure you knocked it down by at least half."

She twisted her lips in that way she had and opened the bag and peeled three C-notes and four fifties off a roll that would choke a tuba. I accepted the bills and riffled through them and stuck the wad in my inside breast pocket.

"How's Paul?" I asked.

"He's in Vegas," she answered automatically. Then she looked up at me quickly and pursed her lips. I cut her off.

"The cops know about you and old Peter Venito, may he rest in peace. The word on the street is young Paul inherited everything."

"Not everything."

I was lighting a cigarette and so didn't bother to shrug. I flipped the match into an ashtray. "Dave Tillet."

"I liked Dave. He wasn't like the others that worked for Paul.

He wanted to get out. He was all set to take the CPA exam in May."

"He didn't just like you," I said. "He was planning to marry you."

She raised her eyebrows. They were darker than her hair, two inverted commas over eyes that I saw now were ringed with red under her makeup. "I didn't know," she said quietly.

"Who dropped the dime on him?"

Now her face took on the hard sheen of polished metal. "All right, so you tricked me into admitting I knew Paul Venito. That doesn't mean I know the heavyweights he hires."

"You've answered my question. When a bookkeeper for the Mob starts making leaving noises, his employers start wondering where he's going with what he knows. What'd Venito do to get you to set up Dave?"

"I didn't set him up!"

I smoked and waited. In the silence she looked at the wall behind me and then at the floor and then at her hands on the purse in her lap and then she drained her glass and refilled it. The neck of the bottle jingled against the rim. She drank.

"Dave went into hiding a week ago because of some threats he said he got over his decision to quit," she said. "None of them came from Paul, but from his own fellow workers. He gave me a number where he could be reached and told me to memorize it and not write it down or give it to anyone else. I'd gone with Paul for a while after old Peter died and Paul knew I was seeing Dave and he came to my apartment yesterday and asked me where he could reach Dave. I wouldn't give him the number. He said he just wanted to talk to him and would I arrange a meeting without saying it would be with Paul. He was afraid Dave's fellow workers had poisoned him against the whole operation. He wanted to make Dave a cash offer to keep quiet about his, Paul's, activities and that if I cared for him and his future I'd agree to help. I said okay. It sounded like the Paul Venito I used to know," she added quickly. "He would spend thousands to avoid hurting someone; he said that was bad business and cost more in the long run."

"Who picked the spot?"

"Paul did. He called it neutral territory, halfway between Dave's place in Southfield and Paul's office downtown."

"It's also handy to expressways out of the city," I said. "So you set up the parley. Then what?"

"I called Paul's office today to ask him if I could sit in on the meeting. His secretary told me he left for Las Vegas last night. That's when I knew he had no intention of keeping his appointment, or of being anywhere near the place when whoever was keeping it for him went in to see Dave. I broke every law driving here, but—"

The metal sheen cracked apart then. She said, "Damn," and dug in her purse for a handkerchief. I watched her pawing blindly through the contents for a moment, then handed her mine. If it was an act it was sweet.

"Did anyone follow you here?" I asked.

She wiped her eyes, blew her nose as discreetly as a thing like that can be done, and looked up. Her cheeks were smeared blue-black. That was when I decided to believe her. You don't look like her and know how to turn the waterworks on and off without knowing how to keep your mascara from running too.

"I don't think so," she said. "I kept an eye out for cops and parked around the corner. Why?"

"Because if what you told me is straight, you're next on Venito's list of Things to Do Today. You're the only one who can connect him to that diner. Have you got a place to stay?"

"I guess one of the girls from the Roost could put me up."

"No, the cops will check them out. They'll hit all the hotels and motels too. You'd better stay here."

"Oh." She gave me her crooked smile. "That plus the five hundred, is that how it goes?"

"I'll toss you for the bed. Loser gets the couch."

"You don't like blonds?"

"I'm not sure I ever met one. But it has something to do with not going to the bathroom where you eat. Give me your keys and I'll stash your car in the garage. Cops'll have a BOL out on it by now."

She was reaching inside her purse when the door buzzer blew us a raspberry. Her hand went to the baby Remington. I touched a finger to my lips and pointed at the bedroom door. She got up clutching her purse and the gun and went into the bedroom and pushed the door shut, or almost. She left a crack. I retrieved my handkerchief stained with her makeup from the chair and put it in a pocket and picked up the Luger and said, "Who is it?"

"Alderdyce."

I opened the door. He glanced down at the gun as if it were a loose button on my jacket and walked around me into the living room. "Expecting trouble?"

"It's a way of life in this town." I safetied the Luger and returned it to the table.

"You alone?" He looked around.

"Who's asking, you or the department?"

He said nothing, circling the living room with his hands in his pockets. He stopped near the bedroom door and sniffed the air. "Nice cologne. A little feminine."

"Even detectives have a social life," I said.

"You couldn't prove it by me."

I killed my cigarette butt and fought the tug to reach for a replacement. "You didn't come all this way to do 'Who's on First' with me."

"We tracked down Paul Venito. I thought you'd want to know."

"In Vegas?"

He moved his large close-cropped head from side to side slowly. "At Detroit Metropolitan Airport. Stiff as a stick in the trunk of a stolen Oldsmobile."

6

The antique clock my grandfather bought for his mother knocked
out the better part of a minute with no competition. I shook out
my last Winston and smoothed it between my fingers. "Shot?"

"Three times with a twenty-two. Twice in the chest, once in
the ear. Sound familiar?"

"Yeah." I speared my lips with the cigarette and lit up. "How
long's he been dead?"

"That's up to the M.E. Twelve hours anyway. He was a cold
cut long before Tillet bought it."

"Which means what?"

He shook his head again. His coarse face was drawn in the
light of the one lamp I had burning.

"My day rate's two-fifty," I said. "If you're talking about consulting."

"I'm talking about withholding evidence and obstruction of justice. The Murrow woman is getting to be important, and I think
you know where she is."

I smoked and said nothing.

"It's this tingly feeling I get," he said. "Happens every time a
case involves a woman and Amos Walker too."

"Christ, John, all I did was order the chicken on a roll."

"I hope that's all you did. I sure hope."

We watched each other. Suddenly he seized the knob and
pushed open the bedroom door, scooping his police special out of his
belt holster. I lunged forward, then held back. The room was empty.

He went inside and looked out the open window and checked
the closet and got down in push-up position to peer under the bed.
Rising, he holstered the .38 and dusted his palms off against each
other. "Perfume's stronger in here," he observed.

"I told you I was a heartbreaker."

"Make sure that's all you're breaking."

"Is this where you threaten to trash my license?"

"That's up to the state police," he said. "What I can do is tank you and link your name to that diner shoot for the reporters until little old ladies in Grosse Pointe won't trust you to walk their poodles."

On that chord he left me. John and I had been friendly a long time. But no matter how long you are something, you are not that something a lot longer.

7

So far I had two corpses and no Rena Murrow. It was time to punt. I dialed Great Lakes Importers, Paul Venito's legitimate front, but there was no answer. Well, it was way past closing time; in an orderly society even the crooks keep regular hours. I thawed something out for supper and watched an old Kirk Douglas film on television and turned in.

The next morning was misty gray with the bitter-metal smell of rain in the air. I broke out the foul-weather gear and drove to the Great Lakes building on East Grand River.

The reception area, kept behind glass like expensive cigars in a tobacco shop, was oval shaped with passages spiking out from it, decorated in orange sherbet with a porcelain doll seated behind a curved desk. She wore a tight pink cashmere sweater and a black skirt slit to her ears.

"Amos Walker to see Mr. Venito," I said.

"I'm sorry. Mr. Venito's suffered a tragic accident." Her voice was honey over velvet. It would be.

"Who took his place?"

"That would be Mr. DeMarco. But he's very busy."

"I'll wait." I pulled a thermos bottle full of hot coffee out of the slash pocket of my trench coat and sat down on an orange couch across from her desk.

The porcelain doll lifted her telephone receiver and spoke into it. A few minutes later, two men in tailored blue suits came out of one of the passages and stood over me, and that was when the front crumbled.

"Position."

I wasn't sure which of them had spoken. They looked alike down to the scar tissue over their eyes. I screwed the top back on the thermos and stood and placed my palms against the wall. One of them kicked my feet apart and patted me down from tie to socks, removing my hat last and peering inside for atomic devices. I wasn't carrying. He replaced the hat.

"Okay, this way."

I accompanied them down the passage with a man on either side. We went through a door marked P. VENITO into an office the size of Hart Plaza with green wall-to-wall carpeting and one wall that was all glass, before which stood a tall man with a fringe of gray hair and a neat Vandyke beard. His suit was tan and clung like sunlight to his trim frame.

"Mr. Walker?" he said pleasantly. "I'm Fred DeMarco. I was Mr. Venito's associate. This is a terrible thing that's happened."

"More terrible for him than you," I said.

He cocked his head and frowned. "This office, you mean. It's just a room. Paul's father had it before him and someone will have it after me. I recognized your name from the news. Weren't you involved in the shooting of this Tillet person yesterday?"

I nodded. "If you call being a witness involved. But you don't have to call him 'this Tillet person.' He worked for you."

"He worked for Great Lakes Importers, like me. I never knew him. The firm employs many people, most of whom I haven't had the chance to meet."

"My information is he was killed because he was leaving Great Lakes and someone was afraid he'd peddle what he knew."

"We're a legitimate enterprise, Mr. Walker. We have nothing to hide. Tillet was let go. Our accounting department is handled mostly by computers now and he elected not to undergo retraining. Whatever he was involved with outside the firm that led to his death has nothing to do with Great Lakes."

"For someone who never met him you know a lot about Tillet," I said.

"I had his file pulled for the police."

"Isn't it kind of a big coincidence that your president and one of your bookkeepers should both be shot to death within a few hours of each other, and with the same caliber pistol?"

"The police were here again last night to ask that same question," DeMarco said. "My answer is the same. If, like Tillet, Paul had dangerous outside interests, they are hardly of concern here."

I got out a Winston and tapped it on the back of my hand. "You've been on the laundering end too long, Mr. DeMarco. You think you've gotten away from playing hardball. Just because you can afford a tailor and a better barber doesn't mean you aren't still Freddy the Mark, who came up busting heads for Peter Venito in the bad old days."

One of the blue suits backhanded the cigarette out of my mouth as I was getting set to light it. "Mr. DeMarco doesn't allow smoking."

"That's enough, Andy." DeMarco's tone was even. "I was just a boy when Prohibition ended, Walker. Peter took me in and almost adopted me. I learned the business and when I got back from the war and college I showed him how to modernize, cut expenses, and increase profits. For thirty years I practically ran the organization. Then Peter died and his son took over and I was back to running errands. But for the good of the firm I drew my pay and kept my mouth shut. We're legitimate now and I mean for it to stay that way. I wouldn't jeopardize it for the likes of Dave Tillet."

"I think you would do just that. You remember a time when no one quit the organization, and when Tillet gave notice and you found out young Paul had arranged to buy his silence instead of making dead sure of it, you took Paul out of the way and then slammed the door on Tillet."

"You're fishing, Walker."

"Why not? I've got Rena Murrow for bait."

The room got quiet. Outside the glass, fourteen floors down, traffic glided along Grand River with all the noise of fish swimming in an aquarium.

"She set up the meet with Tillet for Venito," I went on. "She can tie Paul to that diner at Eight Mile and Dequindre and with a little work the cops will tie you to that trunk at Metro Airport. She can finger your two button men. Looking down the wrong end of life in Jackson, they'll talk."

"Get him out of here," DeMarco snarled.

The blue suits came toward me. I got out of there. I could use the smoke anyway.

8

I was closing my front door behind me when Rena came out of the bedroom. She had fixed her makeup since the last time I had seen her, but she had on the same navy suit and it was starting to look like a navy suit she had had on for two days.

I said, "You remembered to relock the door this time."

She nodded. "I stayed in a motel last night. The cops haven't got to them all yet. But I couldn't hang around. They get suspicious when you don't have luggage."

"You can't stay here. I just painted a bull's-eye on my back for Fred DeMarco." I told her what I'd told him.

"I can't identify the men who killed Dave," she protested.

"Freddy the Mark doesn't know that." I lifted the telephone. "I'm getting you a cab ride to police headquarters and then I'm calling the cops. Things are going to get interesting as soon as DeMarco gets over his mad."

The doorbell buzzed. This time I didn't have to tell her. She went into the bedroom and I got my Luger off the table and opened the door on a man who was a little shorter than I, with gray eyes like nickels on a pad. He had traded his windbreaker for a brown leather jacket but it looked like the same .22 target pistol in his right hand. Without the ski mask he looked about my age, with streaks of premature gray in his neat brown hair.

I waved the Luger and said, "Mine's bigger."

"Old movie line," he said with a sigh. "Take a gander behind you."

That was an old movie line too. I didn't turn. Then someone gasped and I stepped back and moved my head just enough to get the corner of my eye working. A man a little taller than Gray Eyes, with black hair to his collar and a handlebar mustache, stood behind Rena this side of the bedroom door with a squat .38 planted against her neck. His other hand was out of sight and the way Rena was standing said he had her left arm twisted behind her back. He too had ditched his windbreaker and was in shirtsleeves. The lighter-caliber gun he had used on Tillet and probably on Paul Venito would be scrap by now.

It seemed I was the only one who needed a key to get into my house.

"Two beats one, Zorro." Gray Eyes's tone remained tired and I figured out that was his normal voice. He stepped over the threshold and leaned the door shut. "Let's have the Heine." He held out his free hand.

"Uh-uh," I said. "I give it to you and then you shoot us."

"You don't, we shoot the girl first. Then you."

"You'll do that anyway. This way maybe I shoot you too."

Mustache shifted his weight. Rena shrieked. My eyes flickered that way. Gray Eyes swept the barrel of the .22 across my face and grasped the end of the Luger. I fired. The report gulped up all the sound in the room. Mustache let go of Rena and swung the .38 my way. She knocked up his arm and red flame streaked ceilingward. Rena dived for her blue bag on the easy chair. Mustache aimed at her back. I swung the Luger, but Gray Eyes was still standing and fired the .22. Something plucked at my left bicep. The front window exploded then, and Mustache was lifted off his feet and flung backward against the wall, his gun flying. The nasty cracking report followed an instant later.

I looked at Gray Eyes, but he was down now, his gun still in his hand but forgotten, both hands clasped over his abdomen with the blood dark between his fingers. I relieved him of the weapon and put it with the Luger on the table. Rena was half-reclining in the easy chair with her skirt hiked up over one long leg and her .32 Remington in both hands pointing at Mustache dead on the floor. She hadn't fired.

"Walker?"

The voice was tinny and artificially loud. But I recognized it.

"We're all right, John," I called. "Put down that bullhorn and come in." I told Rena to drop the automatic. She obeyed, in a daze.

Alderdyce came in with his gun drawn and looked at the man still alive at his feet and across at the other man who wasn't and at Rena. I introduced them. "She didn't set up Tillet," I added. "Fred DeMarco bought the hit, not Venito. This one will get around to telling you that if you stop gawking and call an ambulance before he's done bleeding into his belly."

"For you too, maybe." Alderdyce picked up the telephone.

He'd seen me grasping my left arm. "Just a crease," I said. "Like in the cowboy pictures."

"You're lucky. I know you, Walker. It's your style to set yourself up as the goat to smoke out a guy like DeMarco. I had men watching the place and had you tailed to and from Great Lakes. When the girl broke in we loaded the neighborhood. Then these two showed—" He broke off and started speaking into the mouthpiece.

I said, "My timing was off. I'm glad yours was better."

The bearded black sergeant came in with some uniformed officers, one of whom carried a 30.06 rifle with a mounted scope. "Nice shooting," Alderdyce told him, hanging up. "What's your name?"

"Officer Carl Breen, Lieutenant." He spelled it.

"Okay."

I let go of my arm and wiped the blood off my hand with my handkerchief and got out my wallet, counting out two hundred and fifty dollars, which I held out to Rena. "My day rate's two-fifty."

She was sitting up now, looking at the money. "Why'd you ask for five hundred?"

"You had your mind made up about me. It saved a speech."

"Keep it. You earned it and a lot more than I can pay."

I folded the bills and stuck them inside the outer breast pocket of her navy jacket. "I'd just blow it on cigarettes and whiskey."

"Who's the broad?" demanded the sergeant.

I thought of telling him that's what a dulcinea was, but the joke was old. We waited for the ambulance.

The surviving gunman's name was Richard Bledsoe. He had two priors in the Detroit area for ADW, one conviction, and after he was released from the hospital into custody he turned state's evidence and convicted Fred DeMarco on two counts of conspiracy to commit murder. DeMarco's appeal is still pending. The dead man went by Austin Grant and had done seven years in San Quentin for second-degree homicide knocked down from murder one. The Detroit police worked a deal with the Justice Department and got Rena Murrow relocation and a new identity to shield her from DeMarco's friends. I never saw her again.

I never ate in Butch's diner again, either. These days you can't get in the place without a reservation.

· ROB KANTNER ·

Fly Away Home

From 1986 through 1989 Rob Kantner took home three of four possible Shamus Awards for best paperback PI novel. In 1986 he also won the Shamus for best short story. That feat—winning two awards in one year—has only been duplicated by Lawrence Block in 1993. Kantner is, therefore, along with Lawrence Block, a four-time winner.

THE PIGEONS DESCEND IN TWOS AND THREES, LIGHTING ON THE short ledge at the edge of the roof. They flutter and strut among the debris and droppings, warbling deep in their throats. Occasionally two or three collide, and there is a squawking, flap-winged argument, with the loser taking wing in a shallow dive off the ledge.

I watch them intently, a cigarette smoldering in one hand, a coffee cup steaming black in the other. It is early summer and early in the morning in Detroit. The city comes awake with increasing sounds of traffic from fourteen floors below. To the south the heavily industrialized Zug Island sends smoke into the air to war with the haze. To the east freighters bay on the Detroit River. Up here I am alone with my coffee and my cigarette, dressed as always in white shirt, neatly clipped tie, dark pants, and black wing-tipped shoes. I look like a clerk, which I am; and I look like I'm about to begin another routine workday, which I am not.

The pigeons descend in twos and threes, lighting on the ledge at the edge of the roof. The turnover is constant, new birds descending to the ledge, others dropping away. Where do they go? A phrase comes to mind from nowhere: fly away home. Fly away home. I think it's a nursery rhyme. Probably recited to me by my grandmother many years ago. I cannot remember the rest of the poem. I do remember my grandmother, and I see her fresh in my mind's eye, kneeling at her flower bed, short spade in hand, straightening and smiling and rising as she watches me approach. . . .

Footsteps sound from behind me, ascending the seldom-used stairwell that rises from the guts of the building to the roof. I turn impatiently, waiting to see who is coming. It was the sound of footsteps like these that started the mess, just a week ago. . . .

I turned as the footsteps reached the top of the stairs and crushed out my cigarette as Connie came through the door. She was a big, beefy bull of a woman, dressed in an immense purple balloon of a dress, with dark brown hair permed high on her head. She had a happy, goofy, angelic face, except when she was forced to talk to me. "Someone to see you," she said flatly, standing at the door to the stairway as if afraid to come out on the roof toward me.

I glanced at my watch. "Well, *who*, Connie? The workday doesn't start for fifteen minutes."

"Maurie's lawyer," she said through a pinched mouth. "And she's brought some kind of detective with her. You'd better get down there. They're going to interview everybody today, in alphabetical order."

That put me first on the list. Bad luck. I huffed a sigh and followed Connie down the dark stairwell. As we approached the heavy fire door leading into our company's suite of offices, she turned to me, face softer and somewhat scared, and said, "You don't think Maurie did it, do you?"

"I'm sure of it," I said sincerely.

Connie's meaty, clownish face looked somber. "Mo was such a nice girl. Maurie is, too. I just can't believe Maurie would kill her. Think there's a chance the lawyer can get her off?"

"There's always a chance, Connie," I said heavily. We entered the suite, air-conditioning gushing coolly against my hot, moist skin. "Where are they waiting?"

Before my eyes, as if she realized who she was talking to, Connie's face changed back to that look, that look that women always had for me: suspicion, contempt, loathing. "Conference B," she answered through pinched lips, and swept away from me.

I headed over there.

I entered the room, closed the door behind me, and stood still, feet apart, hands clasped at my waist in front of me, a polite smile on my face. To my left, at the head of the conference table sat a tall blond woman in her mid-thirties, dressed in a navy blue skirt, matching jacket, and white blouse with spaghetti-thin ties down the front. She had dark eyes, a creamy complexion, and a snub nose, plus a look of competent self-importance. A thin hand-tooled leather briefcase sat open on the table in front of her.

To her right sat a broad-shouldered, very tan, very fit-looking man in his early forties. His full head of thick black hair swept back along the sides and down to the collar. His dark blue eyes shone brightly from the deep tan of his face, and he had a variety of laugh and squint lines to go with the broken nose, broad forehead, and squarish jaw; but mostly he looked sleepy, cynical, contemptuous, inimical. His short-sleeved chambray shirt revealed hard, tanned, heavily muscled arms matted thickly with black hair; intermittently, whitish scars showed against the tan. Below, he wore jeans. In appearance and dress he looked better suited to mowing lawns or digging graves than to presenting himself for discussions in a professional place of business.

Taking the bit in my teeth, I introduced myself and went on. "The lawyer and the detective. Which, may I ask, is which?"

The man looked bored, the woman amused. "I'm Carole Somers, Maureen Frye's attorney." She tipped her head toward the man. "This is the private detective I've retained to assist me in the case. Ben Perkins."

The detective's eyes locked on mine, and instantly I knew him. I knew those men, all of them. Muscled and tanned, with full heads of hair, big white smiles, hearty laughs, and slaps on the rumps, jokes and repartee that turned English into a foreign language. Oh, yes, I knew those men. The high school jocks who stared through their intellectual superiors as if they were bugs, who drove fast cars, joked easily with big-busted girls, and were handy with tools. I knew those men, all right. The slow-moving, lazy hunks who cluttered dark after-hours bars, who bought lottery tickets and cheap beer in dozen lots, who wolfed down ground rounds and watched big-TV sports with packs of their fellows in bowling alley cocktail lounges.

If Perkins read anything in my face—something I worked hard to avoid—he didn't show it. He nodded at me, extracted a short cork-tipped cigar from his shirt pocket, and with the snap of a wood match on his thumbnail began filling the conference room with an evil stench.

Carole Somers said briskly, "Please be seated. We'll try not to take up too much of your time."

I took a chair and composed myself neatly, watching the two as Somers took a yellow legal pad out of her briefcase and Perkins smoked his cigar. I wondered if they had gone to bed together, and then I was sure they had, probably many times.

Somers looked at me, face expectant, professional. "Maureen Stevens: 'Mo.' Maureen Frye: 'Maurie.' " She paused. "Tell me about them, please."

I shrugged. Under the stares of the lawyer and the detective, my palms became moist; to dry them off, I placed them on the padded arms of the chair. "I don't know much. They worked here together. They shared an apartment. They were close friends and well enough liked by everyone who knew them. This past Monday, Mo was found bludgeoned to death here in the office. The police have arrested Maurie and charged her with murder." I smiled indulgently. "Maurie has retained you to help her. You have retained this man to help you." I raised my now-dry hands palms up. "Not much help, I'm afraid."

"You're doing fine," Somers said without raising her eyes from her notes. "Do you personally believe that Maurie killed Mo?"

"No." Palms dry now, heart pounding steadily, mind icily calm, I felt gutsy, daring, brave. "I am convinced she did not."

Somers's eyes met mine. "The police have what they believe is a strong case. During nonworking hours, only authorized personnel are permitted access to the offices. They must sign in at the security guard's desk downstairs. Mo was here very early in the morning, as was her habit; and during the time she was here, only Maurie signed in downstairs. Further, the police theorize, there was some competition between the two—competition for men, leading possibly to a motive of jealousy."

"Certainly Maurie denies that," I said stoutly.

"Of course." Far as Somers was concerned, the detective, Perkins, was not in the room, which would have been fine with me. She was cute. "Maurie says she stopped at the office to pick up some proofs that had to be at the printer first thing in the morning. She swears that Mo was alive when she got there, that she talked with her, that Mo was alive and well when she left. She saw no one else in the office or elsewhere in the building except for the security guard. Further, while both women were single and, ah, fairly active in their involvement with men, there was total openness and communication between the two, and no jealousy between them as far as Maurie was concerned."

I ignored the vacant stare of the beefy detective and kept my eyes candid and friendly on the luscious Carole Somers. "That is consistent with my observations," I said. As usual, particularly when talking to a woman, I felt I sounded stilted and pompous, but Carole did not seem to notice.

She leaned back in her chair and studied me. "In your observation, would you characterize Mo and Maurie as, shall we say, fast women?"

"Nice girls, both of them," I retorted.

She smiled. "Please. There is already evidence on record attesting to a certain level of what some would characterize as promiscuity. It speaks well for you that you defend your friends, but what I think of you personally is irrelevant. I remind you that Maurie is charged with first-degree murder, and if I'm to defend her adequately, I must have the truth."

"Well." I adjusted myself in my chair, studied the backs of my hands, found the detective's flat, vacant stare, and turned my eyes to the lawyer. "You're interviewing everyone in the office today, so I might as well be the one to tell you. Mo and Maurie were—how shall I phrase this?—cheerfully voracious where men were concerned. One heard . . . jokes about them. Some referred to them as 'The Maureens.' As in, 'The Maureens are looking for a few good men.'" I smiled sadly. "I felt that such jokes were in the worst possible taste. Not at all what I consider appropriate in a professional setting." I felt perfectly composed now, strong, confident, secure.

Ben Perkins began to stub out his filthy-smelling cigar in an ashtray and spoke for the first time. "You get any of that?"

"I'm sorry?" I asked politely.

His eyes stayed on his cigar as he crushed it. "Either one of them. Or both."

I played dumb. "I'm afraid I don't follow you."

Perkins finished snuffing his cigar and rubbed his jaw with the back of a heavily knuckled hand as he fixed his blue eyes on me. "What I'm asking you is, was one of those 'few good men' you?"

Irrelevantly, I detected a trace of a southern accent in his heavy, husky voice. I brought myself up straight in my chair and looked at Carole Somers. Rather than giving Perkins an annoyed look, she was watching me expectantly. So.

"I'm a married man," I said, allowing some heat to enter my voice.

"So?" Perkins responded, the syllable a Neanderthal grunt.

I gnawed my lip impatiently. "Certainly not."

Perkins did not change expression. He leaned forward, elbows on knees, eyes on me. "Worked here long?"

"Many years."

"Associate with either Maureen away from the office?"

"I believe it imprudent to develop personal relationships with coworkers. That is my rule."

Paper ripped as Carole Somers tore a blank sheet of paper off her pad. She slid it over to me, along with a pen. "Write something."

Smooth team. Smooth team. But so stupid. They watched me as I selected a pen from the plastic carrier in my pocket and, without a word of protest, wrote the standard "quick brown fox" sentence on the paper. "Satisfied?"

"Right-handed," Perkins told Carole Somers.

"Brilliant deduction, Ben," she answered sarcastically.

That would have angered me, but Perkins only grinned. To me he said with infuriating jauntiness, "Medical examiner says whoever beat Mo to death was left-handed. How they figure that kind of thing I'll never know."

"And you suspect *me*," I said stiffly.

Carole Somers said evenly, "I have an obligation to my client to conduct a full investigation."

"Seems to me that's a job for the police."

Perkins snorted. "Police already figure they got their perp. Maurie's left-handed. She can be placed at the scene at the approximate time of the murder. Motive can be presumed. Detroit's finest are overworked, understaffed; they'll grab the path of least resistance and go for it."

I consciously steadied myself down, forced myself to relax in the chair. Somers and Perkins watched me blandly. I made a smile and said, "Certainly no one would be more happy to see Maurie cleared than myself. I do not doubt that she is innocent." I scratched the bare skin on the side of my head. "But, Mr. Perkins, what makes *you* think she's innocent?"

Perkins leaned back in his chair and crossed an ankle over his knee. Eyes empty, he answered quite lazily, "Yeah, well, number one, I'm being paid to think so. Plus, I've talked to her, and I really do believe it."

Carole Somers had her elegant hands folded over her pad. Obviously she was finished questioning me, and I wanted to be gone, but Perkins kept talking. "Anyway, these things generally get sorted out if someone who gives a damn goes to work on 'em. Guys like me, who make a living asking around and checking up, get a feel for this stuff, get experience, whereas guys who do murder tend not to do it but once, so they don't get experience, and they leave tracks. See? I'll mess with it awhile and get it sorted out."

The big, hard-muscled man sounded so matter-of-fact, so confident, so strong, that I felt loathing rise in me like a gorge. I consciously willed it from showing on my face. Of Somers I asked, "Is there any other way I can be of service?"

"No. You're excused. And many thanks for your help." She gave me a sincere, radiant smile, but it was too late; my interest in her was gone; she'd blown it; anybody who'd go to bed with a man like Perkins could be of no use to me.

"Thank *you.*" I went to the conference room door and, before leaving, turned back toward Perkins. "Any theories as to the actual murderer?"

Perkins was lighting another filthy cigar. "Nary a one." He puffed. "I don't work that way; I start out clean. One thing, though." He pulled the cigar from his mouth and looked at me. "Judging from the pics of the stiff, whoever did her must have had one hell of a reason."

He was certainly right about that. But where did it begin?

Perhaps at home, with Pam. Married eleven years; friends for, perhaps, the first seven. It did not change overnight. As our jobs got worse, and the money tighter, the economy sank its teeth into us. We got older and heavier, less vigorous and more bored. Friends and colleagues moved up in their careers and away to the coasts, leaving us behind; or they bought houses in the suburbs, began to rear fat babies, and preferred to associate with others like them rather than us.

And the guerrilla warfare began. The ambushes. From in the kitchen, or over the phone, or in bed at night. "Why don't you get a better job? Why don't you fight for a promotion? When are you going to stand up for yourself? That piece-of-junk car of mine is going; what are you going to do about *that*? I need *money*. We'll *never* be able to buy a house, *never*. Everybody has nice houses. Everybody has nice cars. Everybody goes on nice vacations. Everybody else but *us*. And all *you* do is sit here with your nose stuck in a book. When are you going to *do* something? When? When? *When?*"

I was a good husband and provider. I changed jobs and worked desperately hard to improve my position and advance myself. I did it all for her and it was never enough. And the time came when I realized that if there was to be a reward, I would have to get it for myself. I had earned it, and I was going to get it.

That was when I decided on Mo Stevens. Everyone else enjoyed her. Why not me?

As the two-day computer seminar in Cleveland drew near, I made it a point to stop by her desk frequently. I was clumsy and shy, as always, but she, unlike the other women at the company, was offhand and friendly, with lots of secretive smiles and casual, seemingly accidental brushings.

On the first day of the seminar, we sat at opposite sides of the classroom. Among the forty other attendees and the droning instructor, in the hot, stuffy August heat, our glances met many times. I felt alone with her. I felt eager and energized for the first time in years.

That night I asked her to dinner. She pleaded a headache and said she'd stay in her room, but she smiled regretfully and, before retiring, gave my arm a warm squeeze that lasted the rest of the night.

The second evening—our last in Cleveland—we had drinks and then dinner. We talked about everything but the real subject. I strolled back to her room with her. She got out her key. I reached for the key and took her hand instead, awkwardly. She faced me, a searching, speculative look on her face. Then she leaned forward and kissed me. I moved against her and kissed her hard. Her arms went around me, the key clinking against my back. She pulled back, a secretive, knowing smile on her face, and said, "B plus." Then she unlocked her door, swung it open, and beckoned me in.

Back home in Detroit, I spent the next two days—Saturday and Sunday—waiting for Monday, waiting to see Mo at the office. It was terribly hot, and Pam was at her vicious best, but for once she didn't get to me. Because now I had Mo. I wanted to call her right away but didn't dare; I respected the fact that she'd want our relationship to be kept a deadly secret. So I waited, strung out with happy, excited anticipation.

On Monday morning I found her at her desk. She smiled at me but kept her manner cool and professional. Good lass, I thought; good lass. Casually I invited her to lunch. She declined, pleading a doctor's appointment.

On Tuesday I went out during my lunch hour and rented a room at the Sheraton Cadillac. I called home and informed Pam that a business emergency required me to go to Toledo that night. Back at the office I wrote a brief note, sealed it in an envelope, and left it on Mo's desk. At quitting time I fairly flew to the Sheraton, ate a quick dinner, then went to the room and waited. I waited till past eleven o'clock, and Mo never arrived.

Mo wasn't at her desk much on Wednesday. I finally encountered her emerging from the conference room. Placing myself between her and the others, I clumsily asked her what had gone wrong the night before. Her face froze, she stared through me, then she made an icy smile, shook her head, and walked away.

She didn't come to work on Thursday. I did my work in a state of nervous, preoccupied dread. At lunchtime I called Mo's apartment. When she heard my voice, she hung up.

The next day I felt none of the usual end-of-the-week relief. I stayed in my cubicle, sorting and shuffling my papers and typing my forms, feeling strangely immobile and detached, dreading going home, dreading staying in the office. Just before lunchtime, I heard voices in the passageway outside my cubicle, and Mo glanced in at me. She turned to her companion, excused herself, then entered, set a file down on the table before me, opened it, and bent down as if to discuss something in the file with me.

But what she said, in a voice light and airy enough to have caused no interest in anyone who couldn't understand the words, was: "Listen, you warped little creep, maybe Cleveland gave you the wrong idea. That was a one-shot, you understand? A whim. The fact is, you make my skin crawl. There is no way it will ever happen again, because even standing this close to you makes me want to puke. Is that clear? Have I made myself very, very clear now?" She closed the file, gave me a casual wave for public consumption, and left. I sat there, a noise like a waterfall roaring in my head.

The noise roared in my head through the weekend and was still there the following Monday, very, very early in the morning, as I stood with my back to the wall, around the corner from Mo and Maurie as they chatted lightly in the deserted office. When Maurie left, I walked around the corner and toward Mo's desk. She jumped when she saw me, her eyes flashed briefly, then her face paled as I brought the short length of lead pipe from behind me and tapped its end lightly in my palm.

I asked, "Am I too close now, Mo? You feel like puking, maybe?"

She slowly rolled on her chair back from her desk. Her eyes

grew and grew, and she started to say something, but her mouth was too dry.

I kept approaching her, tapping the pipe. "How about your skin? Is it crawling now, Mo?"

She lunged clumsily up from her chair. I took a final step, gripped the pipe with both hands, and swung in a flat, arm's-length arc. I didn't feel the impact, but she flew back as if jerked off her feet by a rope around her neck and sprawled with a blaze of tan legs and white underwear over her chair. The roaring in my head built suddenly to full gain as I kicked her chair aside, straddled her like a runner in the starting blocks, and dealt her the two-handed swing again, again, again, again. Over the roaring I heard my own voice: "Made myself clear now, Mo? How about it, Pam? Have I made myself clear? How about it, Mo?" And then it was just the two names, Mo, Pam, Mo, Pam, as if I didn't know who it was.

In the days that followed my interview with Carole Somers and Ben Perkins, I saw the detective around a few times.

I saw him one afternoon in the pub on the ground floor of our building, drinking beer (naturally) and chatting with a handful of people from our company. He gave me a sober-faced wave and nod, nothing more.

I saw him in one of the back halls of our office suite as I was sweeping up the shards of a coffee carafe that one of our clumsy secretaries had dropped on the way to the conference room. As he passed me, Perkins gave me a crooked grin and a nod, nothing more.

I saw him at the curb of Congress Street, leaning out the window of his souped-up blue Mustang (naturally), chatting with Bernie, an elderly, humpbacked man who from time immemorial had been a private message runner and one-man delivery service for downtown companies. Perkins didn't see me that time.

Otherwise I knew nothing about Perkins's "investigation." And I didn't think about it. My plan had been sound, the execution flawless. No subeducated, inarticulate grunt was going to make a case on me. Besides, my thoughts centered on my other problem. The one with Pam's name on it.

I stare impatiently at the stairwell as Ben Perkins emerges onto the sun-drenched roof. He squints from the light but seems unsurprised to see me. He says, "Told you I'd sort it out."

Does he really think I'm such a fool? "I don't want to hear about it." I flick away my half-smoked cigarette.

"Sure you do." Perkins grins. "They all do." Today he's as well dressed as he probably ever gets, in a blue blazer, matching slacks, open-collar white dress shirt. The warm morning breeze whips his thick black hair as the pigeons wheel in the air above us, light on the ledge to my left, and drop into space to fly away home.

Perkins glances around the roof, probably looking for a place to sit. There is none, except the ledge, so instead he leans against the wall and with a big, knuckly hand fetches one of his short cigars out of his blazer pocket. "I found that other way into the building, the one you used to get past the security guard."

I stare at him. The front of my face feels numb. "You think I killed Mo?"

He flares a wood match on his thumbnail, applies the flame to the end of his cigar, and nods as he puffs. "Oh yeah," he answers casually, waving the match out and tossing it. "See, I talked to old Bernie, the delivery fella. He's been working these buildings for years, knows 'em better than the rats. This building wasn't always secure; used to be a passageway on the sixth floor between the Olivetti firm's offices and this building. Hardly anybody remembers it now. But you used to work for Olivetti, right?"

I deny him the satisfaction of changing expression. He shrugs easily. "Show me how you bat," he says casually.

Defiantly I start into the stance, then freeze and straighten again. Perkins's eyes are cold and assured. "Lefty," he murmurs. "You write right-handed, sure. But I saw you swinging a broom the other day. You're sort of ambidextrous. For some reason, lefty's the way you swing a bat, a broom, an ax—and a club. Right?"

I hear the pigeons flapping off the ledge. Traffic noise builds from fourteen floors below as the morning rush hour begins. I sneer at Perkins. "Not precisely what I'd call hanging evidence, Perkins."

"Hey, man's got to try." He puffs on his cigar, studying me. "That Mo, she liked action, right? What'd she do? Turn you down? Or tumble and then dump you? It's an old story, man. A real old story."

As if Perkins cares. I notice that he has positioned himself near the door, as if to intercept me should I try to escape. Fool.

Perkins folds his arms across his chest with his cigar jutting from two fingers, and yawns. "Anyway, I talked it over with the detectives. They got a search warrant last night for your house. They're there right now. Checking your clothes and stuff. For evidence and that. Routine."

My eyes close for just an instant, and in that instant I see what the police will find. Mo, Pam! Mo, Pam!

I turn and stroll casually to the ledge. Pigeons glare and scatter with fluttering squawks as I sit on the ledge with my forearms on my knees, facing the detective. He's stood and taken a couple of steps toward me, eyes narrow. I smile at him. The narrow, tense expression wipes away, and he says, "Well, that about covers it. Come on, let's go downstairs. It's getting right hot up here."

I feel the empty air behind me. Now I can hear the traffic much clearer from the street fourteen floors down. Perkins stands fifteen, twenty feet away from me, waiting for an answer that does not come. Through my mind runs the litany: fly away, fly away, fly away home. Then I remember: it's about a ladybug. Figures. Helpless insect, eaten alive by stronger ones.

Perkins says in a low, calm voice, "You know, once some wise men got together to come up with an absolutely universal truth, and what they came up with was, 'This, too, shall pass.' "

"So?"

He smiles in what I imagine to be a friendly fashion, but I

know better; he's no friend. Men like him never are. He says, "You can get past this, pal."

I'm too tired to argue. I simply say, "No."

"You don't want to die. No matter how bad things are, you don't really want to die. Nobody does. You know why? Because there's nothing then. No rushing wind, no blinding light, no incredible feeling of peace, no welcoming faces of the previously departed. There's absolute, stone-cold nothing."

Fresh in my mind's eye I see my grandmother, kneeling at her flower bed, short spade in hand, straightening and smiling and rising as she watches me approach. I snarl at Perkins, "Spare me your supermarket-tabloid shrink shtick, Perkins."

His voice is still gentle. "Come on, walk back over here."

"No."

His face changes, goes dark and angry, the tendons showing against the tan skin as his jaw tightens. "Okay, so what the hell do *I* care? Go ahead, jump. World could sure use one less sniveling, twisted, four-eyed pukebag. Only thing, I hope you don't land on some innocent citizen down there. Be a real shame if a normal person got hurt by a sick piece of worthless garbage like you. Go ahead, jump! Have a nice trip!"

I grin with contempt at this futile stratagem. He wants to anger me, make me attack him so he can drag me away from the ledge. Even if I hadn't seen *Dirty Harry* and known how the con is supposed to work, it wouldn't have, because all my rage is gone. I am harmless now and know what I am going to do, and no one can stop me, most particularly this son of a bitch.

In the long pause, the traffic noise builds from the amphitheater far, far below. Perkins knots his fists. "What are ya, chicken? Need a hand? Well, buddy, happy to oblige. Call me a public-spirited citizen." He starts for me.

I tease him and play with him and tempt him, sitting still, letting him think I'm so stupid I'll let him grab me and pull me away from the ledge. Just as he lunges for me, I tumble over backward and leave the ledge.

And get just a glimpse of Perkins's reaction, which fills me with joy. His face is a mask of shock, horror, fear, despair.

The wind tears at my clothes and blinds my eyes as I laugh soundlessly. I've beaten him! I've won! I've—

Grandmother?

GRANDMOTHER?

· ED GORMAN ·

Turn Away

Ed Gorman wears many hats, but none so well fitted as short story writer. Already with two individual collections under his belt he is well respected for his abilities in many different genres. His earlier works, however, appeared in the PI genre, such as this gem.

O
N THURSDAY SHE WAS THERE AGAIN. (THIS WAS ON A SOAP opera he'd picked up by accident looking for a western movie to watch because he was all caught up on his work.) Parnell had seen her Monday but not Tuesday then not Wednesday either. But Thursday she was there again. He didn't know her name, hell it didn't matter, she was just this maybe twenty-two twenty-three-year-old who looked a lot like a nurse from Enid, Oklahoma, he'd dated a couple of times (Les Elgart had been playing in the Loop) six seven months after returning from WWII.

Now this young look-alike was on a soap opera and he was watching.

A frigging soap opera.

He was getting all dazzled up by her, just as he had on Monday, when the knock came sharp and three times, almost like a code.

He wasn't wearing the slippers he'd gotten recently at Kmart so he had to find them, and he was drinking straight from a quart of Hamm's so he had to put it down. When you were the manager of an apartment building, even one as marginal as the Alma, you had to go to the door with at least a little "decorousness," the word Sergeant Meister, his boss, had always used back in Parnell's cop days.

It was 11:23 A.M. and most of the Alma's tenants were at work. Except for the ADC mothers who had plenty of work of their own kind what with some of the assholes down at Social Services, not to mention the sheer simple burden of knowing the sweet innocent little child you loved was someday going to end up just as blown-out and bitter and useless as yourself.

He went to the door, shuffling in his new slippers which he'd bought two sizes too big because of his bunions.

The guy who stood there was no resident of the Alma. Not with his razor-cut black hair and his three-piece banker's suit and the kind of melancholy in his pale blue eyes that was almost sweet and not at all violent. He had a fancy mustache spoiled by the fact that his pink lips were a woman's.

"Mr. Parnell?"

Parnell nodded.

The man, who was maybe thirty-five, put out a hand. Parnell took it, all the while thinking of the soap opera behind him and the girl who looked like the one from Enid, Oklahoma. (Occasionally he bought whack-off magazines but the girls either looked too easy or too arrogant so he always had to close his eyes anyway and think of somebody he'd known in the past.) He wanted to see her, fuck this guy. Saturday he would be sixty-one and about all he had to look forward to was a phone call from his kid up the Oregon coast. His kid, who, God rest her soul, was his mother's son and not Parnell's, always ran a stopwatch while they talked so as to save on the phone bill. Hi Dad Happy Birthday and It's Been Really Nice Talking to You. I-Love-You-Bye.

"What can I do for you?" Parnell said. Then as he stood there watching the traffic go up and down Cortland Boulevard in baking July sunlight, Parnell realized that the guy was somehow familiar to him.

The guy said, "You know my father."

"Jesus H. Christ—"

"—Bud Garrett—"

"—Bud. I'll be goddamned." He'd already shaken the kid's hand and he couldn't do that again so he kind of patted him on the shoulder and said, "Come on in."

"I'm Richard Garrett."

"I'm glad to meet you, Richard."

He took the guy inside. Richard looked around at the odds and ends of furniture that didn't match and at all the pictures of dead people and immediately put a smile on his face as if he just couldn't remember when he'd been so enchanted with a place before, which meant of course that he saw the place for the dump Parnell knew it to be.

"How about a beer?" Parnell said, hoping he had something besides the generic stuff he'd bought at the 7-Eleven a few months ago.

"I'm fine, thanks."

Richard sat on the edge of the couch with the air of somebody waiting for his flight to be announced. He was all ready to jump up. He kept his eyes downcast and he kept fiddling with his wedding ring. Parnell watched him. Sometimes it turned out that way. Richard's old man had been on the force with Parnell. They'd been best friends. Garrett, Sr., was a big man, six-three and fleshy but strong, a brawler and occasionally a mean one when the hootch didn't settle in him quite right. But his son . . . Sometimes it turned out that way. He was manly enough, Parnell supposed, but there was an air of being trapped in himself, of petulance, that put Parnell off.

Three or four minutes of silence went by. The soap opera ended with Parnell getting another glance of the young lady. Then a "CBS Newsbreak" came on. Then some commercials. Richard didn't seem to notice that neither of them had said anything for a long time. Sunlight made bars through the venetian blinds. The refrigerator thrummed. Upstairs but distantly a kid bawled.

Parnell didn't realize it at first, not until Richard sniffed, that Bud Garrett's son was either crying or doing something damn close to it.

"Hey, Richard, what's the problem?" Parnell said, making sure to keep his voice soft.

"My, my dad."

"Is something wrong?"

"Yes."

"What?"

Richard looked up with his pale blue eyes. "He's dying."

"Jesus."

Richard cleared his throat. "It's how he's dying that's so bad."

"Cancer?"

Richard said, "Yes. Liver. He's dying by inches."

"Shit."

Richard nodded. Then he fell once more into his own thoughts. Parnell let him stay there awhile, thinking about Bud Garrett. Bud had left the force on a whim that all the cops said would fail. He started a rent-a-car business with a small inheritance he'd come into. That was twenty years ago. Now Bud Garrett lived up in Woodland Hills and drove the big Mercedes and went to Europe once a year. Bud and Parnell had tried to remain friends but beer and champagne didn't mix. When the Mrs. had died Bud had sent a lavish display of flowers to the funeral and a note that Parnell knew to be sincere but they hadn't had any real contact in years.

"Shit," Parnell said again.

Richard looked up, shaking his head as if trying to escape the aftereffects of drugs. "I want to hire you."

"Hire me? As what?"

"You're a personal investigator aren't you?"

"Not anymore. I mean I kept my ticket—it doesn't cost that much to renew it—but hell I haven't had a job in five years." He waved a beefy hand around the apartment. "I manage these apartments."

From inside his blue pin-striped suit Richard took a sleek wallet. He quickly counted out five one-hundred-dollar bills and put them on the blond coffee table next to the stack of Luke Short paperbacks. "I really want you to help me."

"Help you do what?"

"Kill my father."

Now Parnell shook his head. "Jesus, kid, are you nuts or what?"

Richard stood up. "Are you busy right now?"

Parnell looked around the room again. "I guess not."

"Then why don't you come with me?"

"Where?"

When the elevator doors opened to let them out on the sixth floor of the hospital, Parnell said, "I want to be sure that you understand me."

He took Richard by the sleeve and held him and stared into his pale blue eyes. "You know why I'm coming here, right?"

"Right."

"I'm coming to see your father because we're old friends. Because I cared about him a great deal and because I still do. But that's the only reason."

"Right."

Parnell frowned. "You still think I'm going to help you, don't you?"

"I just want you to see him."

On the way to Bud Garrett's room they passed an especially good-looking nurse. Parnell felt guilty about recognizing her beauty. His old friend was dying just down the hall and here Parnell was worrying about some nurse.

Parnell went around the corner of the door. The room was dark. It smelled sweet from flowers and fetid from flesh literally rotting.

Then he looked at the frail yellow man in the bed. Even in the shadows you could see his skin was yellow.

"I'll be damned," the man said.

It was like watching a skeleton talk by some trick of magic.

Parnell went over and tried to smile his ass off but all he could muster was just a little one. He wanted to cry until he collapsed. You son of a bitch, Parnell thought, enraged. He just wasn't sure who he was enraged with. Death or God or himself—or maybe even Bud himself for reminding Parnell of just how terrible and scary it could get near the end.

"I'll be damned," Bud Garrett said again.

He put out his hand and Parnell took it. Held it for a long time.

"He's a good boy, isn't he?" Garrett said, nodding to Richard.

"He sure is."

"I had to raise him after his mother died. I did a good job, if I say so myself."

"A damn good job, Bud."

This was a big private room that more resembled a hotel suite. There was a divan and a console TV and a dry bar. There was a Picasso lithograph and a walk-in closet and a deck to walk out on. There was a double-sized water bed with enough controls to drive a spaceship and a big stereo and a bookcase filled with hardcovers. Most people Parnell knew dreamed of living in such a place. Bud Garrett was dying in it.

"He told you," Garrett said.

"What?" Parnell spun around to face Richard, knowing suddenly the worst truth of all.

"He told you."

"Jesus, Bud, you sent him, didn't you?"

"Yes. Yes, I did."

"Why?"

Parnell looked at Garrett again. How could somebody who used to have a weight problem and who could throw around the toughest drunk the barrio ever produced get to be like this. Nearly every time he talked he winced. And all the time he smelled. Bad.

"I sent for you because none of us is perfect," Bud said.

"I don't understand."

"He's afraid."

"Richard?"

"Yes."

"I don't blame him. I'd be afraid too." Parnell paused and stared at Bud. "You asked him to kill you, didn't you?"

"Yes. It's his responsibility to do it."

Richard stepped up to his father's bedside and said, "I agree with that, Mr. Parnell. It is my responsibility. I just need a little help is all."

"Doing what?"

"If I buy cyanide, it will eventually be traced to me and I'll be tried for murder. If you buy it, nobody will ever connect you with my father."

Parnell shook his head. "That's bullshit. That isn't what you want me for. There are a million ways you could get cyanide without having it traced back."

Bud Garrett said, "I told him about you. I told him you could help give him strength."

"I don't agree with any of this, Bud. You should die when it's your time to die. I'm a Catholic."

Bud laughed hoarsely. "So am I, you asshole." He coughed and said, "The pain's bad. I'm beyond any help they can give me. But it could go on for a long time." Then, just as his son had an hour ago, Bud Garrett began crying almost imperceptibly. "I'm scared, Parnell. I don't know what's on the other side but it can't be any worse than this." He reached out his hand and for a long time Parnell just stared at it but then he touched it.

"Jesus," Parnell said. "It's pretty fucking confusing, Bud. It's pretty fucking confusing."

Richard took Parnell out to dinner that night. It was a nice place. The tablecloths were starchy white and the waiters all wore shiny shoes. Candles glowed inside red glass.

They'd had four drinks apiece, during which Richard told Parnell about his two sons (six and eight respectively) and about the perils and rewards of the rent-a-car business and about how much he liked windsurfing even though he really wasn't much good at it.

Just after the arrival of the fourth drink, Richard took something from his pocket and laid it on the table.

It was a cold capsule.

"You know how the Tylenol Killer in Chicago operated?" Richard asked.

Parnell nodded.

"Same thing," Richard said. "I took the cyanide and put it in a capsule."

"Christ. I don't know about it."

"You're scared too, aren't you?"

"Yeah, I am."

Richard sipped his whiskey and soda. With his regimental striped tie he might have been sitting in a country club. "May I ask you something?"

"Maybe."

"Do you believe in God?"

"Sure."

"Then if you believe in God, you must believe in goodness, correct?"

Parnell frowned. "I'm not much of an intellectual, Richard."

"But if you believe in God, you must believe in goodness, right?"

"Right."

"Do you think what's happening to my father is good?"

"Of course I don't."

"Then you must also believe that God isn't doing this to him—right?"

"Right."

Richard held up the capsule. Stared at it. "All I want you to do is give me a ride to the hospital. Then just wait in the car down in the parking lot."

"I won't do it."

Richard signaled for another round.

"I won't goddamn do it," Parnell said.

By the time they left the restaurant Richard was too drunk to drive. Parnell got behind the wheel of the new Audi. "Why don't you tell me where you live? I'll take you home and take a cab from there."

"I want to go to the hospital."

"No way, Richard."

Richard slammed his fist against the dashboard. "You fucking owe him that, man!" he screamed.

Parnell was shocked, and a bit impressed, with Richard's violent side. If nothing else, he saw how much Richard loved his old man.

"Richard, listen."

Richard sat in a heap against the opposite door. His tears were dry ones, choking ones. "Don't give me any of your speeches." He wiped snot from his nose on his sleeve. "My dad always told me what a tough guy Parnell was." He turned to Parnell, anger in him again. "Well, I'm not tough, Parnell, and so I need to borrow some of your toughness so I can get that man out of his pain and grant him his one last fucking wish. *Do you goddamn understand me?*"

He smashed his fist on the dashboard again.

Parnell turned on the ignition and drove them away.

When they reached the hospital, Parnell found a parking spot and pulled in. The mercury vapor lights made him feel as though he were on Mars. Bugs smashed against the windshield.

"I'll wait here for you," Parnell said.

Richard looked over at him. "You won't call the cops?"

"No."

"And you won't come up and try to stop me?"

"No."

Richard studied Parnell's face. "Why did you change your mind?"

"Because I'm like him."

"Like my father?"

"Yeah. A coward. I wouldn't want the pain either. I'd be just as afraid."

All Richard said, and this he barely whispered, was "Thanks."

While he sat there Parnell listened to country-western music and then a serious political call-in show and then a call-in show where a lady talked about Venusians who wanted to pork her and then some salsa music and then a religious minister who sounded like Foghorn Leghorn in the old Warner Brothers cartoons.

By then Richard came back.

He got in the car and slammed the door shut and said, completely sober now, "Let's go."

Parnell got out of there.

They went ten long blocks before Parnell said, "You didn't do it, did you?"

Richard got hysterical. "You son of a bitch! You son of a bitch!"

Parnell had to pull the car over to the curb. He hit Richard once, a fast clean right hand, not enough to make him unconscious but enough to calm him down.

"You didn't do it, did you?"

"He's my father, Parnell. I don't know what to do. I love him so much I don't want to see him suffer. But I love him so much I don't want to see him die, either."

Parnell let the kid sob. He thought of his old friend Bud Garrett and what a good goddamn fun buddy he'd been and then he started crying, too.

———

When Parnell came down Richard was behind the steering wheel.

Parnell got in the car and looked around the empty parking lot and said, "Drive."

"Any place especially?"

"Out along the East River road. Your old man and I used to fish off that little bridge there."

Richard drove them. From inside his sport coat Parnell took the pint of Jim Beam.

When they got to the bridge Parnell said, "Give me five minutes alone and then you can come over, okay?"

Richard was starting to sob again.

Parnell got out of the car and went over to the bridge. In the hot night you could hear the hydroelectric dam half a mile downstream and smell the fish and feel the mosquitoes feasting their way through the evening.

He thought of what Bud Garrett had said, "Put it in some whiskey for me, will you?"

So Parnell had obliged.

He stood now on the bridge looking up at the yellow circle of moon thinking about dead people, his wife and many of his WWII friends, the rookie cop who'd died of a sudden tumor, his wife with her rosary-wrapped hands. Hell, there was probably even a chance that nurse from Enid, Oklahoma, was dead.

"What do you think's on the other side?" Bud Garrett had asked just half an hour ago. He'd almost sounded excited. As if he were a farm kid about to ship out with the merchant marines.

"I don't know," Parnell had said.

"It scare you, Parnell?"

"Yeah," Parnell had said. "Yeah it does."

Then Bud Garrett had laughed. "Don't tell the kid that. I always told him that nothin' scared you."

Richard came up the bridge after a time. At first he stood maybe a hundred feet away from Parnell. He leaned his elbows on the concrete and looked out at the water and the moon. Parnell watched him, knowing it was all Richard, or anybody, could do.

Look out at the water and the moon and think about dead people and how you yourself would soon enough be dead.

Richard turned to Parnell then and said, his tears gone completely now, sounding for the first time like Parnell's sort of man, "You know, Parnell, my father was right. You're a brave son of a bitch. You really are."

Parnell knew it was important for Richard to believe that— that there were actually people in the world who didn't fear things the way most people did—so Parnell didn't answer him at all.

He just took his pint out and had himself a swig and looked some more at the moon and the water.

· LOREN D. ESTLEMAN ·

The Crooked Way

This is Loren D. Estleman's second Shamus-winning short story, also featuring his Detroit-based PI Amos Walker, who some think is the one true heir to Chandler's Philip Marlowe. Walker certainly shares a moral code with Chandler's famous shamus. Loren also writes westerns and has won many awards in that genre, including the Western Writers of America's Golden Spur Award for best novel.

YOU COULDN'T MISS THE INDIAN IF YOU'D WANTED TO. HE WAS sitting all alone in a corner booth, which was probably his idea, but he hadn't much choice because there was barely enough room in it for him. He had shoulders going into the next county and a head the size of a basketball, and he was holding a beer mug that looked like a shot glass between his callused palms. As I approached the booth he looked up at me—not very far up—through slits in a face made up of bunched ovals with a nose like the corner of a building. His skin was the color of old brick.

"Mr. Frechette?" I asked.

"Amos Walker?"

I said I was. Coming from him my name sounded like two

stones dropping into deep water. He made no move to shake hands, but he inclined his head a fraction of an inch and I borrowed a chair from a nearby table and joined him. He had on a blue shirt buttoned to the neck, and his hair, parted on one side and plastered down, was blue-black without a trace of gray. Nevertheless he was about fifty.

"Charlie Stoat says you track like an Osage," he said. "I hope you're better than that. I couldn't track a train."

"How is Charlie? I haven't seen him since that insurance thing."

"Going under. The construction boom went bust in Houston just when he was expanding his operation."

"What's that do to yours?" He'd told me over the telephone he was in construction.

"Nothing worth mentioning. I've been running on a shoestring for years. You can't break a poor man."

I signaled the bartender for a beer and he brought one over. It was a workingman's hangout across the street from the Ford plant in Highland Park. The shift wasn't due to change for an hour and we had the place to ourselves. "You said your daughter ran away," I said, when the bartender had left. "What makes you think she's in Detroit?"

He drank off half his beer and belched dramatically. "When does client privilege start?"

"It never stops."

I watched him make up his mind. Indians aren't nearly as hard to read as they appear in books. He picked up a folded newspaper from the seat beside him and spread it out on the table facing me. It was yesterday's *Houston Chronicle*, with a banner:

BOYD MANHUNT MOVES NORTHEAST
Bandit's Van Found Abandoned in Detroit

I had read a related wire story in that morning's *Detroit Free Press*. Following the unassisted shotgun robberies of two savings and loan offices near Houston, concerned citizens had reported seeing twenty-two-year-old Virgil Boyd in Mexico and Oklahoma, but his green van with Texas plates had turned up in a city lot five minutes from where we were sitting. As of that morning, Detroit police headquarters was paved with feds and sun-crinkled out-of-state cops chewing toothpicks.

I refolded the paper and gave it back. "Your daughter's taken up with Boyd?"

"They were high school sweethearts," Frechette said. "That was before Texas Federal foreclosed on his family's ranch and his father shot himself. She disappeared from home after the first robbery. I guess that makes her an accomplice to the second."

"Legally speaking," I agreed, "if she's with him and it's her idea. A smart DA would knock it down to harboring if she turned herself in. She'd probably get probation."

"She wouldn't do that. She's got some crazy idea she's in love with Boyd."

"I'm surprised I haven't heard about her."

"No one knows. I didn't report her missing. If I had, the police would have put two and two together and there'd be a warrant out for her as well."

I swallowed some beer. "I don't know what you think I can do that the cops and the FBI can't."

"I know where she is."

I waited. He rotated his mug. "My sister lives in Southgate. We don't speak. She has a white mother, not like me, and she takes after her in looks. She's ashamed of being half Osage. First chance she had, she married a white man and got out of Oklahoma. That was before I left for Texas, where nobody knows about her. Anyway she got a big settlement in her divorce."

"You think Boyd and your daughter will go to her for a get-away stake?"

"They won't get it from me, and he didn't take enough out of Texas Federal to keep a dog alive. Why else would they come here?"

"So if you know where they're headed, what do you need me for?"

"Because I'm being followed and you're not."

The bartender came around to offer Frechette a refill. The big Indian shook his head and he went away.

"Cops?" I said.

"One cop. J. P. Ahearn."

He spaced out the name as if spelling a blasphemy. I said I'd never heard of him.

"He'd be surprised. He's a commander with the Texas state police, but he thinks he's the last of the Texas Rangers. He wants Boyd bad. The man's a bloodhound. He doesn't know about my sister, but he did his homework and found out about Suzie and that she's gone, not that he could get me to admit she isn't away visiting friends. I didn't see him on the plane from Houston. I spotted him in the airport here when I was getting my luggage."

"Is he alone?"

"He wouldn't share credit with Jesus for saving a sinner." He drained his mug. "When you find Suzie I want you to set up a meeting. Maybe I can talk sense into her."

"How old is she?"

"Nineteen."

"Good luck."

"Tell me about it. My old man fell off a girder in Tulsa when I was sixteen. Then I was fifty. Well, maybe one meeting can't make up for all the years of not talking after my wife died, but I can't let her throw her life away for not trying."

"I can't promise Boyd won't sit in on it."

"I like Virgil. Some of us cheered when he took on those bloodsuckers. He'd have gotten away with a lot more from that second job if he'd shot this stubborn cashier they had, but he didn't. He wouldn't hurt a horse or a man."

"That's not the way the cops are playing it. If I find him and don't report it I'll go down as an accomplice. At the very least I'll lose my license."

"All I ask is that you call me before you call the police." He gave me a high school graduation picture of a pretty brunet he said was Suzie. She looked more Asian than American Indian. Then he pulled a checkbook out of his hip pocket and made out a check to me for fifteen hundred dollars.

"Too much," I said.

"You haven't met J. P. Ahearn yet. My sister's name is Harriett Lord." He gave me an address on Eureka. "I'm at the Holiday Inn down the street, room seven-sixteen."

He called for another beer then and I left. Again he didn't offer his hand. I'd driven three blocks from the place when I spotted the tail.

The guy knew what he was doing. In a late-model tan Buick he gave me a full block and didn't try to close up until we hit Woodward, where traffic was heavier. I finally lost him in the grand circle downtown, which confused him just as it does most people from the greater planet earth. The Indians who settled Detroit were being farsighted when they named it the Crooked Way. From there I took Lafayette to I-75 and headed downriver.

Harriett Lord lived in a tall white frame house with blue shutters and a large lawn fenced by cedars that someone had bullied into cone shape. I parked in the driveway, but before leaving the car I got out the unlicensed Luger I keep in a pocket under the dash and stuck it in my pants, buttoning my coat over it. When you're meeting someone they tell you wouldn't hurt a horse or a man, arm yourself.

The bell was answered by a tall woman around forty, dressed in a khaki shirt and corduroy slacks and sandals. She had high cheekbones and slightly olive coloring that looked more like sun than heritage and her short hair was frosted, further reducing the Indian effect. When she confirmed that she was Harriett Lord I gave her a card and said I was working for her brother.

Her face shut down. "I don't have a brother. I have a half brother, Howard Frechette. If that's who you're working for, tell him I'm unavailable." She started to close the door.

"It's about your niece Suzie. And Virgil Boyd."

"I thought it would be."

I looked at the door and got out a cigarette and lit it. I was about to knock again when the door opened six inches and she stuck her face through the gap. "You're not with the police?"

"We tolerate each other on the good days, but that's it."

She glanced down. Her blue mascara gave her eyelids a translucent look. Then she opened the door the rest of the way and stepped aside. I entered a living room done all in beige and white and sat in a chair upholstered in eggshell chintz. I was glad I'd had my suit cleaned.

"How'd you know about Suzie and Boyd?" I used a big glass ashtray on the Lucite coffee table.

"They were here last night." I said nothing. She sat on the beige sofa with her knees together. "I recognized him before I did her. I haven't seen her since she was four, but I take a Texas paper and I've seen his picture. They wanted money. I thought at first I was being robbed."

"Did you give it to them?"

"Aid a fugitive? Family responsibility doesn't cover that even if I felt any. I left home because I got sick of hearing about our proud heritage. Howard wore his Indianness like a suit of armor, and all the time he resented me because I could pass for white. He accused me of being ashamed of my ancestry because I didn't wear my hair in braids and hang turquoise all over me."

"He isn't like that now."

"Maybe he's mellowed. Not toward me, though, I bet. Now his daughter comes here asking for money so she and her desperado boyfriend can go on running. I showed them the door."

"I'm surprised Boyd went."

"He tried to get tough, but he's not very big and he wasn't armed. He took a step toward me and I took two steps toward him and he grabbed Suzie and left. Some Jesse James."

"I heard his shotgun was found in the van. I thought he'd have something else."

"If he did, he didn't have it last night. I'd have noticed, just as I notice you have one."

I unbuttoned my coat and resettled the Luger. I was getting a different picture of "Mad Dog" Boyd from the one the press was painting. "The cops would call not reporting an incident like that being an accessory," I said, squashing out my butt.

"Just because I don't want anything to do with Howard doesn't mean I want to see my niece shot up by a SWAT team."

"I don't suppose they said where they were going."

"You're a good supposer."

I got up. "How did Suzie look?"

"Like an Indian."

I thanked her and went out.

I had a customer in my waiting room. A small angular party crowding sixty wearing a tight gray three-button suit, steel-rimmed glasses, and a tan snap-brim hat squared over the frames. His crisp gray hair was cut close around large ears that stuck out, and he had a long sharp jaw with a sour mouth slashing straight across. He stood up when I entered. "Walker?" It was one of those bitter pioneer voices.

"Depends on who you are," I said.

"I'm the man who ought to arrest you for obstructing justice."

"I'll guess. J. P. Ahearn."

"*Commander* Ahearn."

"You're about four feet short of what I had pictured."

"You've heard of me." His chest came out a little.

"Who hasn't?" I unlocked the inner office door. He marched in, slung a look around, and took possession of the customer's chair. I sat down behind the desk and reached for a cigarette without asking permission. He glared at me through his spectacles.

"What you did downtown today constitutes fleeing and eluding."

"In Texas, maybe. In Michigan there has to be a warrant out first. What you did constitutes harassment in this state."

"I don't have official status here. I can follow anybody for any reason or none at all."

"Is this what you folks call a Mexican standoff?"

"I don't approve of smoking," he snapped.

"Neither do I, but some of it always leaks out of my lungs." I blew some at the ceiling and got rid of the match. "Why don't let's stop circling each other and get down to why you're here?"

"I want to know what you and the Indian talked about."

"I'd show you, but we don't need the rain."

He bared a perfect set of dentures, turning his face into a skull. "I ran your plate with the Detroit police. I have their complete cooperation in this investigation. The Indian hired you to take money to Boyd to get him and his little Osage slut to Canada. You delivered it after you left the bar and lost me. That's aiding and abetting and accessory after the fact of armed robbery. Maybe I can't prove it, but I can make a call and tank you for forty-eight hours on suspicion."

"Eleven."

He covered up his store-boughts. "What?"

"That's eleven times I've been threatened with jail," I said. "Three of those times I wound up there. My license has been swiped at fourteen times, actually taken away once. Bodily harm—you don't count bodily harm. I'm still here, six feet something and one hundred eighty pounds of incorruptible PI with a will of iron and a skull to match. You hard guys come and go like phases of the moon."

"Don't twist my tail, son. I don't always rattle before I bite."

"What's got you so hot on Boyd?"

You could have cut yourself on his jaw. "My daddy helped run Parker and Barrow to ground in '34. *His* daddy fought Geronimo and chased John Wesley Hardin out of Texas. My son's a Dallas city patrolman, and so far I don't have a story to hand him that's a blister on any of those. I'm retiring next year."

"Last I heard Austin was offering twenty thousand for Boyd's arrest and conviction."

"Texas Federal has matched it. Alive *or* dead. Naturally, as a duly sworn officer of the law I can't collect. But you being a private citizen—"

"What's the split?"

"Fifty-fifty."

"No good."

"Do you know what the pension is for a retired state police commander in Texas? A man needs a nest egg."

"I meant it's too generous. You know as well as I do those rewards are never paid. You just didn't know I knew."

He sprang out of his chair. There was no special animosity in his move; that would be the way he always got up.

"Boyd won't get out of this country even if you did give him money," he snapped. "He'll never get past the border guards."

"So go back home."

"Boyd's *mine.*"

The last word ricocheted. I said, "Talk is he felt he had a good reason to stick up those savings and loans. The company was responsible for his father's suicide."

"If he's got the brains God gave a mad dog he'll turn himself in to me before he gets shot down in the street or kills someone and winds up getting the needle in Huntsville. And his squaw right along with him." He took a shabby wallet out of his coat and gave me a card. "That's my number at the Houston post. They'll route your call here. If you're so concerned for Boyd you'll tell me where he is before the locals gun him down."

"Better you than some stranger, that it?"

"Just keep on twisting, son. I ain't in the pasture yet."

After he left, making as much noise in his two-inch cowboy heels as a cruiserweight, I called Barry Stackpole at the *Detroit News.*

"Guy I'm after is wanted for robbery, armed," I said, once the small talk was put away. "He ditched his gun and then his stake didn't come through and now he'll have to cowboy a job for case dough. Where would he deal a weapon if he didn't know anybody in town?"

"Emma Chaney."

"Ma? I thought she'd be dead by now."

"She can't die. The Detroit cops are third in line behind Interpol and customs for her scalp and they won't let her until they've had their crack." He sounded pleased, which he probably was. Barry made his living writing about crime and when it prospered he did, too.

"How can I reach her?"

"Are you suggesting I'd know where she is and not tell the authorities? Got a pencil?"

I tried the number as soon as he was off the line. On the ninth ring I got someone with a smoker's wheeze. "Uh-huh."

"The name's Walker," I said. "Barry Stackpole gave me this number."

The voice told me not to go away and hung up. Five minutes later the telephone rang.

"Barry says you're okay. What do you want?"

"Just talk. It isn't cheap like they say."

After a moment the voice gave me directions. I hung up not knowing if it was male or female.

It belonged to Ma Chaney, who greeted me at the door of her house in rural Macomb County wearing a red Japanese kimono with green parrots all over it. The kimono could have covered a Toyota. She was a five-by-five chunk with marcelled orange hair and round black eyes embedded in her face like nail heads in soft wax. A cigarette teetered on her lower lip. I followed her into a parlor full of flowered chairs and sofas and pregnant lamps with fringed shades. A long strip of pimply blond youth in overalls and no shirt took his brogans off the coffee table and stood up when she barked at him. He gaped at me, chewing gum with his mouth open.

"Mr. Walker, Leo," Ma wheezed. "Leo knew my Wilbur in Ypsi. He's like another son to me."

Ma Chaney had one son in the criminal ward at the Forensic Psychiatry Center in Ypsilanti and another on Florida's death row. The FBI was looking for the youngest in connection with an armored car robbery in Kansas City. The whole brood had come up from Kentucky when Old Man Chaney got a job on the line at River Rouge and stayed on after he was killed in a propane tank explosion. Now Ma, the daughter of a Hawkins County gunsmith, made her living off the domestic weapons market.

"You said talk ain't cheap," she said, when she was sitting in a big overstuffed rocker. "How cheap ain't it?"

I perched on the edge of a hard upright with doilies on the arms. Leo remained standing, scratching himself. "Depends on whether we talk about Virgil Boyd," I said.

"What if we don't?"

"Then I won't take up any more of your time."

"What if we do?"

"I'll double what he's paying."

She coughed. The cigarette bobbed. "I got a business to run. I go around scratching at *re*wards I won't have no customers."

"Does that mean Boyd's a customer?"

"Now, why'd that Texas boy want to come to Ma? He can deal hisself a shotgun at any Kmart."

"He can't show his face in the legal places and being new in town he doesn't know the illegal ones. But he wouldn't have to ask around too much to come up with your name. You're less selective than most."

"You don't have to pussyfoot around old Ma. I don't get a lot of second-timers on account of I talk for money. My boy Earl in Florida needs a new lawyer. But I only talk after, not before. I start setting up customers I won't get no first-timers."

"I'm not even interested in Boyd. It's his girlfriend I want to talk to. Suzie Frechette."

"Don't know her." She rocked back and forth. "What color's your money?"

Before leaving Detroit I'd cashed Howard Frechette's check. I laid fifteen hundred dollars on the coffee table in twenties and fifties. Leo straightened up a little to look at the bills. Ma resumed rocking. "It ain't enough."

"How much is enough?"

"If I was to talk to a fella named Boyd, and if I was to agree to sell him a brand new Ithaca pump shotgun and a P–thirty-eight still in the box, I wouldn't sell them for less than twenny-five hunnert. Double twenny-five hunnert is five thousand."

"Fifteen hundred now. Thirty-five hundred when I see the girl."

"I don't guarantee no girl."

"Boyd then. If he's come this far with her he won't leave her behind."

She went on rocking. "They's a white barn a mile north on this road. If I was to meet a fella named Boyd, there's where I might do it. I might pick eleven o'clock."

"Tonight?"

"I might pick tonight. If it don't rain."

I got up. She stopped rocking.

"Come alone," she said. "Ma won't."

On the way back to town I filled up at a corner station and used the pay telephone to call Howard Frechette's room at the Holiday Inn. When he started asking questions I gave him the number and told him to call back from a booth outside the motel.

"Ahearn's an anachronism," he said ten minutes later. "I doubt he taps phones."

"Maybe not, but motel operators have big ears."

"Did you talk to Suzie?"

"Minor setback," I said. "Your sister gave her and Boyd the boot and no money."

"Tight bitch."

"I know where they'll be tonight, though. There's an old auto court on Van Dyke between Twenty-one and Twenty-two Mile in Macomb County, the Log Cabin Inn. Looks like it sounds." I was staring at it across the road. "Midnight. Better give yourself an hour."

He repeated the information.

"I'm going to have to tap you for thirty-five hundred dollars," I said. "The education cost."

"I can manage it. Is that where they're headed?"

"I hope so. I haven't asked them yet."

I got to my bank just before closing and cleaned out my savings and all but eight dollars in my checking account. I hoped Frechette was good for it. After that I ate dinner in a restaurant and went to see a movie about a one-man army. I wondered if he was available.

The barn was just visible from the road, a moonlit square at the end of a pair of ruts cut through weeds two feet high. It was a chill night in early spring and I had on a light coat and the heater running. I entered a dip that cut off my view of the barn, then bucked up over a ridge and had to stand the Chevy on its nose when the lamps fell on a telephone pole lying across the path. A second later the passenger's door opened and Leo got in.

He had on a mackinaw over his overalls and a plaid cap. His right hand was wrapped around a large-bore revolver and he kept it on me, held tight to his stomach, while he felt under my coat and came up with the Luger. "Drive." He pocketed it.

I swung around the end of the pole and braked in front of the barn, where Ma was standing with a Coleman lantern. She was wearing a man's felt hat and a corduroy coat with sleeves that came down to her fingers. She signaled a cranking motion and I rolled down the window.

"Well, park it around back," she said. "I got to think for you, too?"

I did that and Leo and I walked back. He handed Ma the Luger and she looked at it and put it in her pocket. She raised the lantern then and swung it from side to side twice.

We waited a few minutes, then were joined by six feet and two hundred and fifty pounds of red-bearded young man in faded denim jacket and jeans carrying a rifle with an infrared scope. He had come from the direction of the road.

"Anybody following, Mason?" asked Ma.

He shook his head and I stared at him in the lantern light. He had small black eyes like Ma's with no shine in them. This would be Mace Chaney, for whom the FBI was combing the western states for the Kansas armored car robbery.

"Go on in and warm yourself," Ma said. "We got some time."

He opened the barn door and went inside. It had just closed when two headlamps appeared down the road. We watched them approach and slow for the turn onto the path. Ma, lighting a cigarette off the lantern, grunted.

"Early. Young folks all got watches and they can't tell time."

Leo trotted out to intercept the car. A door slammed. After a pause the lamps swung around the fallen telephone pole and came up to the barn, washing us all in white. The driver killed the lamps and engine and got out. He was a small man in his early twenties with short brown hair and stubble on his face. His flannel shirt and khaki pants were both in need of cleaning. He had scant eyebrows that were almost invisible in that light, giving him a perennially surprised look. I'd seen that look in Frechette's *Houston Chronicle* and in both Detroit papers.

"Who's he?" He was looking at me.

I had a story for that, but Ma piped up. "You ain't paying to ask no questions. Got the money?"

"Not all of it. A thousand's all Suzie could get from the sharks."

"The deal's two thousand."

"Keep the P–thirty-eight. The shotgun's all I need."

Ma had told me twenty-five hundred; but I was barely listening to the conversation. Leo had gotten out on the passenger's side, pulling with him the girl in the photograph in my pocket. Suzie Frechette had done up her black hair in braids and she'd lost weight, but her dark eyes and coloring were unmistakable. With that hairstyle and in a man's work shirt and jeans and boots with western heels she looked more like an Indian than she did in her picture.

Leo opened the door and we went inside. The barn hadn't been used for its original purpose for some time, but the smell of moldy hay would remain as long as it stood. It was lit by a bare bulb swinging from a frayed cord and heated by a barrel stove in a corner. Stacks of cardboard cartons reached almost to the rafters, below which Mace Chaney sat with his legs dangling over the edge of the empty loft, the rifle across his knees.

Ma reached into an open carton and lifted out a pump shotgun with the barrel cut back to the slide. Boyd stepped forward to take it. She swung the muzzle on him. "Show me some paper."

He hesitated, then drew a thick fold of bills from his shirt pocket and laid it on a stack of cartons. Then she moved to cover me. Boyd watched me add thirty-five hundred to the pile.

"What's *he* buying?"

Ma said, "You."

"Cop!" He lunged for the shotgun. Leo's revolver came out. Mace drew a bead on Boyd from the loft. He relaxed.

I was looking at Suzie. "I'm a private detective hired by your father. He wants to talk to you."

"He's here?" She touched Boyd's arm.

He tensed. "It's a damn cop trick!"

"You're smarter than that," I said. "You had to be, to pull those two jobs and make your way here with every cop between here and Texas looking for you. If I were one, would I be alone?"

"Do your jabbering outside." Ma reversed ends on the shotgun for Boyd to take. He did so and worked the slide.

"Where's the shells?"

"That's your headache. I don't keep ammo in this firetrap."

That was a lie, or some of those cartons wouldn't be labeled C-4 Explosives. But you don't sell loaded guns to strangers.

Suzie said, "Virgil, you never load them anyway."

"Shut up."

"Your father's on his way," I said. "Ten minutes, that's all he wants."

"Come on." Boyd took her wrist.

"Stay put."

This was a new voice. Everyone looked at Leo, standing in front of the door with his gun still out.

"Leo, *what* in the *hell*—"

"Ma, the Luger."

She shut her mouth and took my gun out of her right coat pocket and put it on the carton with the money. Then she backed away.

"Throw 'er down, Mace." He covered the man in the loft, who froze in the act of raising the rifle. They were like that for a moment.

"Mason," Ma said.

His shoulders slumped. He snapped on the safety and dropped the rifle eight feet to the earthen floor.

"You, too, Mr. Forty Thousand Dollar Reward," Leo said. "Even empty guns give me the jumps."

Boyd cast the shotgun onto the stack of cartons with a violent gesture.

"That's nice. I cut that money in half if I got to put a hole in you."

"That reward talk's just PR," I said. "Even if you get Boyd to the cops they'll probably arrest you, too, for dealing in unlicensed firearms."

"Like hell. I'm through getting bossed around by fat old ladies. Let's go, Mr. Reward."

"No!" screamed Suzie.

An explosion slapped the walls. Leo's brows went up, his jaw dropping to expose the wad of pink gum in his mouth. He looked down at the spreading stain on the bib of his overalls and fell down on top of his gun. He kicked once.

Ma was standing with a hand in her left coat pocket. A finger of smoking metal poked out of a charred hole. "Dadgum it, Leo," she said, "this coat belonged to my Calvin, rest his soul."

I was standing in front of the Log Cabin Inn's deserted office when Frechette swung a rented Ford into the broken paved driveway. He unfolded himself from the seat and loomed over me.

"I don't think anyone followed me," he said. "I took a couple of wrong turns to make sure."

"There won't be any interruptions, then. The place has been closed a long time."

I led him to one of the log bungalows in back. Boyd's Plymouth, stolen from the same lot where he'd left the van, was parked alongside it facing out. We knocked before entering.

All of the furniture had been removed except a metal bedstead with sagging springs. The lantern we had borrowed from Ma Chaney hung hissing from one post. Suzie was standing next to it. "Papa." She didn't move. Boyd came out of the bathroom with the shotgun. The Indian took root.

"Man said you had money for us," Boyd said.

"It was the only way I could get him to bring Suzie here," I told Frechette.

"I won't pay to have my daughter killed in a shoot-out."

"Lying bastard!" Boyd swung the shotgun my way. Frechette backhanded him, knocking him back into the bathroom. I stepped forward and tore the shotgun from Boyd's weakened grip.

"Empty," I said. "But it makes a good club."

Suzie had come forward when Boyd fell. Frechette stopped her with an arm like a railroad gate. "Take Dillinger for a walk while I talk to my daughter," he said to me.

I stuck out a hand, but Boyd slapped it aside and got up. His right eye was swelling shut. He looked at the Indian towering a foot over him, then at Suzie, who said, "It's all right. I'll talk to him."

We went out. A porch ran the length of the bungalow. I leaned the shotgun against the wall and trusted my weight to the railing. "I hear you got a raw deal from Texas Federal."

"My old man did." He stood with his hands rammed deep in his pockets, watching the pair through the window. "He asked for a two-month extension on his mortgage payment, just till he brought in his crop. Everyone gets extensions. Except when Texas Federal wants to sell the ranch to a developer. He met the dozers with a shotgun. Then he used it on himself."

"That why you use one?"

"I can't kill a jackrabbit. It used to burn up my old man."

"You'd be out in three years if you turned yourself in."

"To you, right? Let you collect that reward." He was still looking through the window. Inside, father and daughter were gesturing at each other frantically.

"I didn't say to me. You're big enough to walk into a police station by yourself."

"You don't know Texas Federal. They'd hire their own prosecutor, see I got life, make an example. I'll die first."

"Probably, the rate you're going."

He whirled on me. The parked Plymouth caught his eye. "Just who the hell are you? And why'd you—" He jerked his chin toward the car.

I got out J. P. Ahearn's card and gave it to him. His face lost color.

"You work for that headhunter?"

"Not in this life. But in a little while I'm going to call that number from the telephone in that gas station across the road."

He lunged for the door. I was closer and got in his way. "I don't know how you got this far with a head that hot," I said. "For once in your young life listen. You might get to like it."

He listened.

"This is Commander Ahearn! I know you're in there, Boyd. I got a dozen men here and if you don't come out we'll shoot up the place!"

Neither of us had heard them coming, and with the moon behind a cloud the thin, bitter voice might have come from anywhere. This time Boyd won the race to the door. He had the reflexes of a deer.

"Kill the light!" I barked to Frechette. "Ahearn beat me to it. He must have followed you after all."

We were in darkness suddenly. Boyd and Suzie had their arms around each other. "We're cornered," he said. "Why didn't that old lady have shells for that gun?"

"We just have to move faster, that's all. Keep him talking. Give me a hand with this window." The last was for Frechette, who came over and worked his big fingers under the swollen frame.

"There's a woman in here!" Boyd shouted.

"Come on out and no one gets hurt!" Ahearn sounded wired.

The window gave with a squawking wrench.

"One minute, Boyd. Then we start blasting!"

I hoped it was enough. I slipped out over the sill.

"The car! Get it!"

The Plymouth's engine turned over twice in the cold before starting. The car rolled forward and began picking up speed down the incline toward the road. Just then the moon came out, illuminating the man behind the wheel, and the night came apart like mountain ice breaking up, cracking and splitting with the staccato rap of handgun fire and the deeper boom of riot guns. Orange flame scorched the darkness. Slugs whacked the car's sheet metal and shattered the windshield. Then a red glow started to spread inside the vehicle and fists of yellow flame battered out the rest of the windows with a *whump* that shook the ground. The car rolled for a few more yards while the shooters, standing now and visible in the light of the blaze, went on pouring lead into it until it came to a stop against a road sign. The flame towered twenty feet above the crackling wreckage.

I approached Ahearn, standing in the overgrown grass with his shotgun dangling, watching the car burn. He jumped a little when I spoke. His glasses glowed orange.

"He made a dash, just like you wanted."

"If you think I wanted this you don't know me," he said.

"Save it for the six o'clock news."

"What the hell are you doing here, anyway?"

"Friend of the family. Can I take the Frechettes home or do you want to eat them here?"

He cradled the shotgun. "We'll just go inside together."

We found Suzie sobbing in her father's arms. The Indian glared at Ahearn. "Get the hell out of here."

"He was a desperate man," Ahearn said. "You're lucky the girl's alive."

"I said get out or I'll ram that shotgun down your throat."

He got out. Through the window I watched him rejoin his men. There were five, not a dozen as he'd claimed. Later I learned that three of them were off-duty Detroit cops and he'd hired the other two from a private security firm.

I waited until the fire engines came and Ahearn was busy talking to the firefighters, then went out the window again and crossed to the next bungalow, set farther back where the light of the flames didn't reach. I knocked twice and paused and knocked again. Boyd opened the door a crack.

"I'm taking Suzie and her father back to Frechette's motel for looks. Think you can lie low here until we come back in the morning for the rent car?"

"What if they search the cabins?"

"For what? You're dead. By the time they find out that's Leo in the car, if they ever do, you and Suzie will be in Canada. Customs won't be looking for a dead bandit. Give everyone a year or so to forget what you look like and then you can come back. Not to Texas, though, and not under the name Virgil Boyd."

"Lucky the gas tank blew."

"I've never had enough luck to trust to it. That's why I put a box of C-four in Leo's lap. Ma figured it was a small enough donation to keep her clear of a charge of felony murder."

"I thought you were some kind of corpse freak." He still had the surprised look. "You could've been killed starting that car. Why'd you do it?"

"The world's not as complicated as it looks," I said. "There's always a good and a bad side. I saw Ahearn's."

"You ever need anything," he said.

"If you do things right I won't be able to find you when I do." I shook his hand and returned to the other bungalow.

———

A week later, after J. P. Ahearn's narrow, jug-eared features had made the cover of *People*, I received an envelope from Houston containing a bonus check for a thousand dollars signed by Howard Frechette. He'd repaid the thirty-five hundred I'd given Ma before going home. That was the last I heard from any of them. I used the money to settle some old bills and had some work done on my car so I could continue to ply my trade along the Crooked Way.

· MICKEY SPILLANE ·

The Killing Man

Mickey Spillane's Mike Hammer has been around for almost fifty years. In 1989 this story showed up in the pages of Playboy *magazine, and was closely followed by the publication of a Mike Hammer novel of the same title. The story captured the Shamus. In 1981 Mickey was awarded the PWA's life achievement award, the Eye, and was gracious and appreciative in his acceptance. After all these years, he is still Mickey.*

SOME DAYS HANG OVER MANHATTAN LIKE A HUGE PAIR OF UN-seen pincers slowly squeezing the city until you can hardly breathe. A low growl of thunder echoed up the cavern of Fifth Avenue, and I looked up to where the sky started at the seventy-first floor of the Empire State Building. I could smell the rain. It was the kind that hung above the orderly piles of concrete until it was soaked with dust and debris, and when it came down, it wasn't rain at all but the sweat of the city.

When I reached my corner, I crossed against the light and ducked into the ground-level arcade of my office building. It wasn't often that I bothered coming in on Saturdays, but my client couldn't make it any time other than noon today, and from what Velda had told me, he was representing some pretty big interests. I punched my button and rode the elevator up to the eighth floor.

On an ordinary day, the corridor would have been filled with the early-lunch crowd, but now the emptiness gave the place an eerie feeling, as though I were a trespasser and hidden eyes were watching me. Except that I was the only one there, and the single sign of life was the light behind my office door.

I turned the knob, pushed the door open, and just stood there a second because something was wrong, sure as hell wrong, and the silence was as loud as a wild scream. I had the .45 in my hand and I crouched and edged to one side, listening, waiting, watching.

Velda wasn't at her desk. Her pocketbook sat there, and a paper cup of coffee had spilled over and stained the sheaf of papers before dripping to the floor. And I didn't have to move far before I saw her body crumpled up against the wall, half of her face a bloody mass of clotted blood that seeped from under her hair.

The door to my office was partially open and there was somebody still in there, sitting at my desk, part of his arm clearly visible. I couldn't play it smart. I had to explode and ram through the door in a blind fury, ready to blow somebody into a death full of bloody, flying parts. . . . Then I stopped, my breath caught in my throat, because it had already been done.

The guy sitting there had been taped to my chair, his body immobilized. The wide splash of adhesive tape across his mouth had immobilized his voice, too, but all the horror that had happened was still there in his glazed, dead eyes that stared at hands whose fingertips had been amputated at the first knuckle and lay in neat order on the desktop. A dozen knife slashes had cut open the skin of his face and chest, and his clothes were a sodden mass of congealed blood.

But the thing that had killed him was the note spike I kept my expense receipts on. Somebody had slipped them all off the six-inch steel nail, positioned it squarely in the middle of the guy's forehead, and pounded it home with the bronze paperweight that held my folders down.

I ran back to Velda. Her pulse was weak, but it was there, and when I lifted her hair, there was a huge hematoma above her ear, the skin split wide from the vicious swelling of it. Her breathing was shallow and her vital signs weren't good. I grabbed her coat off the rack, draped it around her, stood up and forced the rage to leave me, then found the number in my phone book and dialed it.

The nurse said, "Dr. Reedey's office."

"Meg, this is Mike Hammer," I told her. "Burke in?"

"Yes, but—"

"Listen, call an ambulance and get a stretcher up here right away and get Burke to come up *now*. Velda's been hurt badly."

While she dialed, she said, "Don't move her. I'll send the doctor right up. Keep her warm and—" I hung up in midsentence.

Pat Chambers wasn't home, but his message service said he could be reached at his office. The sergeant at the switchboard answered, took my name, put me through, and when Pat said, "Captain Chambers," I told him to get to my office with a body bag. I wasn't about to waste time with explanations while Velda could be dying right beside me.

Her skin was clammy and her pulse was getting weaker. The frustration I felt was the kind you get in a dream when you can't run fast enough away from some terror that is chasing you. And now I had to stay here and watch Velda slip away from life while some bastard was out there getting farther and farther away all the time.

There were hands around my shoulders that yanked me away from her, and Burke said, "Come on, Mike, let me get to her."

I almost swung on him before I realized who he was. When he saw my face, he said, "You all right?"

After a moment, I said, "I'm all right," and moved back out of the way.

Burke Reedey was a doctor who had come out of the slaughter

of Vietnam with all the expertise needed to handle an emergency like this. He and his nurse moved swiftly and the helpless feeling I had before abated and I moved the desk to give him room, trying not to listen to their comments. There was something in their tone of voice that had a desperate edge to it. Almost on cue, the ambulance attendants arrived, visibly glad to see a doctor there ahead of them, and carefully, they got Velda onto the stretcher and out of the office, Burke going with them.

"What happened, Mike?" asked Meg.

"I don't know yet." I pointed to the door of my office. "Go look in there."

A worried look touched her eyes and she walked to the door and opened it. I didn't think old-time nurses could gasp like that. Her hand went to her mouth and I saw her head shake in horror. "Mike . . . you didn't mention—"

"He's dead. Velda wasn't. The cops will take care of that one."

She backed away from the door, turned and looked at me. "That's the first . . . deliberate murder . . . I've ever seen." Slowly, very slowly, her eyes widened.

I shook my head. "No, I didn't do it, Meg. Whoever hit Velda did that, too."

The relief in her expression was plain. "Do you know why?"

"Not yet."

When she left, I walked over to the miniature bar by the window and picked up a glass. Hell, this was no time to take a drink. I put the glass back and went into my office.

The dead guy was still looking at his mutilated hands, seemingly ignoring the spike driven into his skull until the ornamental base of it indented his skin. The glaze over his eyes seemed thicker.

I heard the front door open and Pat shouted my name. I called back, "In here."

Pat was a cop who had seen it all. This one was just another on his list. But the kill wasn't what disturbed him. It was where it had happened. He turned to the uniform at the door. "Anybody outside?"

"Only our people. They're shortstopping everybody at the elevators."

"Good, keep everybody out for five minutes. Our guys, too."

"Got it," the cop said and turned away.

"Let's talk," Pat said.

It didn't take long. "I was to meet a prospective client at noon in my office. Velda went ahead to open up and get some other work out of the way. I walked in a few minutes before twelve and found her on the floor and the guy dead."

"And you touched nothing?"

"Not in here, Pat. I wasn't about to wait for you to show before I got a doctor for Velda."

Pat looked at me with the same old look.

"Okay," he said. His eyes looked tired. "Let's get our guys in here."

While the photographer shot the corpse from all angles and did close-ups on the mutilation, Pat and I went into Velda's office, where the plainclothes officers were dusting for prints and vacuuming the area for any incidental evidence. Pat had already jotted down what I had told him. Now he said, "Give me the entire itinerary of your day, Mike. Start from when you got up this morning, and I'll check everything out while it's fresh."

"I got up at seven. I showered, dressed and went down to the deli for some rolls, picked up the paper, went back to the apartment, ate, read the news, and took off for the gym."

"Which one?"

"Bing's Gym. I got to the office a few minutes before twelve and walked into . . . this." I waved my hand at the room. "Burke Reedey will give you the medical report on Velda and the M.E. will be able to pinpoint the time of death pretty well, so don't get me mixed up in suspect status."

Pat finished writing, tore a leaf out of the pad, and closed the book. He called one of the detectives over and handed him the slip, telling him to check out all the details of my story. "Let's just keep straight with the system, buddy. Face it; you're not one of its favorite people."

Pat bent over and examined the body carefully. His arm brushed the dead man's coat and pushed it open. Sticking up out of the shirt pocket was a Con Edison bill folded in half. When Pat straightened it out, he looked at the name and said, "Anthony DiCica." He held it out for me to look at. "You know him, Mike?"

"Never saw him before."

"DiCica was an enforcer for the New York Mob. He was a suspect in four homicides, never got tapped for any of them, and gained a reputation of being a pretty efficient workman."

"Then?"

"Simple. Somebody cracked his skull open in a street brawl and he came all unraveled. He was in a hospital and left with severely impaired mental faculties."

"Who sponsored him?"

"Nobody took him in. He remembered very little of his past, but he could handle uncomplicated things."

"What's the tag line, Pat?"

"He could have made enemies. Somebody saw him and came after him."

"In my office?"

"Okay, Mike, who would want *you* dead?"

"Nobody I can think of."

"Hell, somebody wants you even better than dead. They want you all chopped up and with a spike through your head. Somebody had a business engagement with you at noon, got here early, took out Velda and didn't have to wait for you because there was a guy in your office he thought was you and he nailed that poor bastard instead."

"I've thought of that," I said.

I picked up the phone and called the building super. I told him I needed the place cleaned up and what had happened. He said he'd do it personally. I thanked him and hung up.

Pat said, "Let's go get something to eat. You'll feel better. Then we'll go to the hospital."

"I don't want to eat. I'll tell you what you can do, though."

"What's that?"

"Station a cop at her door. Somebody missed Velda, and they may want another go when they find out what happened."

Pat had called ahead, and the cop at Velda's door looked at my ID and let me in. The hospital room was in a deep gloom, only a small night-light on the wall, making it possible to see the outlines of the bed and the equipment. When the door snicked shut, I picked up the straight-backed chair by the sink, went to the bed, and sat down beside her.

Velda. Beautiful, gorgeous Velda. Those deep brown eyes and that full, full mouth. Shimmering auburn hair that fell in a pageboy around her shoulders.

Now her face was a bloated black-and-blue mask on one side, one eye totally closed under the bulbous swelling, the other a flat slit. Her hair was gone around the bandaged area and her upper lip was twice its normal size.

I put my hand over hers and whispered, "Damn it, kitten. . . ."

Then her wrist moved and her fingers squeezed mine gently. "Are you . . . all right?" she asked me softly.

"I'm fine, honey, I'm okay. Now, don't talk. Just take it easy. All I want is to be here with you. That's enough."

I just sat there, and in a minute, she said, "I can . . . listen, Mike. Please tell me . . . what happened."

I played it back without building it up. I didn't tell her the details of the kill and hinted that it was strictly the work of a nut, but she knew better.

Under my fingers, I could feel her pulse. It was steady. Her hand squeezed mine again. "They came in . . . very fast. One had a hand over his face . . . and he was . . . swinging at me . . . with the other. I . . . never saw a face at all." Remembering it hadn't excited her. The pulse rate hadn't changed.

I said, "Okay, honey, that's enough. You're supposed to take it real easy awhile."

But she insisted, "Mike . . ."

"What, kitten?"

"If the police . . . ask questions . . ."

I knew what she was thinking. In her mind, she had already put it on a case basis and filed it for immediate activity.

"Play sick," I said.

Until she made a statement, everything was up in the air. She was still alive, so there was a possibility that she could have seen the killers. They couldn't afford any witness at all, but if they tried to erase her, they'd be sitting ducks themselves. From here on, there would be a solid cover on the hospital room. The killers were going to sweat a little more now.

I thought I saw the good corner of her mouth twitch in a smile, and again, I got the small finger squeeze. "Be careful," she said. Her voice was barely audible and she was slipping back into a sleep once more. "I want . . . you back."

Her fingers loosened and her hand slipped out of mine. She didn't hear me when I said, "I want you back, too, baby."

Outside the door, a cop said, "How is she?"

"Making it." He was a young cop, this one. He still had that determined look. He had the freshness of youth, but his eyes told me he had seen plenty of street work since he left the academy. "Did Captain Chambers tell you what this is about?" I asked.

"Only that it was heavy. The rest I got through the grapevine."

"It's going to get rougher," I said. "Don't play down what you're doing."

He grinned at me. "Don't worry, Mike, I'm not jaded yet."

"Take care of my girl in there, will you?"

His face suddenly went serious. "You got it, Mike."

Downstairs, another shift was coming on, fresh faces in white uniforms replacing the worn-out platoon that had gone through a rough offense on the day watch. The interns looked too young to be doctors, but they already had the wear and tear of their profession etched into them. One had almost made it to the door when the hidden PA speaker brought him up short, and with an expression of total fatigue, he shrugged and went back inside.

I cut around the little groups and pushed my way through the outside door. The rain had stopped, but the night was clammy, muting the street sounds and diffusing the light of the buildings. Nights like this stank. There were no incoming taxis and it was a two-block walk to where they might cruise by. There was no other choice, so I went down to the street.

I thought the little guy in the oddball suit who shuffled up to me on the street outside my apartment was another panhandler. He peered at me, a grin twisting his mouth, and said, "Remember me? I'm Ambrose."

"Ambrose who?"

"How many people with a name like that you know? From Charlie the Greek's place, man. Charlie says he wants you to give him a call."

"Why?"

"Beats me, man. He just told me to tell you that. And the sooner the better. It's important."

I told him okay, handed him two bucks, and watched him scuttle away. When I got upstairs, I dug out the old phone book, looked up the Greek's place, and called Charlie. His raspy voice started chewing me out for not stopping by the past six months, and when he was finished, he said, "There's a gent that wants to meet with you, Mike."

Charlie was an old-fashioned guy. When he said gent, it was with quotation marks around it, printed in red. Any gent would be somebody in the chain of command that led to the strange avenues of what they deny is organized crime. He wasn't connected; he was simply a useful tool in the underworld apparatus.

"He got a name, Charlie?"

"Sure, I guess. But I don't know it."

"What's the deal?"

"Like tonight. Can you make it down here tonight?"

I looked at my watch. "Okay, give me thirty. You think I need some backup?"

"Naw. This guy's clean."

"Tell him to sit at the bar."

"You got it, Mike."

The Greek's place was just a run-down old saloon in a neighborhood that was going under the wrecker's ball little by little. Half of the places had been abandoned, but Charlie's joint was near the corner, got a regular trade and a lot of daytime transients, but from four to seven every evening, the gay crowd took over like a swing shift, then left abruptly and everything went back to sloppy normalcy.

A pair of old biddies were sipping beer at the end of the bar and right in the center was a middle-aged portly guy in a dark suit having a highball. His eyes had picked me up in the back bar when I'd come in and we didn't have to be introduced. He waved Charlie over. I said, "Canadian Club and ginger," then we picked up the drinks and went to a table across the room.

"Appreciate your coming," he said.

"No trouble. What's happening?"

"There are some people interested in Tony DiCica's death."

"Pretty messy subject. You know what happened to him?"

He bobbed his head. "Tough."

"Yeah. He sure as hell messed up my office. But that's not what you want to know. Let's get something squared away here. You guys don't give a shit whether DiCica is dead or alive, do you?" I snarled.

"Couldn't care less."

"You mean *unless* he told my secretary what you wanted."

After thinking about it, he acknowledged the point. "Something like that."

I said, "You know, I don't give a rat's ass what Tony had. I don't have it and she doesn't either."

"Some people aren't going to look at it that way," he told me. "Until they are absolutely satisfied, you're going to have a problem."

"There's one hell of a hole in your presentation, fella," I said. "Tony's been running loose a long time. If he had something, why didn't they get it from him when he was alive?"

"You know about Tony's history?"

"I know."

"If you guess the answer, I'll tell you if it's right."

Hell, there could be only one answer. I said, "Tony had something he could hang somebody with." The guy kept watching me. "He had permanent amnesia after getting his head bashed in and didn't remember having it or putting it somewhere." The eyes were still on mine. The story line started to open up now. "Just lately, he said or did something that might have indicated a sudden return of memory." The eyes narrowed and I knew I had it.

When he put his drink away in two quick swallows, he rolled the empty glass between his fingers a moment and said, "A week ago, he suddenly recognized somebody—he called him by his right name."

"Then he relapsed into amnesia again?"

"Nobody knows that."

"So?"

"You have your fingers in all kinds of shit. You move with the clean guys and you go with the dirty ones just as easy. Nobody likes to mess with you because you've blown a few asses off with that cannon of yours and you got buddies up in Badgeville, where it counts. So you'd be just the kind of guy Tony DiCica would run to with a story that would keep his head on his shoulders."

"Crazy," I said.

"He went to your office to arrange something with you. Before you got there, somebody showed up and did the job, expecting to walk away with the information. He didn't have it on him."

This thing was really coming back at me. "Okay, what's my part?"

"He is your client, Mr. Hammer. He told you all in return for an escape route you were to furnish."

"That's a lot of bullshit, you know."

A gesture of his hands meant it didn't make any difference. "You see, as far as certain people are concerned, you're in until they say you're out. The information Tony had can be worth a lot of money and can cause a lot of killing. One way or another, they expect to get it back."

"What happens if the cops get it first?"

"Nobody really expects that to happen," he said. He pulled his cuff back and looked at his watch.

I took one more sip of my drink and stood up. "I guess somebody wants me to talk."

"Certain people are giving you a few days to make a decision."

I could feel my lips pulling back in controlled anger and knew it wasn't a nice grin at all. I pulled the .45 out and watched his eyes go blank until I flipped out the clip and fingered a shell loose. I handed it to him. "Give them that," I said.

"What's this supposed to mean?"

"They'll know," I told him.

I called Pat the next day. "What have you got on DiCica?"

"Interesting history. I'm going off duty. How about a beer?"

"How can you go off duty? It's afternoon."

"I'm the boss, that's how."

"I'll meet you downtown."

Over the beer, Pat told me about Anthony DiCica. He had a listing of all his arrests, convictions that were a laugh, and the victims he was suspected of killing. Every dead guy was involved in the Mob scene, and two of them were really big-time. Those two had been hit simultaneously while they were eating in a small Italian restaurant. DiCica, after shooting both parties in the head twice, made off with an envelope that had been seen on the table by a waiter. Following the hit, there had been an ominous quiet in the city for a week, then several other persons in the organization died. It was two weeks later that Anthony DiCica's head collided with a pipe in a street brawl.

"They went a little overboard in bringing him in and cracked his skull. After that, he was no good to anybody. They still needed his goods and had to wait for him to come out of his memory loss before they could move. . . ."

Pat lifted his beer and made a silent toast. "We really took his place apart, you know."

"No, I didn't know. What did you find?"

"Zilch. There were no hiding places. We even tried the cellar area. If he had anything at all, it's someplace else. End of case. It died with Anthony."

"The hell it did," I said. "Somebody in the organization thinks DiCica suddenly remembered and dropped his secret on me."

"Brother!"

I nodded. "The bastards as much as said it's my ass if I don't produce."

"Shake you up?"

"I've been in the business too long, kiddo. I just get more cautious and keep my forty-five on half cock."

He watched me, frowning, grouping his thoughts. "That mutilation of DiCica could have been a message to you, then."

"It's beginning to look like it," I said.

"What do you do now?"

"See how far I can go before I touch a trip wire."

"You don't give a damn, do you?" he said.

"About what?"

"Anything at all. You don't want any backup, no protection . . . you want to be out there all alone like a first-class idiotic target."

I shrugged.

"There's a lot more of them than there are of you."

I watched him and waited.

He finally said, "They know how you are, Mike. You're leaving yourself wide open."

I felt a tight grin stretch across my lips and said, "That's the trip wire *I* set out."

They knew me at the hospital but wanted to see my ID anyway. The cop at the door scanned my PI ticket and driver's license, checking my face against the photo before letting me into Velda's room.

"Hey, kid," I said softly. In the dim light, I saw her head turn slowly and knew she was awake. They had propped her up, the sheet lying lightly across her breasts, her arms outside it. The facial swelling had lessened, but the discoloration still put a dark shadow on her face. One eye still was closed and I knew smiling wasn't easy.

"Do I look terrible?"

I let out a small laugh and walked to the bed. "I've seen you when you looked better." I took her hand in mine and let the warmth of her seep into me. Inside, I could feel a madness clawing at my guts, scratching at my mind because somebody had done this to her. They had taken soft beauty and a loving body and tried to smash it into a lifeless hulk because it was there and killing was the simple way of moving it.

"Mike, don't," she said.

I sucked my breath in, held it, then eased out. I was squeezing her hand too hard and relaxed my fingers. "Everything okay, kitten?"

"Yes. They are taking care of me." She tilted her head up. "What's happening?"

I filled her in with some of the general information, but she stopped me. She wanted details, so I gave them to her.

I put my hands on the mattress and bent down so my face was close to hers. Her tongue slipped between her lips, wetting them, and as my mouth touched hers, she closed one eye. A kiss is strange. It's a living thing, a communication, a whole wild emotion expressed in a simple moist touch and, when her tongue barely met mine, a silent explosion. We felt, we tasted, then, satisfied, we separated.

"You know what you do to me?" I asked.

She smiled.

"Now I'm as horny as hell and I can't go out in the hall like this. Not yet."

"You can kiss me again while you're waiting."

"No. I'll need a cold shower if I do." I stood up, still feeling her mouth on mine. "I'll be back tomorrow, kitten."

Her smile was crooked and her eye laughed. "What are you going to do with . . . that?" she asked me.

"Hold my hat over it," I told her.

I had the cabby drop me at the corner and picked up a late-evening paper at the kiosk. There was a mist in the air and the streetlights had a soft glow around them and lighted windows in the apartments were gently blurred. It was the kind of night that dampened street sounds and put a dull slick on the pavement.

The doorman at my place generally paced under the marquee, but tonight I couldn't blame him for staying inside. I hugged the side of the building out of the wind, moved around the garbage pails outside the areaway that ran to the rear, and saw the feet inside the glass doors as the guy jumped me from behind.

Damn.

One arm grabbed me around the throat and a fist was ready to slam into my kidneys, but I was twisting and dropping at the same time, so fast that the fucker lost his rhythm and went down with me. His arm came loose and he rolled free, and I forgot all about him because the other one had come out of the hallway with a sap in his hand, ready to lay my skull open. I let the swing go past my face and threw a right smack into his nose, saw his head snap back, then put another into his gut.

Everything was working right. The guy behind me came off the sidewalk thinking he had me nailed. I didn't want any broken knuckles. I just drove my fist into his neck under his chin and didn't wait to see what would happen. The boy with the sap was still standing there, nose stunned, blood all over his face but not out of it.

You don't have to waste any skin on guys like that. I kicked him in the balls, and the pain-instinct reaction was so fast he nearly locked onto my foot. His mouth made silent screaming motions and he went down on his knees, his supper foaming out of his mouth.

I went inside. The doorman was just coming out of it, a lump already growing on the side of his head. "Can you hear me, Jeff?" I said.

He grimaced, his eyes opened and he nodded. "That bastard . . ."

"I have them outside. You give the cops a call."

"Yeah. Damn right."

The big guy I had rapped in the throat was trying to get away. He was on all fours, scratching toward the car at the curb. I took out the .45, let him hear me jack a shell into the chamber, and he stopped cold. That old army automatic can have a deadly sound to it. I walked over to him, knelt down, and poked the muzzle against his head.

"Who sent you?"

He shook his head.

I thumbed the hammer back. That sound, the double click, was even deadlier.

"We . . . was to . . . rough you up." His voice was hardly understandable.

"Who sent you?"

His head dropped, spit ran out of his mouth, and he shook his head again.

"Why?" I asked him. I kept the tone nasty.

All the big slob had in his eyes was fear. "You sent . . . the guys . . . a bullet."

I heard the siren of a squad car coming up Third Avenue. "How much did they pay you?"

"Five hundred . . . each."

"Asshole," I said. I eased the hammer back on half cock and

took the rod away from his head. A grand for a mugging meant that the victim would be wary and dangerous, and these two slobs hadn't given it a thought. I gave him a kick in the side and told him to get over beside his buddy. I didn't have to tell him twice.

Wheels squealing, a car turned at the corner and the floodlight hit me while it was still rolling. The cameraman came out, turning film, a girl in a flapping trench coat right behind him, giving into a hand mike a rapid, detailed description of what was going on, and I even let New York City's favorite on-the-spot TV team catch me giving the guy another boot just for the hell of it.

When the squad car got there, I identified myself, gave a statement, and let the doorman fill in the rest. The two guys had waited near the curb nearly an hour, spotted me at the corner, then one had gone in, grabbed the doorman, then waited until the other had jumped me to lay a sap on his head before joining the fun. Luckily, the sweatband of the doorman's uniform cap had softened the blow. Both of the clowns had knives in their pockets along with the old standbys, brass knuckles and a blackjack. It took one radio call to get an ID on them and they were shoved, handcuffed, into the rear of the squad car.

Enough of the crowd had collected to make it an interesting spot in the late news coming up, and the reporter said, "Any further comment on this, Mr. Hammer?"

At least she'd remembered my name.

"They just tried to mug the wrong guy," I said. Then I winked into the lens and walked away.

Upstairs, I called Pat. I ran through the story again, then added, "It's all coming back to DiCica, buddy. They're making sure I know they're watching."

"You don't scare them, Mike."

"If they think I have access to what Anthony had, I can sure shake them up. What have you got?"

"Something extremely interesting. My boys came up with another lead, an old dealer who is straight now and doesn't want his name mentioned in any way. You're right. It all comes back to when DiCica shot those two gang leaders and picked up that envelope."

"And you know what was in it?"

"Yes. Directions."

"To what?"

"A truckload of cocaine."

"Do you realize how much stuff that is?"

"In dollars, the street value is incredible. Anyway, it came up via Route Ninety-five into the New York area. The trailer was delivered to a depot in Brooklyn, all the paperwork completed, and the next day, another tractor signed for it, hauled it out, and it hasn't been seen to this day."

"But *somebody* would know where the cargo went to."

"Sure," Pat said. "The drivers would have known."

"So they were the only ones who knew?"

"Why not? The fewer the better. They picked their own hiding spot for the shipment, made up a map, and delivered it to the bosses. On the way out, they were followed by hit men and taken out in a supposed accident. The bosses didn't want anybody knowing where the stuff went. Unfortunately, they were in line for a hit themselves that night. And DiCica got the map."

"Tell me something. How much is the street value of the junk today?"

He told me. I let out a low whistle. Nine-digit figures are understandable. When they reach ten, it's almost unbelievable.

"Mike, unless we find that cargo, nothing will ever end."

"Are you checking out all the leads?"

"The trailer would take a certain-size building to be concealed in. We're working on the assumption that something was bought, rather than leased. By now, taxes would be owing, and if anything matches, we'll be on it."

"You don't have that much time."

"Any other options?"
"A lot of luck."

Sickness and injury never stop in the big city. It was a bloody night
in the emergency room, spatters of red on the walls, trails stringing
along the floors, smeared where feet had skidded in its sticky vis-
cosity. The walking wounded were crowded by stretchers and
wheelchairs and my shortcut to Velda's floor was blocked.

When I reached her floor, I pushed through the steel fire door
into the corridor and the wave of quiet was a soft kiss of relief. The
nurse's desk was to my left, the white tip of the attendant's hat
bobbing behind the counter. Someplace, a phone rang and was
answered. Halfway down the hall, a uniformed officer was standing
beside a chair, his back against the wall, reading a paper.

The nurse didn't look up, so I went by her. Two of the rooms
I passed had their doors open, and in a half-lit room, I could see
the forms of the patients, deep in sleep. The next two doors were
closed and so was Velda's.

Until I was ten feet away, the cop didn't give me a tumble,
then he turned and scowled at me. This was a new one on the night
shift and he pulled back his sleeve and gave a deliberate look at his
wristwatch, as if to remind me of the time.

I said, "Everything okay?"

For a second, the question seemed to confuse him. Then he
nodded. "Sure," he replied. "Of course."

All I could do was nod back, like it was stupid of me to ask,
and I let him go back to leaning against the wall. At the desk, the
nurse glanced up. She recognized me and smiled. "Mr. Hammer,
good evening."

"How's my doll doing?"

"Just fine, Mr. Hammer. Dr. Reedey was in twice today. Her
bandages have been changed and one of the nurses has even helped
her with cosmetics."

"Is she moving around?"

"Oh, no. The doctor wants her to have complete bed rest for

now. It will be several days before she'll be active at all." She stopped, suddenly realizing the time herself. "Aren't you a little early?"

"I hope not." Something was bothering me. Something was grating at me and I didn't know what it was. "Nothing out of order on the floor?"

She seemed surprised. "No, everything is quite calm, fortunately."

A small timer on her desk pinged and she looked at her watch. "I'll be back in a few minutes, Mr. Hammer. . . ."

Now I knew what the feeling was. That cop had looked at his watch, too, and his was a Rolex Oyster, a big, fat, expensive watch street cops don't wear on duty. But the real kicker was his shoes. They were regulation black, but they were wing tips. The son of a bitch was a phony, but his rod would be for real and whatever was going down would be just as real.

I said, "How long has that cop been on her door?"

"Oh . . . he came in about fifteen minutes ago."

It was two hours too soon for a shift change.

"Did you see the other one check out?"

"Well, no, but he could have gone—"

"They always take the elevators down, don't they?"

She nodded, consternation showing in her eyes. She got the picture all at once and asked calmly, "What shall I do?"

"Give me the phone and you beat it. Don't look back. Do things the way you always do."

She patted her hair in place, went around the counter, and stepped on down the hall. She didn't look back. I pulled her call sheet over where I could see it and dialed hospital security. The phone rang eight times and nobody answered. I dialed the operator and she tried. Finally she said, "I'll put their code on, sir. The guards must be making their rounds."

Or they're laid out on their backs someplace.

Overhead, the call bell started to ping out a quiet code every few seconds.

I hung up and dialed Pat's office. I said, "Pat, I have no time for talk. I'm at the hospital and everything's breaking loose. There's a phony cop at the door, so the real officer is down somewhere. They're going to try to snatch Velda. Get some cars up here and no sirens. They smell cops and they'll kill her."

"They moving now?"

I heard wheels rolling on the tile and squinted around the wall. Coming out of the last door down on the right was an empty gurney pushed by a man in an orderly's clothes. "They're moving, Pat. Shake your ass."

I hung up and stepped out into the corridor, whistling between my teeth. The guy pushing the gurney stopped and started playing with the mattress. I pushed the button on the elevator, looked down at the cop who was watching me, and waved. The phony cop waved back.

When the elevator halted, I got in, let the doors close, and pushed the Stop button. I stood there, hoping the guy pushing the gurney wouldn't notice the lights over the door standing still. The rubber tires thumped a little louder, passed the elevator, and when I didn't hear them any longer, I pushed the Open button and stared out into the corridor. I took my hat off, dropped it on the floor, and yanked the .45 out of the holster. There was a shell in the chamber and the hammer was on half cock. I thumbed it back all the way and looked down the corridor.

The guy in the orderly's clothes was standing there with an AK-47 automatic rifle cradled in his arms, watching both ends of the hallway. His stance was low, and when he swung, his coat flopped open and it looked like he was wearing upper-body armor. The gurney was sticking out of Velda's door. She was strapped onto the carrier. The man in the uniform came out of her room, a police-service .38 in one hand and one hell of a big bruiser of an automatic in the other. Unless I got some backup, I was totally outgunned and no way could I close in on them without putting Velda's life on the line.

A quiet little code still pinged from the hall bell. Security still hadn't answered.

No wasted moves this time. The pair moved the gurney away from me and I knew they were headed toward the other bank of elevators. The phony orderly had draped a sheet over the gun on his arm. The uniform had hidden the automatic but had placed the .38 on the gurney next to Velda.

I stepped back into the car, let the doors close, pushed the first-floor button, and hoped nobody tried to get on. Like all hospital elevators, this one took forever to pass each level, and before it stopped, I picked my hat up and held it over my .45. When it reached the first floor, I stepped out. This time, I didn't run. The gurney would be moving at proper walking speed, seemingly going through a normal routine, and as long as I hurried, I could meet it outside the building. There was no way this play could be stopped without some kind of shooting, and I didn't want anybody else in the way.

They came out of the elevator just as I stepped outside, and now I felt better. They had turned toward the walkway door and I was waiting out there in the dark. There were only a few seconds to look around for their probable course and find cover. The walkway curved down to the street, but the parking places were filled with off-street overnighters, and the cars there couldn't handle a limp patient. Unless they had planned on a mobile van or a station wagon, any transportation would have to be farther down the line, out of sight from where I was standing.

I moved on down the walk, reached the parked cars, and got into the street behind them. The doors of the hospital swung inward. The guy in the orderly uniform came out first, the AK-47 under his arm, still covered. He never took his eyes off the area in front of him, pulling the gurney forward with one hand while the other man pushed from behind.

The gurney finally slid through the doors and now the phony cop had the oversized automatic in his hand.

I let them pass me, crouching down behind the cars, and when they were about ten feet in front of me, I kept pace with their movements.

A car turned up the road, momentarily lighting the area. It swept over the gurney, but the two went on in a normal manner. I stepped between the parked cars and let it pass. It was a civilian car with a woman at the wheel. It seemed like an hour had passed, but it had been only a few minutes.

Hell, the traffic was light. A squad car could have been here by now. Another set of lights turned up and a truck dropped down a gear and lumbered up the hill. I moved down two car lengths, still staying close, still silently swearing at the frustrating delays in emergency police actions. A car made a U-turn at the hospital and came toward me from the other direction, and only when it got past me did a raucous blast from the loud-hailer yell, "Freeze, police!" and the power lights from the truck turned night into day, blinding the two men in the glare.

Everything happened so quickly that there was a hesitancy in the movements the men made. The phony orderly wasted one second trying to strip the sheet from the AK-47 and a pair of rapid blasts took him down and out. The phony cop jammed himself down in a crouch and his gun came up to shoot through the bottom of the gurney. He was out of the others' sight but not out of mine, and I squeezed off a single round that took him in the shoulder and spun him around like a rag doll.

I was standing and had my hands over my head so the cops wouldn't take me out with a wild shot, figuring me for the other side. Pat came running up, a snub-nosed .38 in his fist, and said, "You okay, Mike?"

"No sweat." I took my hands down in time to yell and point behind Pat, and he turned and fired at the phony cop, who was about to let go at the gurney again. Pat put one into the side of his head, blowing his brains all over the sidewalk. They all came out one side, so his face was gory but still recognizable.

The area was cordoned off so fast no spectators had a chance to get near the bodies. Two cops took the gurney out to the truck and lifted it into the back, and the lady cop from the first car got in with Velda and the truck lurched ahead, made a turn in the street, and headed west.

Pat took my arm and hustled me toward his own marked cruiser that was close by. I said, "Where did you guys come from?"

"Come on, pal, I alerted this team as soon as you headed over here." He yanked a portable radio from his pocket and said into it, "Charlie squad, what do you have?"

There was a click and a hum, and a flat voice answered with, "One officer down in the patient's room, Captain. We have a doctor here who says he was sapped, then drugged. There are two syringes on the bed table, both empty."

"Is the officer okay?"

"Vital signs okay, doc says."

I tapped Pat on the shoulder. "Tell him to check the last room down the hall on the right."

He passed the message on, and a minute later, the receiver hummed and the voice said, "Got a nurse down in there, too, Captain. She got the same treatment. The patient who was there is gone."

"He sure is," Pat told him.

As we got into the car, the radio came alive again. Pat barked a go-ahead, and the cop on the other end said, "Captain, four hospital-security guys just got here. They answered a call in the basement and wound up locked in a storeroom."

"Good. Get a statement from them."

"Roger, Captain."

He turned the key and put the car in gear. Up ahead, the truck was turning the corner and he leaned on the gas to catch up to it. "Mind telling me where we're going?" I asked.

"For tonight, you're going fancy. I'm putting you up in my apartment. We'll hold you there overnight and get you squared away tomorrow. If you weren't a friend, I'd slap you in a prison ward to keep you out of trouble."

"Did you get a good look at the guy you shot?"

"I got a good look at both of them."

"Make 'em?"

He yanked the wheel, going around a car and pulling up directly behind the truck. "The slob playing cop was Nolo Abberniche. He started out as a kid with the Costello bunch. That bastard has knocked off a half dozen guys and all he has is three arrests on petty offenses."

"You seem to have a good line on him."

"Plenty of fliers, nationwide inquiries. Pal, you are traveling in some pretty heavy company. That other guy was Marty Santino. He's another hit man, but he likes fancy jobs. This one was right up his alley."

"Who's paying for it, Pat?"

"That died with those hoods. You know damn well we won't find anything to tie them in directly with any of the Mob boys."

"Beautiful," I said. "We wait for them to make another run on us."

"Not this time, Mike."

"What's that supposed to mean?" I asked him.

"Simple, pal. We have the location of the truck. It's in a barn on a farm north of Lake Hopatcong, New Jersey, on Route Ninety-four, just before Hamburg. Because it's an interstate operation, the FBI can get on this from their local offices a lot faster. And we're taking you and Velda out of the action. You're too important as witnesses and possible targets to be exposed during the mop-up. I know damn well you're not going to let her out of your sight, so we're setting both of you up at a safe house of our choosing. Any objections?"

"No."

"Good. I thought you'd do it my way for once. You'll be covering Velda and we'll be covering both of you, just in case. It may seem redundant, but we don't want to take any chances. Once we haul in that trailer, I expect things will quiet down."

"Things are never quiet around me, Pat. You should know that by now."

"Just shoulder the piece, Mike. You've had your revenge."

Out of the corner of my eye, I caught Pat grinning at me. We both laughed, while the buildings of the city passed by.

· MARCIA MULLER ·

Final Resting Place

In 1977 Marcia Muller's first Sharon McCone book, Edwin of the Iron Shoes, *was published. These days that establishes her as the mother of the series female PI in her present form (G. G. Fickling and Honey West notwithstanding). In 1990 she was awarded the Shamus for this story. In 1993 she was presented with the PWA's life achievement award, the Eye, the first woman so honored.*

THE VOICES OF THE WELL-DRESSED LUNCH CROWD REVERBER-ated off the chromium and Formica of Max's Diner. Busy waiters made their way through the room, trays laden with meat loaf, mashed potatoes with gravy, and hot turkey sandwiches. The booths and tables and counter seats of the trendy restaurant—one of the forerunners of San Francisco's fifties revival—were all taken, and a sizable crowd awaited their turn in the bar. What I waited for was Max's famous onion rings, along with the basket of sliders—little burgers—I'd just ordered.

I was seated in one of the window booths overlooking Third Street with Diana Richards, an old friend from college. Back in the seventies, Diana and I had shared a dilapidated old house a few blocks from the UC Berkeley campus with a fluctuating group of anywhere from five to ten other semi-indigent students, but nowadays we didn't see much of each other. We had followed very different paths since graduation: She'd become a media buyer with the city's top ad agency, drove a new Mercedes, and lived graciously in one of the new condominium complexes near the financial district; I'd become a private investigator with a law cooperative, drove a beat-up MG, and lived chaotically in an old cottage that was constantly in the throes of renovation. I still liked Diana, though—enough that when she'd called that morning and asked to meet with me to discuss a problem, I'd dropped everything and driven downtown to Max's.

Milk shakes—the genuine article—arrived. I poured a generous dollop into my glass from the metal shaker. Diana just sat there, staring out at the passersby on the sidewalk. We'd exchanged the usual small talk while waiting for a table and scanning the menu ("Have you heard from any of the old gang?" "Do you still like your job?" "Any interesting men in your life?"), but then she'd grown uncharacteristically silent. Now I sipped and waited for her to speak.

After a moment she sighed and turned her yellow eyes toward me. I've never known anyone with eyes so much like a cat's; their color always startles me when we meet to renew our friendship. And they are her best feature, lending her heart-shaped face an exotic aura and perfectly complementing her wavy light brown hair.

She said, "As I told you on the phone, Sharon, I have a problem."

"A serious one?"

"Not serious, so much as . . . nagging."

"I see. Are you consulting me on a personal or a professional basis?"

"Professional, if you can take on something for someone who's not an All Souls client." All Souls is the legal cooperative where I work; our clients purchase memberships, much as they would in a health plan, and pay fees that are scaled to their incomes.

"Then you actually want to hire me?"

"I'd pay whatever the going rate is."

I considered. At the moment my regular caseload was exceptionally light. And I could certainly use some extra money; I was in the middle of a home-repair crisis that threatened to drain my checking account long before payday. "I think I can fit it in. Why don't you tell me about the problem."

Diana waited while our food was delivered, then began: "Did you know that my mother died two months ago?"

"No, I didn't. I'm sorry."

"Thanks. Mom died in Cabo San Lucas, at this second home she and my father have down there. Dad had the cause of death hushed up; she'd been drinking a lot and passed out and drowned in the hot tub."

"God."

"Yes." Diana's mouth pulled down grimly. "It was a horrible way to go. And so unlike my mother. Dad naturally wanted to keep it from getting into the papers, so it wouldn't damage his precious reputation."

The bitterness and thinly veiled anger in her voice brought me a vivid memory of Carl Richards: a severe, controlling man, chief executive with a major insurance company. When we'd been in college, he and his wife, Teresa, had crossed the Bay Bridge from San Francisco once a month to take Diana and a few of her friends to dinner. The evenings were not great successes; the restaurants the Richardses chose were too elegant for our preferred jeans and T-shirts, the conversations stilted to the point of strangulation. Carl Richards made no pretense of liking any of us; he used the dinners as a forum for airing his disapproval of the liberal political climate at Berkeley, and boasted that he had refused to pay more than Diana's basic expenses because she'd insisted on enrolling there. Teresa Richards tried hard, but her ineffectual social flutterings reminded me of a bird trapped in a confined space. Her husband often mocked what she said, and it was obvious she was completely dominated by him. Even with the nonwisdom of nineteen, I sensed they were a couple who had grown apart, as the man made his way in the world and the woman tended the home fires.

Diana plucked a piece of fried chicken from the basket in front of her, eyed it with distaste, then put it back. I reached for an onion ring.

"Do you know what the San Francisco Memorial Columbarium is?" she asked.

I nodded. The columbarium was the old Odd Fellows mausoleum for cremated remains, in the Inner Richmond district. Several years ago it had been bought and restored by the Neptune Society—a sort of All Souls of the funeral industry, specializing in low-cost cremations and interments, as well as burials at sea.

"Well, Mom's ashes are interred there, in a niche on the second floor. Once a week, on Tuesdays, I have to consult with a major client in South San Francisco, and on the way back I stop in over the noon hour and . . . visit. I always take flowers—carnations, they were her favorite. There's a little vaselike thing attached to the wall next to the niche where you can put them. There were never any other flowers in it until three weeks ago. But then carnations, always white ones with a dusting of red, started to appear."

I finished the onion ring and started in on the little hamburgers. When she didn't go on, I said, "Maybe your father left them."

"That's what I thought. It pleased me, because it meant he missed her and had belatedly come to appreciate her. But I had my monthly dinner with him last weekend." She paused, her mouth twisting ruefully. "Old habits die hard. I suppose I do it to keep up the illusion we're a family. Anyway, at dinner I mentioned how glad I was he'd taken to visiting the columbarium, and he said he hadn't been back there since the interment."

The man certainly didn't trouble with sentiment, I thought. "Well, what about another relative? Or a friend?"

"None of our relatives live in the area, and I don't know of any close friend Mom might have had. Social friends, yes. The wives of other executives at Dad's company, the neighbors on Russian Hill, the ladies she played bridge with at her club. But no one who would have cared enough to leave flowers."

"So you want me to find out who is leaving them."

"Yes."

"Why?"

"Because since they've started appearing it's occurred to me that I never really knew my mother. I loved her, but in my own way I dismissed her almost as much as my father did. If Mom had that good a friend, I want to talk with her. I want to see my mother through the eyes of someone who *did* know her. Can you understand that?"

"Yes, I can," I said, thinking of my own mother. I would never dismiss Ma—wouldn't *dare* dismiss the hundred-and-five-pound dynamo who warms and energizes the McCone homestead in San Diego—but at the same time I didn't really know much about her life, except as it related to Pa and us kids.

"What about the staff at the columbarium?" I asked. "Could they tell you anything?"

"The staff occupy a separate building. There's hardly ever anyone in the mausoleum, except for occasional visitors, or when they hold a memorial service."

"And you've always gone on Tuesday at noon?"

"Yes."

"Are the flowers you find there fresh?"

"Yes. And that means they'd have to be left that morning, since the columbarium's not open to visitors on Monday."

"Then it means this friend goes there before noon on Tuesdays."

"Yes. Sometime after nine, when it opens."

"Why don't you just spend a Tuesday morning there and wait for her?"

"As I said, I have regular meetings with a major client then. Besides, I'd feel strange, just approaching her and asking to talk about Mom. It would be better if I knew something about her first.

That's why I thought of you. You could follow her, find out where she lives and something about her. Knowing a few details would make it easier for me."

I thought for a moment. It was an odd request, something she really didn't need a professional investigator for, and not at all the kind of job I'd normally take on. But Diana was a friend, so for old times' sake . . .

"Okay," I finally said. "Today's Monday. I'll go to the columbarium at nine tomorrow morning and check it out."

Tuesday dawned gray, with a slowly drifting fog that provided the perfect backdrop for a visit to the dead. Foghorns moaned a lament as I walked along Loraine Court, a single block of pleasant stucco homes that dead-ended at the gates of the park surrounding the columbarium. The massive neoclassical building loomed ahead of me, a poignant reminder of the days when the Richmond district was mostly sand dunes stretching toward the sea, when San Franciscans were still laid to rest in the city's soil. That was before greed gripped the real-estate market in the early decades of the century, and developers decided the limited acreage was too valuable to be wasted on cemeteries. First cremation was outlawed within the city, then burials, and by the late 1930s the last bodies were moved south to the necropolis of Colma. Only the columbarium remained, protected from destruction by the Homestead Act.

When I'd first moved to the city I'd often wondered about the verdigrised copper dome that could be glimpsed when driving along Geary Boulevard, and once I'd detoured to investigate the structure it topped. What I'd found was a decaying rotunda with four small wings jutting off. Cracks and water stains marred its facade; weeds grew high around it; one stained-glass window had buckled with age. The neglect it had suffered since the Odd Fellows had sold it to an absentee owner some forty years before had taken its full toll.

But now I saw the building sported a fresh coat of paint: a medley of lavender, beige, and subdued green highlighted its ornate architectural details. The lawn was clipped, the surrounding fir trees pruned, the names and dates on the exterior niches newly lettered and easily readable. The dome still had a green patina, but somehow it seemed more appropriate than shiny copper.

As I followed the graveled path toward the entrance, I began to feel as if I were suspended in a shadow world between the past and the present. A block away Geary was clogged with cars and trucks and buses, but here their sounds were muted. When I looked to my left I could see the side wall of the Coronet Theater, splattered with garish, chaotic graffiti; but when I turned to the right, my gaze was drawn to the rich colors and harmonious composition of a stained-glass window. The modern-day city seemed to recede, leaving me not unhappily marooned on this small island in time.

The great iron doors to the building stood open, inviting visitors. I crossed a small entry and stepped into the rotunda itself. Tapestry-cushioned straight chairs were arranged in rows there, and large floral offerings stood next to a lectern, probably for a memorial service. I glanced briefly at them and then allowed my attention to be drawn upward, toward the magnificent round stained-glass window at the top of the dome. All around me soft, prismatic light fell from it and the other windows.

The second and third floors of the building were galleries— circular mezzanines below the dome. The interior was fully as ornate as the exterior and also freshly painted, in restful blues and white and tans and gilt that highlighted the bas-relief flowers and birds and medallions. As I turned and walked toward an enclosed staircase to my left, my heels clicked on the mosaic marble floor; the sound echoed all around me. Otherwise the rotunda was hushed and chill; as near as I could tell, I was the only person there.

Diana had told me I would find her mother's niche on the second floor, in the wing called Kepheus—named, as the others were, after one of the four Greek winds. I climbed the curving staircase and began moving along the gallery. The view of the rotunda floor, through railed archways that were banked with philodendrons, was dizzying from this height; the wall opposite the arches was honeycombed with niches. Some of them were covered with plaques engraved with people's names and dates of birth and death; others were glass-fronted and afforded a view of the funerary urns. Still others were vacant, a number marked with red tags— meaning, I assumed, that the niche had been sold.

I found the name Kepheus in sculpted relief above an archway several yards from the entrance to the staircase. Inside was a small-ish room—no more than twelve by sixteen feet—containing per-haps a hundred niches. At its front were two marble pillars and steps leading up to a large niche containing a coffin-shaped box; the ones on the walls to either side of it were backed with stained-glass windows. Most of the other niches were smaller and contained urns of all types—gold, silver, brass, ceramics. Quickly I located Teresa Richards's: at eye level near the entry, containing a simple jar of hand-thrown blue pottery. There were no flowers in the metal holder attached to it.

Now what? I thought, shivering from the sharp chill and glanc-ing around the room. The reason for the cold was evident: part of the leaded-glass skylight was missing. Water stains were prominent on the vaulted ceiling and walls; the pillars were chipped and cracked. Diana had mentioned that the restoration work was being done piecemeal, because the Neptune Society—a profit-making organization—was not eligible for funding usually available to those undertaking projects of historical significance. While I could appre-ciate the necessity of starting on the ground floor and working upward, I wasn't sure I would want my final resting place to be in a structure that—up here, at least—reminded me of Dracula's castle.

And then I thought, Just listen to yourself. It isn't as if you'd be peering through the glass of your niche at your surroundings! And just think of being here with all the great San Franciscans— Adolph Sutro, A. P. Hotaling, the Stanfords and Folgers and Mag-nins. Of course, it isn't as if you'd be creeping out of your niche at night to hold long, fascinating conversations with them, either. . . .

I laughed aloud. The sound seemed to be sucked from the room and whirled in an inverted vortex toward the dome. Quickly I sobered and considered how to proceed. I couldn't just be standing here when Teresa Richards's friend paid her call—*if* she paid her call. Better to move about on the gallery, pretending to be a history buff studying the niches out there.

I left the Kepheus Room and walked around the gallery, glancing at the names, admiring the more ornate or interesting urns, peering through archways. Other than the tapping of my own heels on the marble, I heard nothing. When I leaned out and looked down at the rotunda floor, then up at the gallery above me, I saw no one. I passed a second staircase, wandered along, glanced to my left, and saw familiar marble pillars. . . .

What is this? I wondered. How far have I walked? Surely I'm not already back where I started.

But I was. I stopped, puzzled, studying what I could discern of the columbarium's layout.

It was a large building, but by virtue of its imposing architecture it seemed even larger. I'd had the impression I'd only traveled partway around the gallery, when in reality I'd made the full circle.

I ducked into the Kepheus Room to make sure no flowers had been placed in the holder at Teresa Richards's niche during my absence. Disoriented as I'd been, it wouldn't have surprised me to find that someone had come and gone. But the little vase was still empty.

Moving about, I decided, was a bad idea in this place of illusion and filtered light. Better to wait in the Kepheus Room, appearing to pay my respects to one of the other persons whose ashes were interred there.

I went inside, chose a niche belonging to someone who had died the previous year, and stood in front of it. The remains were those of an Asian man—one of the things I'd noticed was the ethnic diversity of the people who had chosen the columbarium as their resting place—and his urn was of white porcelain, painted with one perfect, windblown tree. I stared at it, trying to imagine what the man's life had been, its happiness and sorrows. And all the time I listened for a footfall.

After a while I heard voices, down on the rotunda floor. They boomed for a moment, then there were sounds as if the tapestried chairs were being rearranged. Finally all fell as silent as before. Fifteen minutes passed. Footsteps came up the staircase, slow and halting. They moved along the gallery and went by. Shortly after that there were more voices, women's, that came close and then faded.

Was it always this deserted? I wondered. Didn't anyone visit the dead who rested all alone?

More sounds again, down below. I glanced at my watch, was surprised to see it was ten-thirty.

Footsteps came along the gallery—muted and squeaky this time, as if the feet were shod in rubber soles. Light, so light I hadn't heard them on the staircase. And close, coming through the archway now.

I stared at the wind-bent tree on the urn, trying to appear reverent, oblivious to my surroundings.

The footsteps stopped. According to my calculations, the person who had made them was now in front of Teresa Richards's niche.

For a moment there was no sound at all. Then a sigh. Then noises as if someone was fitting flowers into the little holder. Another sigh. And more silence.

After a moment I shifted my body ever so slightly. Turned my head. Strained my peripheral vision.

A figure stood before the niche, head bowed as if in prayer. A bunch of carnations blossomed in the holder—white, with a dusting as red as blood. The figure was clad in a dark blue windbreaker, faded jeans, and worn athletic shoes. Its hands were clasped behind its back.

It wasn't the woman Diana had expected I would find. It was

a man, slender and tall, with thinning gray hair. And he looked
very much like a grieving lover.

At first I was astonished, but then I had to control the urge to laugh
at Diana's and my joint naïveté. A friend of mine has coined a
phrase for that kind of childlike thinking: "teddy bears in the brain."
Even the most cynical of us occasionally falls prey to it, especially
when it comes to relinquishing the illusion that our parents—while
they may be flawed—are basically infallible. Almost everyone seems
to have difficulty setting that idea aside, probably because we fear
that acknowledging their human frailty will bring with it a terrible
and final disappointment. And that, I supposed, was what my discovery would do to Diana.

But maybe not. After all, didn't this mean that someone had
not only failed to dismiss Teresa Richards, but actually loved her?
Shouldn't Diana be able to take comfort from that?

Either way, now was not the time to speculate. My job was to
find out something about this man. Had it been the woman I'd
expected, I might have felt free to strike up a conversation with
her, mention that Mrs. Richards had been an acquaintance. But with
this man, the situation was different: he might be reluctant to talk
with a stranger, might not want his association with the dead
woman known. I would have to follow him, use indirect means to
glean my information.

I looked to the side again; he stood in the same place, staring
silently at the blue pottery urn. His posture gave me no clue as to
how long he would remain there. As near as I could tell, he'd given
me no more than a cursory glance upon entering, but if I departed
at the same time he did, he might become curious. Finally I decided
to leave the room and wait on the opposite side of the gallery.
When he left, I'd take the other staircase and tail him at a safe
distance.

I went out and walked halfway around the rotunda, smiling
politely at two old ladies who had just arrived laden with flowers.
They stopped at one of the niches in the wall near the Kepheus

Room and began arguing about how to arrange the blooms in the vase, in voices loud enough to raise the niche's occupant. Relieved that they were paying no attention to me, I slipped behind a philodendron on the railing and trained my eyes on the opposite archway. It was ten minutes or more before the man came through it and walked toward the staircase.

I straightened and looked for the staircase on this side. I didn't see one.

That can't be! I thought, then realized I was still a victim of my earlier delusion. While I'd gotten it straight as to the distance around the rotunda and the number of small wings jutting off it, I hadn't corrected my false assumption that there were two staircases instead of one.

I hurried around the gallery as fast as I could without making a racket. By the time I reached the other side and peered over the railing, the man was crossing toward the door. I ran down the stairs after him.

Another pair of elderly women were entering. The man was nowhere in sight. I rushed toward the entry, and one of the old ladies glared at me. As I went out, I made mental apologies to her for offending her sense of decorum.

There was no one near the door, except a gardener digging in a bed of odd, white-leafed plants. I turned left toward the gates to Loraine Court. The man was just passing through them. He walked unhurriedly, his head bent, hands shoved in the pockets of his windbreaker.

I adapted my pace to his, went through the gates, and started along the opposite sidewalk. He passed the place where I'd left my MG and turned right on Anza Street. He might have parked his car there, or he could be planning to catch a bus or continue on foot. I hurried to the corner, slowed, and went around it.

The man was unlocking the door of a yellow VW bug three spaces down. When I passed, he looked at me with that blank, I'm-not-really-seeing-you expression that we city dwellers adopt as protective coloration. His face was thin and pale, as if he didn't spend a great deal of time outdoors; he wore a small beard and mustache, both liberally shot with gray. I returned the blank look, then glanced at his license plate and consigned its number to memory.

"It's a man who's been leaving the flowers," I said to Diana. "Gordon DeRosier, associate professor of art at SF State. Fifty-three years old. He owns a home on Ninth Avenue, up the hill from the park in the area near Golden Gate Heights. Lives alone; one marriage, ended in divorce eight years ago, no children. Drives a 1979 VW bug, has a good driving record. His credit's also good—he pays his bills in full, on time. A friend of mine who teaches photography at State says he's a likable enough guy, but hard to get to know. Shy, doesn't socialize. My friend hasn't heard of any romantic attachments."

Diana slumped in her chair, biting her lower lip, her yellow eyes troubled. We were in my office at All Souls—a big room at the front of the second floor, with a bay window that overlooks the flat Outer Mission district. It had taken me all afternoon and used up quite a few favors to run the check on Gordon DeRosier; at five Diana had called wanting to know if I'd found out anything, and I'd asked her to come there so I could report my findings in person.

Finally she said, "You, of course, are thinking what I am. Otherwise you wouldn't have asked your friend about this DeRosier's romantic attachments."

I nodded, keeping my expression noncommittal.

"It's pretty obvious, isn't it?" she added. "A man wouldn't bring a woman's favorite flowers to her grave three weeks running if he hadn't felt strongly about her."

"That's true."

She frowned. "But why did he start doing it now? Why not right after her death?"

"I think I know the reason for that: he's probably done it all along, but on a different day. State's summer class schedule just began; DeRosier is probably free at different times than he was in the spring."

"Of course." She was silent a moment, then muttered, "So that's what it came to."

"What do you mean?"

"My father's neglect. It forced her to turn to another man." Her eyes clouded even more, and a flush began to stain her cheeks. When she continued, her voice shook with anger. "He left her alone most of the time, and when he was there he ignored or ridiculed her. She'd try so hard—at being a good conversationalist, a good hostess, an interesting person—and then he'd just laugh at her efforts. The bastard!"

"Are you planning to talk with Gordon DeRosier?" I asked, hoping to quell the rage I sensed building inside her.

"God, Sharon, I can't. You know how uncomfortable I felt about approaching a woman friend of Mom's. This . . . the *implications* of this make it impossible for me."

"Forget it, then. Content yourself with the fact that someone loved her."

"I can't do that, either. This DeRosier could tell me so much about her."

"Then call him up and ask to talk."

"I don't think . . . Sharon, would you—"

"Absolutely not."

"But you know how to approach him tactfully, so he won't resent the intrusion. You're so good at things like that. Besides, I'd pay you a bonus."

Her voice had taken on a wheedling, pleading tone that I remembered from the old days. I recalled one time when she'd convinced me that I really *wanted* to get out of bed and drive her to Baskin-Robbins at midnight for a gallon of pistachio ice cream. And I don't even like ice cream much, especially pistachio.

"Diana—"

"It would mean so much to me."

"Dammit—"

"Please."

I sighed. "All right. But if he's willing to talk with you, you'd better follow up on it."

"I will, I promise."

Promises, I thought. I knew all about promises. . . .

"We met when she took an art class from me at State," Gordon DeRosier said. "An oil-painting class. She wasn't very good. Afterward we laughed about that. She said she was always taking classes in things she wasn't good at, trying to measure up to her husband's expectations."

"When was that?"

"Two years ago last April."

Then it hadn't been a casual affair, I thought.

We were seated in the living room of DeRosier's small stucco house on Ninth Avenue. The house was situated at the bottom of a dip in the road, and the evening fog gathered there; the branches of an overgrown plane tree shifted in a strong wind and tapped at the front window. Inside, however, all was warm and cozy. A fire burned on the hearth, and DeRosier's paintings—abstracts done in reds and blues and golds—enhanced the comfortable feeling. He'd been quite pleasant when I'd shown up on his doorstep, although a little puzzled because he remembered seeing me at the columbarium that morning. When I'd explained my mission, he'd agreed to talk with me and graciously offered me a glass of an excellent zinfandel.

I asked, "You saw her often after that?"

"Several times a week. Her husband seldom paid any attention to her comings and goings, and when he did, she merely said she was pursuing her art studies."

"You must have cared a great deal about her."

"I loved her," he said simply.

"Then you won't mind talking with her daughter?"

"Of course not. Teresa spoke of Diana often. Knowing her will be a link to Teresa—something more tangible than that urn I visit every week."

I found myself liking Gordon DeRosier. In spite of his ordinary appearance, there was an impressive dignity about the man, as well as a warmth and genuineness. Perhaps he could become a friend to Diana, someone who would make up in part for losing her mother before she really knew her.

He seemed to be thinking along the same lines, because he said, "It'll be good to finally meet Diana. All the time Teresa and I were together I'd wanted to, but she was afraid Diana wouldn't accept the situation. And then at the end, when she'd decided to divorce Carl, we both felt it was better to wait until everything was settled."

"She was planning to leave Carl?"

He nodded. "She was going to tell him that weekend, in Cabo San Lucas, and move in here the first of the week. I expected her to call on Sunday night, but she didn't. And she didn't come over as she'd promised she would on Monday. On Tuesday I opened the paper and found her obituary."

"How awful for you!"

"It was pretty bad. And I felt so . . . shut out. I couldn't even go to her memorial service—it was private. I didn't even know how she had died—the obituary merely said 'suddenly.'"

"Why didn't you ask someone? A mutual friend? Or Diana?"

"We didn't have any mutual friends. Perhaps that was the bond between us; neither of us made friends easily. And Diana . . . I didn't see any reason for her ever to know about her mother and me. It might have caused her pain, colored her memories of Teresa."

"That was extremely caring of you."

He dismissed the compliment with a shrug and asked, "Do you know how she died? Will you tell me, please?"

I related the circumstances. As I spoke DeRosier shook his head as if in stunned denial.

When I finished, he said, "That's impossible."

"Diana said something similar—how unlike her mother it was. I gather Teresa didn't drink much—"

"No, that's not what I mean." He rose and began to pace, extremely agitated now. "Teresa did drink too much. It started during all those years when Carl alternately abused her and left her alone. She was learning to control it, but sometimes it would still control her."

"Then I imagine that's what happened that weekend down in Cabo. It would have been a particularly stressful time, what with having to tell Carl she was getting a divorce, and it's understandable that she might—"

"That much is understandable, yes. But Teresa would *not* have gotten into that hot tub—not willingly."

I felt a prickly sense of foreboding. "Why not?"

"Teresa had eczema, a severe case, lesions on her wrists and knees and elbows. She'd suffered from it for years, but shortly before her death it had spread and become seriously aggravated. Water treated with chemicals, as it is in hot tubs and swimming pools, makes eczema worse and causes extreme pain."

"I wonder why Diana didn't mention that."

"I doubt she knew about it. Teresa was peculiar about illness—it stemmed from having been raised a Christian Scientist. Although she wasn't religious anymore, she felt physical imperfection was shameful and wouldn't talk about it."

"I see. Well, about her getting into the hot tub—don't you think since she was drunk, she might have anyway?"

"No. We had a discussion about hot tubs once, because I was thinking of installing one here. She told me not to expect her to use it, that she had tried the one in Cabo just once. Not only had it aggravated her skin condition, but it had given her heart palpitations, made her feel she was suffocating. She hated that tub. If she really did drown in it, she was put in against her will. Or after she passed out from too much alcohol."

"If that was the case, I'd think the police would have caught on and investigated."

DeRosier laughed bitterly. "In Mexico? When the victim is the wife of a wealthy foreigner with plenty of money to spread around, and plenty of influence?" He sat back down, pressed his hands over his face, as if to force back tears. "When I think of her there, all alone with him, at his mercy . . . I never should have let her go. But she said the weekend was planned, that after all the years she owed it to Carl to break the news gently." His fist hit the arm of the chair. "*Why* didn't I stop her?"

"You couldn't know." I hesitated, trying to find a flaw in his logic. "Mr. DeRosier, why would Carl Richards kill his wife? I know he's a proud man, and conscious of his position in the business and social communities, but divorce really doesn't carry any stigma these days."

"But a divorce would have denied him the use of Teresa's money. Carl had done well in business, and they lived comfortably. But the month before she died, Teresa inherited a substantial fortune from an uncle. The inheritance was what made her finally decide to leave Carl; she didn't want him to get his hands on it. And, as she told me in legalese, she hadn't commingled it with what she and Carl held jointly. If she divorced him immediately, it wouldn't fall under the community property laws."

I was silent, reviewing what I knew about community property and inheritances. What Teresa had told him was valid—and it gave Carl Richards a motive for murder.

DeRosier was watching me. "We could go to the police. Have them investigate."

I shook my head. "It happened on foreign soil; the police down there aren't going to admit they were bribed, or screwed up, or whatever happened. Besides, there's no hard evidence."

"What about Teresa's doctor? He could substantiate that she had severe eczema and wouldn't have gotten into that tub voluntarily."

"That's not enough. She was drunk; drunks do irrational things."

"Teresa wasn't an irrational woman, drunk or sober. Anyone who knew her would agree with me."

"I'm sure they would. But that's the point: You knew her; the police didn't."

DeRosier leaned back, deflated and frustrated. "There's got to be some way to get the bastard."

"Perhaps there is," I said, "through some avenue other than the law."

"How do you mean?"

"Well, consider Carl Richards: He's very conscious of his social position, his business connections. He's big on control. What if all of that fell apart—either because he came under suspicion of murder or if he began losing control because of psychological pressure?"

DeRosier nodded slowly. "He *is* big on control. He dominated Teresa for years, until she met me."

"And he tried to dominate Diana. With her it didn't work so well."

"Diana . . ." DeRosier half rose from his chair.

"What about her?"

"Shouldn't we tell her what we suspect? Surely she'd want to avenge her mother somehow. And she knows her father and his weak points far better than you or I."

I hesitated, thinking of the rage Diana often displayed toward Carl Richards. And wondering if we wouldn't be playing a dangerous game by telling her. Would her reaction to our suspicions be a rational one? Or would she strike out at her father, do something crazy? Did she really need to know any of this? Or did she have a right to the knowledge? I was ambivalent: On the one hand, I wanted to see Carl Richards punished in some way; on the other, I wanted to protect my friend from possible ruinous consequences.

DeRosier's feelings were anything but ambivalent, however; he waited, staring at me with hard, glittering eyes. I knew he would embark on some campaign of vengeance, and there was nothing to stop him from contacting Diana if I refused to help. Together their rage at Richards might flare out of control, but if I exerted some sort of leavening influence . . .

After a moment I said, "All right, I'll call Diana and ask her to come over here. But let me handle how we tell her."

It was midnight when I shut the door of my little brown-shingled cottage and leaned against it, sighing deeply. When I'd left Gordon DeRosier's house, Diana and he still hadn't decided what course of action to pursue in regard to Carl Richards, but I felt certain it would be a sane and rational one.

A big chance, I thought. That's what you took tonight. Did you really have a right to gamble with your friend's life that way? What if it had turned out the other way?

But then I pictured Diana and Gordon standing in the doorway of his house when I'd left. Already I sensed a bond between them, knew that they'd forged a united front against a probable killer. Old Carl would get his, one way or the other.

Maybe their avenging Teresa's death wouldn't help her rest more easily in her niche at the columbarium, but it would certainly salve the pain of the two people who remembered and loved her.

· NANCY PICKARD ·

Dust Devil

Not generally known for PI stories, Nancy Pickard nevertheless picked up this award in 1991 for this story, which appeared in the pages of the Armchair Detective, *not well known for its fiction. It seems the two made a great team. Nancy has won countless awards, including the Anthony and the Agatha. That's a triple crown that may never be repeated.*

THE FATHER OF THE CHILD PULLED BACK THE VERTICAL BLINDS that hung at the window of his law office, and stared at the merciless sky that glared back at him from above downtown Kansas City. The sun was a branding iron, scorching the Midwest wherever its rays touched the earth. In this, the hottest August on record, the temperature had broken one hundred degrees for twenty-one days running. Newspapers warned parents not to leave their children or pets in cars, the city pools were so full a person couldn't dive under water without hitting somebody's legs, in airless rooms old people died for lack of fans.

The private investigator who was seated in the room inquired, "Look like it could rain?"

The man at the window, Chad Peters, didn't bother to answer the question that was on everybody's lips. He wasn't looking for rain. He was looking for his three-month-old son, Brook.

"My wife stole him from the hospital," Peters said, as if the private investigator hadn't spoken.

"Your wife's name?"

"Diane." His voice was hard and cracked, like the scorched earth, and it shook with a rage that rivaled the heat of the drought. "Diane Peters. If she's still using my name. If not, she might use her maiden name, Brewer. Diane Brewer. She was going to abort, but I got a court order preventing her from doing it. By the time her lawyers got that reversed, she was too far along in her pregnancy. And then what does she do, she steals the baby she didn't want to begin with. I'm the one who wanted the baby, not her. My son Brook wouldn't be alive if it weren't for me. I don't even know if he is still alive. . . ." He let the blinds fall, plunging his office into artificial coolness and light, and he turned his face away.

The private investigator watched him. He judged Chad Peters to be around forty years old, already a full partner with his name on the door. Peters was tall, slim, a good-looking man, but not likable in his grief; he held himself upright and rigid as a dam, as if afraid that if somebody touched him it would poke a hole in his defenses, and all of his emotions would come rushing out in a drowning flood. The private investigator didn't like him, but he felt sorry for him, all the same. Losing a child to the other parent, that was tough on anybody. When the man had himself under control once again, he looked back at the private investigator. Peters's eyes were red-rimmed, but his flushed cheeks were dry, as if the heat of his anger had dried his tears before they could fall.

"Find them for me," he said. "I'll give you your advance, and expenses, and whatever it costs beyond that, but I'll tell you, the last investigator I hired took my money and ran with it. I never heard from him again after the first couple of phone calls. What I figure is that he found her, and that Diane talked him into letting her go. She's capable of that. Diane would screw an ax murderer if she thought it would hurt me somehow." His glance at the private investigator was aggressive, offensive. "How do I know you won't screw me, too?"

"You don't, but I won't."

Peters shrugged, as if he were past the point of expecting any good to come of anything. "What's your name again?"

"Ken, Mr. Peters. I'm Ken Meredith."

"I can't remember anything anymore. I don't know where to tell you to look, either. I'll give you the names of her family and friends, everything I gave the other guy, I'll give you any information you need, and I'll warn you as I warned him—"

Meredith cocked his head, always interested in warnings.

"Diane is nuts. She's an overgrown flower child, a twenty-seven-year-old hippie who's too young even to know what that means. She didn't want me, she didn't want our child. Too conventional. Too bourgeois. Of course, she also didn't want to use birth control pills while we were married," he said, bitterly. "Too much risk of cancer, she said. You run a greater risk of getting run over by a truck on the highway, I said. It's not your body, she said. Which is the same thing she said when I stopped her from having the abortion. It may not be my body, I said, but it's sure as hell my child. I don't know how far she'll go to spite me, but . . ." Peters shook his head. "I'm afraid. . . ."

"Of what, exactly?"

"That Diane will abandon my son. Or kill him."

"Kill her own child?"

There was a moment of silence, and then Peters said, "What do you think abortion is, Mr. Meredith?"

"What do I do when I find them?"

"Call me, but not if it means letting her out of your sight. If you so much as suspect that she'll run with him again, then take him."

"Steal the baby, just grab him? I can't—"

Peters interrupted him. "She has no rights."

Meredith was not convinced, but he thought of something else that settled the argument for him. "Okay, but it'll cost a lot more if I have to do it that way."

"Of course." The father of the child pulled back a slat of the vertical blinds and stared outside again. Meredith could barely hear his next words. "Everything costs more than you think it will."

The grandmother of the child, on the father's side, showed the private investigator her son's baby book.

"This is Chad as a baby, I'm showing you this because he looked just like my grandson. I got to see Brook in the hospital before she stole him away. Brook is a beautiful baby, just like his daddy was—look at all of that dark hair! I remember the doctor joking, he said, 'Mrs. Peters, if we'd given him a haircut, you wouldn't have had to have a C-section!' Take this picture with you, Mr. Meredith. If you find a baby who looks like this, it's Brook." She was a young and pretty grandmother, and she gazed at him with sad hope in her eyes. "Maybe you could have some copies made? Put them up in truck stops, or something?"

"Where do you think she took him, Mrs. Peters?"

She sighed, and he watched the hope fade from her eyes as the breath escaped from her mouth. "If there were still such a thing as a Haight-Ashbury, she would have taken him there. She was so strange and emotional all the time, Mr. Meredith, I always suspected she must be on drugs. I don't know why Chad married her, although she's pretty, I'd have to say that she's very pretty. Chad always wanted a family, especially children. That could be one reason he married a woman so much younger than he is. And maybe he thought she was fun for a while, so much younger and freer in her behavior, you know."

She was working her wedding band, rubbing it up and down on her finger. Her eyes filled and her voice cracked on her next words.

"I think my worst fear is that she'll sell him, for money, for drugs."

"She isn't a very responsible person," her best friend confided to the private investigator as they sat together in her kitchen drinking sun tea from an iced pitcher she had set on the table between them. "I told the other guy that, too. I'll be straight with you, like I was with him. I love her like a sister, but she was always a little crazy. Like she'd fall for these guys, and she'd just move in with them after one date! Crazy. Nobody does that anymore. It's not . . . responsible. AIDS, and herpes and serial killers and all that. You can't trust people like you used to. But Diane always trusted everybody." Her mouth twisted into an expression of wry bitterness. "At least she did until she met Chad. He taught her that there are people in this world you can only trust to use you. He's like that, incredibly controlling. You'll do things Chad's way, or else. Diane was always so flaky, she must have looked like somebody he could mold, you know? Like turn her into this sweet, obedient little wife." The best friend looked up at Meredith, and laughed. "Boy, was he wrong."

"Why didn't she want to have the baby?"

"Why should she?"

"What?"

"I said, why should she want to have one?"

"I don't know. I thought every woman did."

"No." She didn't say it in an unfriendly way, but just as a statement of fact. He felt a little amazed at that.

"Then why did she keep it and run away with it?"

Her best friend smiled. "He was really cute."

"The baby? Is that the reason, because he was so cute?"

"I don't know, it could be. You probably think she's a bad person because she didn't want to have a baby and because she wanted to abort it. But she isn't. She didn't love Chad and she didn't want to have a baby, especially with him, that's all. You could say that when she *met* her baby, she fell for him." Her best friend grinned. "I told you, she was always falling in love at first sight. So just because she didn't want him before doesn't mean she might not want him when he got here. Sure, she ran away with him, but it wouldn't be the first time she ran off with some guy."

Ken Meredith found himself feeling very confused, as if he'd wandered into a thicket of femaleness where he was lost without a map. He thought of the first PI, and pictured him running off with nutty Diane Peters and her baby. She'd keep him around only until they spent the money, that's what she'd do, and then she'd split again. Although, if she was half as good-looking as her pictures, maybe that wasn't such a bad way for a guy to make a fool of himself, even if it was just for just a little while. Meredith felt like laughing. The heat was getting to him, he decided. He sucked an ice cube into his mouth, to chill himself back into reality.

"But she took him away from his father," he said, talking around the melting cube.

"Well, of course," her best friend said, and then leaned forward to add patiently, as though to someone slow and stupid, "Chad's a lawyer, you know. Chad got custody, in the divorce settlement, and Diane gave up all visitation rights, because she didn't think she wanted the baby. He would have taken the baby away from her forever."

"The baby she didn't want, right?"

"Before. Not after." She screwed up her face so that she looked very intense, as if she were trying to convince him of something. "Mr. Meredith, can you imagine how it'd feel if other people *made* you grow a baby inside of you?" She touched her hands to her abdomen. "It'd be horrible." Her long fingernails scraped the fabric of her yellow shorts. "You'd feel like you wanted to tear it out of you with your bare hands."

"Then why didn't she just go ahead and abort it?"

"Chad told her he'd send her to prison."

Meredith doubted that could happen, but he wasn't sure, so he just said, "Where'd she go with the baby?"

The best friend leaned back, and grinned again. "I'm going to tell you?"

Meredith sighed. He wondered if the other PI had also felt like strangling this woman, if she had said that to him, too.

"No, really," she said, quickly, as if sensing that she'd gone too far. "Honestly, I don't know, although it's true that I wouldn't tell you if I did. But I don't, really."

"What's she using for money?"

The best friend shrugged. "From the divorce. And she's got a car, she could go a long way." The last phrase was accompanied by a swift, sly glance, as if she hoped to persuade him that it was useless to look.

"Mr. Peters is afraid she might abandon the baby."

She looked angry. "No way."

"His mother thinks she might sell the baby for drugs."

That produced a laugh. "Yeah, right."

"But you said yourself that she's irresponsible."

She rubbed her nose and thought about it. "I guess . . . I guess what I'm afraid of is that she won't have the sense to keep him out of this heat. What if she goes into a grocery store, or something, and she leaves him sleeping in her car? You know what she said to me one time? She said, I don't see why you couldn't just leave a baby in the house for ten minutes while you ran to the grocery store. Can you believe that? My God, I told her, in ten minutes— less than that—a house could burn down!" The best friend nibbled on her lower lip. "What if Diane does something dumb like that? He could . . . die. . . ." She looked up at him, the laughter gone. "Okay. Well, I don't know where she went, but she loves nature. She always wanted to live on a farm, out in the country. You might look there."

He thought of all of the Midwest, most of it countryside, all of it baking under the 104-degree sun, and he shook his head, and smiled. "You couldn't be a little more specific?"

"Well, you might try the Flint Hills," she said. "Diane thinks it's beautiful out there." The best friend shuddered. "Gives me the creeps, all that open space."

"Thanks," he said, getting up. By advising him to "try the Flint

Hills," she had narrowed it down to only about a couple of million acres of open country.

"How'd you get to be a private eye?" she asked him.

Abruptly, he sat down again. The best friend was attractive and he was divorced and loathe to go out into the hundred-plus heat again. "I ought to warn you that I'm not really a very nice person," he said, surprising both of them. "What I do, sometimes it's shitty, like spying on unsuspecting people, like that. You might think, well, if a husband's playing around, he's got it coming, but you might be surprised to find out that he's the nice one, and the wife who hired me, she's the bitch. Or maybe it's the husband who hired me and he's a jerk, and his wife, the one I'm following around, she's okay. But I'm working for whoever's paying me, that's the bottom line for me."

"You think Chad's a jerk?" she asked him, smiling a little.

"No, no, I didn't say that. You wouldn't have a beer, would you?"

Ken Meredith figured that the first investigator had also gotten a line on the possibility that the mother and child were hiding in the Flint Hills. According to Peters, the first guy had made his last report from a Rodeway Inn on I-35 at Emporia. Said he was following a lead. Meredith had laughed to himself when he heard that: sure, we're all following leads, even when we're sitting on our butts in air-conditioned motel rooms watching HBO. What the first guy had followed was the money, Meredith figured, and he'd followed it right on down the road.

In the first couple of days after getting the job from Chad Peters, Meredith followed his usual routine for disappearances: no moving violations had been issued to her in the three months she had been gone; she wasn't running up any credit card bills; if she was working, which he doubted, because of the infant, Social Security didn't show any sign of it yet. She had been the assistant manager of a health food store in Kansas City, and he doubted there were many of those in the meat-and-potatoes country of the

Flint Hills. If she had been traveling alone, she might have been one of those adults who was nearly impossible to locate because she didn't want to be found. But as long as she kept the baby with her, he thought he had a chance of finding her. Babies needed diapers. And checkups and shots from doctors, maybe even medicine she'd have to buy from a pharmacy.

It was over one hundred degrees for the twenty-fourth day in a row when he drove southwest out of Kansas City. Even though he'd kept his car in his garage overnight, it didn't cool down enough to be comfortable until he reached Olathe. He wore a short-sleeved shirt and a tie, and his suit coat hung on a hanger in the backseat. On his way out of town, he stopped at a Kmart on Shawnee Mission Parkway and bought a car seat, a baby bottle, some formula, and a pacifier, just in case.

The farther south he drove, the farther away from city sprinklers and garden hoses, the drier and browner the state looked. When he stopped outside of Ottawa for an iced tea, he fancied he could smell the earth smoldering, heating up like a compost heap, slowly incinerating itself, smelling of dead baked grass and garbage. Meredith thought to himself: if we don't get rain soon, we'll be toast by September.

At the edge of the beginning of the Flint Hills, he started asking questions. He showed photographs of Diane and Brook to people working in the hospitals, pediatricians' offices, and drugstores in Emporia. When that netted him nothing, he drove deeper into the Flint Hills themselves, where the cattle listlessly swished flies with their tails at dry water holes.

He wished Diane had been deeply religious, so that he might have stood a chance of locating her through one of the many little churches that dotted the region. But unless you counted an interest in astrology, Diane wasn't religious, her husband had said, with a certain bitter wryness. If only she'd been Catholic, Chad Peters had said, and opposed to abortion, she'd have saved them all a lot of trouble. Just for the hell of it, and because you never knew where the oddest facts might lead you, Meredith bought a cheap horoscope book in a drugstore and looked up the Peterses' birth dates in an astrology book: Diane was an Aries and Chad was a Scorpio. The baby was a Cancer. The private investigator was amused to see that, according to the descriptions in the astrology book, it was no wonder that "flighty, passionate" Aries couldn't stay married to "cynical Scorpio." As for the baby, when he read that Cancers were supposed to love family, home, and hearth, he thought: fat chance for this child.

In Council Groves, near the site of a tree stump where there was a plaque commemorating the fact that General George Custer had rested there with his troops before charging on toward Little Big Horn, Meredith stopped at a grocery store for cigarettes.

More out of habit than hope, he showed the photographs to the clerk who checked him out.

"Oh yeah, I seen her, she come in here for diapers one time."

Meredith nearly laughed out loud. Wasn't it always the way that he found what he wanted when he wasn't really looking. All those nurses, all those pharmacists he'd quizzed, and none of them as helpful as this skinny girl with pimples standing beside the cash register and behind the jar of beef jerky. He could have reached across the *People* magazines and kissed her.

Still, he was afraid to hope for much; after all, Diane could have stopped here once before driving on to Texas, or New Mexico, or even old Mexico, for God's sake. But the clerk decided that yes, the woman with the baby had been back a second time. And then Meredith found a Texaco station where they'd changed a tire for her, and then a volunteer at a thrift shop recalled that a young woman looking like Diane's picture had purchased some baby clothes a few weeks ago. But it was at another grocery store, on the main street, that he made the discovery that settled the issue for him: about a month previously Diane had purchased several hundred dollars' worth of canned goods, diet Cokes, and other imperishables.

That told him she was staying around there, somewhere within driving vicinity of Council Groves. To figure out where, he sought the help of the sheriff.

The sheriff showed Ken Meredith a map of the county and pointed out to him the locations of empty and abandoned buildings. "If she's not staying with friends someplace, or if somebody hasn't taken her in, then my bet is that she's holed up with the baby in one of these vacant places," the sheriff said. "Some of them are in falling-down condition, I mean she'd have to be crazy for sure to live in one of them, but one or two of them are nice places that belong to absentee landowners. Like this ranch—" He penciled an X on a thin line of road on the map. "I suppose she could be camped out, but I think somebody'd notice her, where they wouldn't necessarily if she kept inside of one of these old barns or houses."

By the time he was finished at the sheriff's office, Ken Meredith had a map and a list of rural addresses and directions on how to get to each place. He also had instructions to include the sheriff's office in any action he might be forced to take that might require legal, possibly armed, assistance.

It was easy, he thought, as he got back into his car, when you knew how to do it. He was so damned hot, though, and annoyed at this woman for running away and causing him so much aggravation in such miserable weather. He pictured himself spending the next days driving for miles over dirt and gravel roads, raising clouds of brown dust. What if his car overheated out in the middle of nowhere? What if he busted an oil pan or a tire?

Meredith could almost sympathize with the other private investigator for taking off with the money and saying to hell with the selfish bitch.

The mother of the child climbed the hill behind the cabin every day, sometimes carrying Brook to the top in a papoose sack strapped to her back, other times climbing alone while the baby napped in the cabin. The hill was her Indian lookout, where she'd found an arrowhead that she wore around her neck on a string like an amulet.

The cabin she called her "safe" house. When she'd found it, it was empty except for a broken-leg table and a leftover wooden stool. Diane had cleaned its filthy kitchen, the bathroom, and all the rest of it. There she settled in with Brook, stocking the cupboards with the pans, food, and supplies she purchased after she fled from the hospital, making beds on the floor for both of them out of stolen hospital blankets and thrift store sheets.

Nobody bothered them. Sometimes she longed for the sound of traffic, for a telephone, and especially for a television. At those moments, she felt ashamed of her weakness. Then she reminded herself that she loved the cabin, its isolation, the eerie quiet, the pitch-dark nights that made her feel as if she were as courageous as the early prairie mothers.

She even loved the drought.

It seemed, on some days, to evaporate her, so that she felt as if she'd disappeared entirely. On other days, it baked her into a calm, stolid passivity that felt like endurance.

"We're blessed," she whispered to the baby. "Thank the stars for these blessings, my little one."

The two of them, mother and child, had themselves and Diane's full breasts and canned goods in the cupboards and the cabin and the enveloping, comforting heat. During the days, she felt safe. But at night, waves of emotion—love, hate, fear—swept over Diane like terrifying, psychedelic waves of shimmering, pulsating heat.

One day after lunch, in the third month of their disappearance, when the baby was asleep in the cabin, Diane climbed to the top of the hill. The brown grass, hard and prickly as straight pins, crackled under her tennis shoes so that she felt as if she were climbing a tinfoil mountain.

As she climbed, the sun felt like a warm body pressed against her, sweating against her, and it filled her with a different, but very familiar, kind of longing. At the top, she stripped out of her halter top, her jeans, her panties, even her shoes. Stepping carefully on the flint pebbles and the grass that cut her feet, she stood on the hilltop, feeling like a tiny, invisible speck of life in an immense, dying landscape.

She could see no one.

No one could see her.

She lifted her arms above her head, so her hair fell down her back, and she closed her eyes and faced the sun. She hummed, the sort of tuneless song she thought an Indian woman might have hummed, a propitiation, and a prayer of gratitude to the sun.

The heat embraced her.

After a moment, she turned her face away from the sun and opened her eyes.

Down the dirt lane, dust was moving.

A deer? Diane lowered her arms to her sides, smiling at the thought of a deer—perhaps the antlered stag she had seen—and herself alone on the prairie, two natural creatures in a wilderness. . . .

The dust moved, and cleared, and she saw a man walking down the dirt road.

The shock of seeing a human being on the lane was so great that for a moment she didn't move. Then she dropped to the ground, wincing as the sharp grass and rocks bit her bare skin. Frantic with haste and fear, she worked herself back into the halter, jeans, and shoes, leaving the panties where they lay. When she looked up again, the man was closer, walking without any sound she could hear, keeping to the shade of the cottonwood trees, but coming steadily, as if he had a purpose in mind.

From behind the old tractor, with shaking hands and racing heart, she observed him.

He was tall, thin, with straight brown hair that shone when the sun hit it, as if it were greasy. The man wore city shoes and cheap-looking trousers and a short-sleeved blue shirt, opened three buttons at the neck so that his white T-shirt showed beneath it. He kept to the shadows, walking with his eyes on his shoes, except that every few seconds, he glanced up at the cabin. He didn't look at the top of the hill. Was that because he had already spied her there?

"Who are you?" she whispered, her mouth gone as dry as the ground around her.

With a single long stride, the man stepped out from the shade of the cottonwoods and began the long walk up the driveway. Diane strained to hear the sound of gravel under his shoes. Why would a stranger walk up her gravel drive in the middle of the broiling day? There were many possible reasons, but only one likely one. She stared at him so hard her eyes squinted to slits in the sun, as if she were trying to probe through that long skull into the reasons he held in his brain, as if she were trying to will him away, away! He had a long, tired face, and he looked angry, as if the heat had provoked him.

She watched him walk up the two steps to the back door.

Now he stood between her and the baby, and she felt it acutely. The three of them were in a line now—Diane crouching at the top of the rise, the stranger at the door, and the baby sleeping in the cabin.

Ken Meredith cupped his hands, making binoculars out of them, and peered through the window that was set into the back door of the little cabin. He couldn't see into the dark interior, so he drew back and walked around the house, trying to look into the other windows. But they were all curtained against the sun. Or against somebody looking in them, and maybe seeing something hidden in there?

Instead of knocking, he placed his hand on the door knob.

"What are you doing!"

Startled, he turned quickly and looked toward the sound of the woman's voice. He saw her now, standing at the top of the rise behind the cabin. At first, he thought he was hallucinating in the heat, because what he thought he saw was a wild-haired, copper-skinned Indian woman above him. But then he saw that it was Diane

Peters, all right, and that she was holding a good-sized rock in her right hand.

He held his hands high, open wide, to display innocence.

He had the unnerving feeling of having aroused something ancient and primitive from deep within the Flint Hills of the prairie. He was not normally an introspective man, or even a sensitive one, but Meredith knew fear when he saw it, and raw, dangerous fury.

He put down his hands, easily, appeasingly.

"Ran out of gas, ma'am. Use your phone?"

His heart beat twice before she said, "You'll have to go somewhere else."

The private investigator pretended to slump against the back door screen. "I don't think I can," he called tiredly up to her, and smiled as charmingly as he knew how. "Ma'am, I've already walked about five miles in these darned shoes, and if I don't get a drink of water, I'm going to die right here on your stoop. Please, if you could even make the call for me, I'll leave, and wait back down the road for the tow truck."

"I thought you said you ran out of gas."

He coughed into his hands before he squinted up at her again. "I don't know for sure that's the problem, ma'am. Could be a dead battery, or maybe it's just this heat that killed it, you know how cars are, they're like us people, can't take too much pressure." He smiled again, inviting her to smile down, to climb down the hill to him.

Instead, she shifted her weight, lifting the rock for a moment as she did so.

Instinctively, Meredith stepped back, though he tried to disguise the movement as meaningless and as casual as a man shaking dirt out of his shoe. But he knew that she had seen it and recognized that no man with just an empty gas tank on his mind would move so quickly, so defensively.

"Go away," she said in a tough voice.

He pursed his lips, as if he were thinking that over, but then he shook his head at her, almost sadly, as if he were disappointed in her.

The man suddenly cocked his head toward the cabin.

Oh my God, Diane thought, he's heard the baby.

One of his hands disappeared from her view, and she realized he was opening the cabin door.

Through the open windows, filtered through the curtains and the dusty screens, came the crying sounds of a baby waking up. The man shot her a look that had cunning in it. Quickly, he turned his back on her and faced the door.

"No!" Diane screamed. "Stay out of there!"

She ran down the hill at him, and reached the stoop just as he was about to shut the door in her face. Diane shoved her weight at the door, forcing it open.

"Damn, lady!"

The door pushed Meredith backward, and he was laughing a little, as though in astonishment at her strength. "Now hold on, Diane, let's just talk about this. . . ." His arms flew up to protect his head as she flung herself at him with the rock. "Your husband's got a right to see his baby. . . ."

The baby began to wail in the bedroom.

"No!" She brought the rock down on the side of Meredith's face. Blood ran into his eyes, blinding him, and then into his open, astonished mouth, choking him. "No, no, no!" With every scream, she struck him, until he slumped to the floor.

Her hands lost their strength, and the rock fell out of them.

The man was still breathing.

After a moment, Diane stepped over him.

She washed her hands at the sink, and then ran to the screaming baby. With the stranger out of her sight, around the bend of the L-shaped room, she nursed Brook back to tranquillity.

"I will never let anyone take you away from me."

She whispered it over and over, in a singsong, like a lullaby.

The idea had come to her as she had lain in her own blood

on the delivery table, the very moment they placed at her breast the baby that Chad had forced her to bear, and which he would force her to give up forever. She had stared at the tiny face and thought: this is what Chad wants more than anything else in the world. And suddenly she had known what to do. She would take the baby. By running away with the child, she could make Chad suffer every day for the rest of his life. Lying on the delivery table with the baby in her arms, filled with hatred for her ex-husband, Diane had felt a stirring of love for the child, as unexpected as a lily floating in a pool of acid. She also experienced an orgasmic-like rush of the vicious, soul-deep satisfaction of perfect revenge. She vowed: no one will ever take this child away from me.

Nobody. Ever.

While the baby kicked his legs happily on the cabin floor, Diane pulled the unconscious man deep into the cold, damp darkness of the storm cellar where the other man's body lay, and then she walked out and bolted the door. This time, she didn't take his wallet to see what his name was, or how old he was, or to see if he had any pictures in his wallet of a wife or little children. This time she didn't want to know anything about him, not even if he carried a private investigator's license, like the first one. She did remove his keys, however, and then set out walking until she found his car a half mile down the road. She drove it into the same barn where her own car was stored, and then abandoned the vehicles to the owls and rats. Back at the cabin, Diane scrubbed the linoleum floor, while her jeans and halter top soaked in cold water in the sink.

In the morning, the baby giggled at the sight of the deer in the pasture.

The drought carried on into September.

In Kansas City, Chad Peters hired a third private eye, this one a former cop by the name of Ed Banks.

In the country, every day after lunch, Diane climbed the rise behind the house. The heat was such that she began taking her clothes off inside the cabin and going naked into the afternoon. The sun baked her skin to brown and warmed the milk in her heavy breasts.

At the top of the rise, she raised her arms to the sun, her hair fell down her back like an Indian blanket, and she closed her eyes. When she opened them, she gazed down, looking for dust devils blowing up the long dirt road.

· BENJAMIN M. SCHUTZ ·

Mary, Mary, Shut the Door

Not only did this story win the Shamus for 1992; it won the MWA Edgar, as well. That had not happened since Lawrence Block did it in 1984 with "By the Dawn's Early Light." This puts Ben Schutz in damned good company. Ben also won the Shamus Award for best novel in 1987 for his Leo Haggerty novel A Tax in Blood. *"Mary, Mary, Shut the Door" also features Haggerty.*

ENZO SCOLARI MOTORED INTO MY OFFICE AND MOTIONED ME to sit. What the hell, I sat. He pulled around to the side of my desk, laced his fingers in his lap, and sized me up.

"I want to hire you, Mr. Haggerty," he announced.

"To do what, Mr. Scolari?"

"I want you to stop my niece's wedding."

"I see. And why is that?"

"She is making a terrible mistake, and I will not sit by and let her do it."

"Exactly what kind of mistake is she making?"

"She knows nothing about him. They just met. She is infatuated, nothing more. She knows nothing about men. Nothing. The first one to pay any attention to her and she wants to get married."

"You said they just met. How long ago, exactly?" Just a little reality check.

"Two weeks. Can you believe it? Two weeks. And I just found out about it yesterday. She brought him to the house last night. There was a party and she introduced him to everyone and told us she was going to marry him. How can you marry someone you've known for two weeks? That's ridiculous. It's a guarantee of failure and it'll break her heart. I can't let that happen."

"Mr. Scolari, I'm not sure we can help you with this. Your niece may be doing something foolish, but she has a right to do it. I understand your concern for her well-being, but I don't think you need a detective, maybe a priest or a therapist. We don't do pre-marital background checks. Our investigations are primarily criminal."

"The crime just hasn't happened yet, Mr. Haggerty. My niece may be a foolish girl, but he isn't. He knows exactly what he's doing."

"And what is that?"

"He's taking advantage of her naïveté, her innocence, her fears, her loneliness, so he can get her money. That's a crime, Mr. Haggerty."

And a damn hard one to prove. "What are you afraid of, Mr. Scolari? That he'll kill her for her money? That's quite a leap from an impulsive decision to marry. Do you have any reason to think that this guy is a killer?"

He straightened up and gave that one some thought. Enzo Scolari was wide and thick with shoulders so square and a head so flat he could have been a candelabra. His snow-white eyebrows and mustache hung like awnings for his eyes and lips.

"No. Not for that. But I can tell he doesn't love Gina. Last night I watched him. Every time Gina left his side his eyes went somewhere else. A man in love, his eyes follow his woman everywhere. No, he's following the maid or Gina's best friend. Gina comes back and he smiles like she's the sunrise. And she believes it.

"He spent more time touching the tapestries than he did holding her hand. He went through the house like a creditor, not a guest. No, he doesn't want Gina, he wants her money. You're right, murder is quite a step from that, but there are easier ways to steal. Gina is a shy, quiet woman who has never had to make any decisions for herself. I don't blame her for that. My sister, God rest her soul, was terrified that something awful would happen to Gina and she tried to protect her from everything. It didn't work. My sister was the one who died and it devastated the girl. Now Gina has to live in the world and she doesn't know how. If this guy can talk her into marrying him so quickly, he'll have no trouble talking her into letting him handle her money."

"How much money are we talking about here?"

"Ten million dollars, Mr. Haggerty." Scolari smiled, having made his point. People have murdered or married for lots less.

"How did she get all this money?"

"It's in a trust for her. A trust set up by my father. My sister and I each inherited half of Scolari Enterprises. When she died, her share went to Gina as her only child."

"This trust, who manages it?"

"I do, of course."

Of course. Motive number two just came up for air. "So, where's the problem? If you control the money, this guy can't do anything."

"I control the money as trustee for my sister. I began that when Gina was still a little girl. Now she is of age and can control the money herself if she wants to."

"So you stand to lose the use of ten million dollars. Have I got that right?"

Scolari didn't even bother to debate that one with me. I liked that. I'll take naked self-interest over the delusions of altruism any day.

"If they've just met, how do you know that this guy even knows that your niece has all this money?"

Scolari stared at me, then spat out his bitter reply. "Why else would he have pursued her? She is a mousy little woman, dull and plain. She's afraid of men. She spent her life in those fancy girls' schools where they taught her how to set the table. She huddled with her mother in that house, afraid of everything. Well, now she is alone and I think she's latched onto the first person who will rescue her from that."

"Does she know how you feel?"

He nodded. "Yes, she does. I made it very clear to her last night."

"How did she take it?"

"She told me to mind my own business." Scolari snorted. "She doesn't even know that that's what I'm doing. She said she loved him and she was going to marry him, no matter what."

"Doesn't sound so mousy to me. She ever stand up to you before?"

"No, never. On anything else, I'd applaud it. But getting married shouldn't be the first decision you ever make."

"Anyone else that might talk to her that she'd listen to?"

"No. She's an only child. Her father died when she was two in the same explosion that killed my father and took my legs. Her mother died in an automobile accident a little over a year ago. I am a widower myself and Gina was never close to my sons. They frightened her as a little girl. They were loud and rough. They teased her and made her cry." Scolari shrugged as if boys would be boys. "I did not like that and would stop it whenever I caught them, but she was such a timid child, their cruelty sprouted whenever she was around. There is no other family."

I picked up the pipe from my desk, stuck it in my mouth, and chewed on it. A glorified pacifier. Kept me from chewing up the inside of my mouth, though. Wouldn't be much of a stretch to take this one on. What the hell, work is work.

"Okay, Mr. Scolari, we'll take the case. I want you to understand that we can't and we won't stop her wedding. There are guys who will do that, and I know who they are, but I wouldn't give you their names. We'll do a background check on this' guy and see if we can find something that'll change her mind or your mind. Maybe they really love each other. That happens, you know. This may be a crazy start, but I'm not sure that's a handicap. What's the best way to run a race when you don't know where the finish is?" I sure didn't have an answer and Scolari offered none.

"Mr. Haggerty, I am not averse to taking a risk, but not a blind one. If there's information out there that will help me calculate the odds, then I want it. That's what I want you to get for me. I appreciate your open mind, Mr. Haggerty. Perhaps you will change my mind, but I doubt it."

"Okay, Mr. Scolari. I need a description of this guy, his name and anything else you know about him. First thing Monday morning, I'll assign an investigator and we'll get on this."

"That won't do, Mr. Haggerty. You need to start on this immediately, this minute."

"Why is that?"

"Because they flew to St. Mary's this morning to get married."

"Aren't we a little late, then?"

"No. You can't apply for a marriage license on St. Mary's until you've been on the island for two days."

"How long to get the application approved?"

"I called the embassy. They say it takes three days to process the application. I'm looking into delaying that, if possible. Once it's issued they say most people get married that day or the next."

"So we've got what, five or six days? Mr. Scolari, we can't run a complete background check in that period of time. Hell, no one can. There just isn't enough time."

"What if you put everyone you've got on this, round the clock?"

"That gets you a maybe and just barely that. He'd have to have a pimple on his backside the size of Mount Rushmore for us to find it that fast. If this guy's the sneaky, cunning opportunist that you think he is, then he's hidden that, maybe not perfectly, but deep enough that six days won't turn it up. Besides, I can't put everyone on this, we've got lots of other cases that need attention."

"So hire more staff, give them the other cases, and put everyone else on this. Money is no object, Mr. Haggerty. I want you to use all your resources on this."

My jaw hurt from clamping on the dead pipe. Scolari was old enough to make a foolish mistake. I told him it was a long shot at best. What more could I tell him? When did I become clairvoyant, and know how things would turn out? Suppose we did find something, like three dead ex-wives? Right! Let's not kid ourselves—all the staff for six days—round the clock—that's serious money. What was it Rocky said? When you run a business, money's always necessary but it's never sufficient. Don't confuse the two and what you do at the office won't keep you up at night.

I sorted everything into piles and then decided. "All right, Mr. Scolari, we'll do it. I can't even tell you what it'll cost. We'll bill you at our hourly rates plus all the expenses. I think a reasonable retainer would be thirty thousand dollars."

He didn't even blink. It probably wasn't a week's interest on ten million dollars.

"There's no guarantee that we'll find anything, Mr. Scolari, not under these circumstances. You'll know that you did everything you could, but that's all you'll know for sure."

"That's all you ever know for sure, Mr. Haggerty."

I pulled out a pad to make some notes. "Do you know where they went on St. Mary's?"

"Yes. A resort called the Banana Bay Beach Hotel. I have taken the liberty of registering you there."

"Excuse me." I felt like something under his front wheel.

"The resort is quite remote and perched on the side of a cliff. I have been assured that I would not be able to make my way around. I need you to be my legs, my eyes. If your agents learn anything back here, someone has to be able to get that information to my niece. Someone has to be there. I want that someone to be you, Mr. Haggerty. That's what I'm paying for. Your brains, your eyes, your legs, to be there because I can't."

I stared at Scolari's withered legs and the motorized wheelchair he got around in. More than that he had money, lots of money. And money's the ultimate prosthetic.

"Let's start at the top. What's his name?"

The island of St. Mary's is one of lush green mountains that drop straight into the sea. What little flat land there is, is on the west coast, and that's where almost all the people live. The central highlands and peaks are still wild and pristine.

My plane banked around the southern tip of the island and headed toward one of those flat spots, the international airport. I flipped through the file accumulated in those few hours between Enzo Scolari's visit and my plane's departure. While Kelly, my secretary, made travel arrangements I called everyone into the conference room and handed out jobs. Clancy Hopper was to rearrange caseloads and hire temporary staff to keep the other cases moving. Del Winslow was to start investigating our man Derek Marshall. We had a name, real or otherwise, an address, and a phone number. Del would do the house-to-house with the drawing we made from Scolari's description. Larry Burdette would be smilin' and dialin'. Calling every computerized data base we could access to get more information. Every time Marshall's name appeared he'd take the information and hand it to another investigator to verify every fact and then backtrack each one by phone or in person until we could re-create the life of Derek Marshall. Our best chance was with the St. Mary's Department of Licenses. To apply for a marriage license Marshall had to file a copy of his passport, birth certificate, decrees of divorce if previously married, death certificate if widowed, and proof of legal name change, if any. If the records were open to the public, we'd get faxed copies or I'd go to the offices myself and look at them personally. I took one last look at the picture of Gina

Dalesandro and then the sketch of Derek Marshall, closed the file, and slipped it into my bag as the runway appeared outside my window.

I climbed out of the plane and into the heat. A dry wind moved the heat around me as I walked into the airport. I showed my passport and had nothing to declare. They were delighted to have me on their island. I stepped out of the airport and the cab master introduced me to my driver. I followed him to a battered Toyota, climbed into the front seat, and stowed my bag between my feet. He slammed the door and asked where to.

"Banana Bay Beach Hotel," I said as he turned the engine on and pulled out.

"No problem."

"How much?" We bounced over a sleeping policeman.

"Eighty ecee."

Thirty-five dollars American. "How far is it?"

"Miles or time?"

"Both."

"Fifteen miles. An hour and a half."

I should have gotten out then. If the road to hell is paved at all, then it doesn't pass through St. Mary's. The coast road was a lattice of potholes winding around the sides of the mountains. There were no lanes, no lights, no signs, and no guardrails. The sea was a thousand feet below and we were never more than a few inches from visiting it.

Up and down the hills, there were blue bags on the trees.

"What are those bags?" I asked.

"Bananas. The bags keep the insects away while they ripen."

I scanned the slopes and tried to imagine going out there to put those bags on. Whoever did it, they couldn't possibly be paying him enough. Ninety minutes of bobbing and weaving on those roads like a fighter on the ropes and I was exhausted from defying gravity. I half expected to hear a bell to end the trip as we pulled up to the resort.

———

I checked in, put my valuables in a safe-deposit box, took my key and information packet, and headed up the hill to my room. Dinner was served in about an hour. Enough time to get oriented, unpack, and shower.

My room overlooked the upstairs bar and dining area and below that the beach, the bay, and the surrounding cliffs. I had a thatched-roof veranda with a hammock and clusters of flamboyant and chenille red-hot cattails close enough to pluck. The bathroom was clean and functional. The bedroom large and sparely furnished. Clearly, this was a place where the attractions were outdoors and rooms were for sleeping in. The mosquito netting over the bed and the coils on the dresser were not good signs. It was the rainy season and Caribbean mosquitoes can get pretty cheeky. In Antigua one caught me in the bathroom and pulled back the shower curtain like he was Norman Bates.

I unpacked quickly and read my information packet. It had a map of the resort, a list of services, operating hours, and tips on how to avoid common problems in the Caribbean such as sunburn, being swept out to sea, and a variety of bites, stings, and inedible fruits. I familiarized myself with the layout and took out the pictures of Gina and Derek. Job one was to find them and then tag along unobtrusively until the home office gave me something to work with.

I showered, changed, and lay down on the bed to wait for dinner. The best time to make an appearance was midway through the meal. Catch the early birds leaving and the stragglers on their way in.

Around eight-thirty, I sprayed myself with insect repellent, slipped my keys into my pocket, and headed down to dinner. The schedule said that it would be a barbecue on the beach.

At the reception area I stopped and looked over the low wall to the beach below. Scolari was right, he wouldn't be able to get around here. The rooms jutted out from the bluff and were connected by a steep roadway. However, from this point on, the hillside was a precipice. A staircase wound its way down to the beach. One hundred and twenty-six steps, the maid said.

I started down, stopping periodically to check the railing. There were no lights on the trail. Late at night, a little drunk on champagne, a new bride could have a terrible accident. I peered over the side at the concrete roadway below. She wouldn't bounce and she wouldn't survive.

I finished the zigzagging descent and noted that the return trip would be worse.

Kerosene lamps led the way to the beach restaurant and bar. I sat on a stool, ordered a yellowbird, and turned to look at the dining area. Almost everyone was in couples, the rest were families. All white, mostly Americans, Canadians, British, and German. At least that's what the brochure said.

I sipped my drink and scanned the room. No sign of them. No problem, the night was young even if I wasn't. I had downed a second drink when they came in out of the darkness. Our drawing of Marshall was pretty good. He was slight, pale, with brown hair parted down the middle, round-rimmed tortoiseshell glasses, and a deep dimpled smile he aimed at the woman he gripped by the elbow. He steered her between the tables as if she had a tiller.

They took a table and I looked about to position myself. I wanted to be able to watch Marshall's face and be close enough to overhear them without looking like it. One row over and two up a table was coming free. I took my drink from the bar and ambled over. The busboy cleared the table and I took a long sip from my drink and set it down.

Gina Dalesandro wore a long flower-print dress. Strapless, she had tan lines where her bathing suit had been. She ran a finger over her ear and flipped back her hair. In profile she was thin-lipped, hook-nosed, and high-browed. Her hand held Marshall's, and then, eyes on his, she pulled one to her and kissed it. She moved from one knuckle to the next, and when she was done she took a finger and slowly slid it into her mouth.

"Gina, please, people will look," he whispered.

"Let them," she said, smiling around his finger.

Marshall pulled back and flicked his eyes around. My waitress had arrived and I was ordering when he passed over me. I had the fish chowder, the grilled dolphin with stuffed christophine, and another drink.

Gina picked up Marshall's hand and held it to her cheek and said something soothing because he smiled and blew her a kiss. They ordered and talked in hushed tones punctuated with laughter and smiles. I sat nearby, watching, waiting, her uncle's gargoyle in residence.

When dessert arrived, Gina excused herself and went toward the ladies' room. Marshall watched her go. I read nothing in his face or eyes. When she disappeared into the bathroom, his eyes wandered around the room, but settled on no one. He locked in on her when she reappeared and led her back to the table with his eyes. All in all it proved nothing.

We all enjoyed the banana cake and coffee and after a discreet pause I followed them back toward the rooms. We trudged silently up the stairs, past the bar and the reception desk, and back into darkness. I kept them in view as I went toward my room and saw that they were in room 7, two levels up and one over from me. When their door clicked closed, I turned around and went back to the activities board outside the bar. I scanned the list of trips for tomorrow to see if they had signed up for any of them. They were down for the morning trip to the local volcano. I signed aboard and went to arrange a wake-up call for the morning.

After a quick shower, I lit the mosquito coils, dialed the lights way down, and crawled under the netting. I pulled the phone and my book inside, propped up the pillows, and called the office. For his money, Scolari should get an answer. He did.

"Franklin Investigations."

"Evening, Del. What do we have on Derek Marshall?"

"Precious little, boss, that's what."

"Well, give it to me."

"Okay, I canvassed his neighborhood. He's the invisible man.

Rented apartment. Manager says he's always on time with the rent. Nothing else. I missed the mailman, but I'll catch him tomorrow. See if he can tell me anything. Neighbors know him by sight. That's about it. No wild parties. Haven't seen him with lots of girls. One thought he was seeing this one particular woman but hasn't seen her around in quite a while."

"How long has he been in the apartment?"

"Three years."

"Manager let you look at the rent application?"

"Leo, you know that's confidential. I couldn't even ask for that information."

"We prosper on the carelessness of others, Del. Did you ask?"

"Yes, and he was offended and indignant."

"Tough shit."

"Monday morning we'll go through court records and permits and licenses for the last three years, see if anything shakes out."

"Neighbors tell you anything else?"

"No, like I said, they knew him by sight, period."

"You find his car?"

"Yeah. Now that was a gold mine. Thing had stickers all over it."

"Such as?"

"Bush-Quayle. We'll check him out with Young Republican organizations. Also, Georgetown Law School."

"You run him through our directories?"

"Yeah, nothing. He's either a drone or modest."

"Call Walter O'Neil, tonight. Give him the name, see if he can get a law firm for the guy, maybe even someone who'll talk about him."

"Okay. I'm also going over to the school tomorrow, use the library, look up yearbooks, et cetera. See if we can locate a classmate. Alumni affairs will have to wait until Monday."

"How about NCIC?"

"Clean. No warrants or arrests. He's good or he's tidy."

"Anything else on the car?"

"Yeah, a sticker for something called Ultimate Frisbee. Nobody here knows anything about it. We're trying to track down an association for it, find out where it's played, then we'll interview people."

"Okay. We've still got three, maybe four days. How's the office doing? Are the other cases being covered?"

"Yeah, we spread them around. Clancy hired a couple of freelancers to start next week. Right now, me, Clancy, and Larry are pulling double shifts on this. Monday when the offices are open and the databases are up, we'll probably put the two new guys on it."

"Good. Any word from the St. Mary's registrar's office?"

"No. Same problem there. Closed for the weekend. Won't know anything until Monday."

"All right. Good work, Del." I gave him my number. "Call here day or night with anything. If you can't get me directly, have me paged. I'll be out tomorrow morning on a field trip with Marshall and Gina, but I should be around the rest of the day."

"All right. Talk to you tomorrow."

I slipped the phone under the netting. Plumped the pillows and opened my book. Living alone had made me a voracious reader, as if all my other appetites had mutated into a hunger for the words that would make me someone else, put me somewhere else, or at least help me to sleep. The more I read, the harder it was to keep my interest. Boredom crept over me like the slow death it was. I was an old jaded john needing ever kinkier tricks just to get it up, or over with. Pretty soon nothing would move me at all. Until then, I was grateful for Michael Malone and the jolts and length of *Time's Witness.*

I woke up to the telephone's insistent ring, crawled out of bed, and thanked the front desk for the call. A chameleon darted out from under the bed and headed out the door. "Nice seeing you," I called out, and hoped he'd had a bountiful evening keeping my room an insect-free zone. I dressed and hurried down to breakfast.

After a glass of soursop, I ordered saltfish and onions with bakes and lots of coffee. Derek and Gina were not in the dining room. Maybe they'd ordered room service, maybe they were sleeping in and wouldn't make it. I ate quickly and kept checking my watch while I had my second cup of coffee. Our driver had arrived and was looking at the activities board. Another couple came up to him and introduced themselves. I wiped my mouth and left to join the group. Derek and Gina came down the hill as I checked in.

Our driver told us that his name was Wellington Bramble and that he was also a registered tour guide with the Department of the Interior. The other couple climbed into the back of the van, then Derek and Gina in the middle row. I hopped in up front, next to Wellington, turned, and introduced myself.

"Hi, my name is Leo Haggerty."

"Hello, I'm Derek Marshall and this is my fiancée, Gina Dalesandro."

"Pleasure to meet you."

Derek and Gina turned and we were all introduced to Tom and Dorothy Needham of Chicago, Illinois.

Wellington stuck his head out the window and spoke to one of the maids. They spoke rapidly in the local patois until the woman slapped him across the forearm and waved a scolding finger at him.

He engaged the gears, pulled away from the reception area, and told us that we would be visiting the tropical rain forests that surround the island's active volcano. All this in perfect English, the language of strangers and for strangers.

Dorothy Needham asked the question on all of our minds. "How long will we be on this road to the volcano?"

Wellington laughed. "Twenty minutes, ma'am, then we go inland to the volcano."

We left the coast road and passed through a gate marked ST. MARY'S ISLAND CONSERVANCY—DEVIL'S CAULDRON VOLCANO AND TROPICAL RAIN FOREST. I was first out and helped the women step down into the muddy path. Wellington lined us up and began to lead us through the jungle, calling out the names of plants and flowers and answering questions.

There were soursop trees, lime trees, nutmeg, guava, bananas, coconuts, cocoa trees, ginger lilies, lobster-claw plants, flamboyant and hibiscus, impression fern, and chenille red-hot cattails. We stopped on the path at a large fern. Wellington turned and pointed to it.

"Here, you touch the plant, right here," he said, pointing at Derek, who eyed him suspiciously. "It won't hurt you."

Derek reached out a finger and touched the fern. Instantly the leaves retracted and curled in on themselves.

"That's Mary, Mary, Shut the Door. As you can see, a delicate and shy plant indeed."

He waved us on and we followed. Gina slipped an arm through Derek's and put her head on his shoulder. She squeezed him once.

"Derek, you know I used to be like that plant. Before you came along. All closed up and frightened if anybody got too close. But not anymore. I am so happy," she said, and squeezed him again.

Other than a mild self-loathing, I was having a good time, too. We came out of the forest and were on the volcano. Wellington turned to face us.

"Ladies and gentlemen, please listen very carefully. We are on top of an active volcano. There is no danger of an eruption, because there is no crust, so there is no pressure buildup. The last eruption was over two hundred years ago. That does not mean that there is no danger here. You must stay on the marked path at all times and be very careful on the sections that have no guardrail. The water in the volcano is well over three hundred degrees Fahrenheit; should you stumble and fall in, you would be burned alive. I do not wish to alarm you unreasonably, but a couple of years ago we did lose a visitor, so please be very careful. Now follow me."

We moved along, single file and well spaced through a setting unlike any other I'd ever encountered. The circular top of the volcano looked like a wound on the earth. The ground steamed and smoked and nothing grew anywhere. Here and there black water leaked out of crusty patches like blood seeping from under a scab. The smell of sulfur was everywhere.

I followed Derek and Gina and watched him stop a couple of times and test the railings before he let her proceed. Caution, Derek? Or a trial run?

We circled the volcano and retraced our path back to the van. As promised, we were back at the hotel twenty minutes later. Gina was flushed with excitement and asked Derek if they could go back again. He thought that was possible, but there weren't any other guided tours this week, so they'd have to rent a car and go themselves. I closed my eyes and imagined her by the side of the road, taking a picture perhaps, and him ushering her through the foliage and on her way to eternity.

We all went in for lunch and ate separately. I followed them back to their room and then down to the beach. They moved to the far end of the beach and sat facing away from everyone else. I went into the bar and worked my way through a pair of long necks.

A couple in the dining room was having a spat, or maybe it was a tiff. Whatever, she called him a *schwein* and really tagged him with an open forehand to the chops. His face lit up redder than a baboon's ass.

She pushed back her chair, swung her long blond hair in an about-face, and stormed off. I watched her go, taking each step like she was grinding out a cigarette under her foot. Made her hips and butt do terrible things.

I pulled my eyes away when I realized I had company. He was leering at me enthusiastically.

I swung around slowly. "Yes?"

It was one of the local hustlers who patrolled the beach, as ubiquitous and resourceful as the coconuts that littered the sand.

"I seen you around, man. Y'all alone. That's not a good thin', man. I was thinkin' maybe you could use some company. Someone to share paradise wit'. Watcha say, man?"

I shook my head. "I don't think so."

He frowned. "I know you ain't that way, man. I seen you watch that blond with the big ones. What'sa matter? What you afraid of?" He stopped and tried to answer that one for me. "She be clean, man. No problem."

When I didn't say anything, he got pissed. "What is it then? You don't fuck strange, man?"

"Watch my lips, bucko. I'm not interested. Don't make more of it than there is."

He sized me up and decided I wasn't worth the aggravation. Spinning off his stool, he called me something in patois. I was sure it wasn't "sir."

I found a free lounge under a *bohio* and kept an eye on Derek and Gina. No sooner had I settled in than Gina got up and headed across the cocoa-colored volcanic sands to the beach bar. She was a little pink around the edges. Probably wouldn't be out too long today. Derek had his back to me, so I swiveled my head to keep her in sight. She sat down and one of the female staff came over and began to run a comb through her hair. Cornrowing. She'd be there for at least an hour. I ordered a drink from a wandering waiter, closed my eyes, and relaxed.

Gina strolled back, her hair in tight little braids, each one tipped with a series of colored beads. She was smiling and kicking up little sprays of water. I watched her take Derek by the hands and pull him up out of his chair. She twirled around and shook her head back and forth, just to watch the braids fly by. They picked up their snorkels and fins and headed for the water. I watched to see which way they'd go. The left side of the bay had numerous warning signs about the strong current including one on the point that said TURN BACK—NEXT STOP PANAMA.

They went right and so did I. Maybe it was a little fear, maybe it was love, but she held on to his hand while they hovered over the reef. I went farther out and then turned back so I could keep them in sight. The reef was one of the richest I'd ever been on and worthy of its reputation as one of the best in the Caribbean.

I kept my position near the couple, moving when they did, just like the school of squid I was above. They were in formation, tentacles tucked in, holding their position by undulating the fins on each lateral axis. When the school moved, they all went at once and kept the same distance from each other. I drifted off the coral to a bed of sea grass. Two creatures were walking through the grass. Gray-green, with knobs and lumps everywhere, they had legs and wings! They weren't toxic-waste mutants, just the flying gurnards. I dived down on them and they spread their violet wings and took off.

When I surfaced, Derek and Gina were heading in. I swam downstream from them and came ashore as they did. Gina was holding her side and peeking behind her palm. Derek steadied her and helped get her flippers off.

"I don't know what it was, Derek. It just brushed me and then it felt like a bee sting. It really burns," Gina said.

I wandered by and said, "Looks like a jellyfish sting. When did it happen?"

"Just a second ago." They answered in unison.

"Best thing for that is papaya skins. Has an enzyme that neutralizes the toxin. The beach restaurant has plenty of them. They keep it just for things like this. You better get right over, though. It only works if you apply it right away."

"Thanks. Thanks a lot," Derek said, then turned to help Gina down the beach. "Yes, thank you," she said over his shoulder.

"You're welcome," I said to myself, and went to dry off.

I sat at the bar, waiting for dinner and playing backgammon with myself. Derek and Gina came in and went to the bar to order. Her dress was a swirl of purple, black, and white and matched the color of the beads in her hair. Derek wore lime green shorts and a white short-sleeved shirt. Drinks in hand, they walked over to me. I stood up, shook hands, and invited them to join me.

"That tip of yours was a lifesaver. We went over to the bar and got some papaya on it right away. I think the pain was gone in maybe five minutes. How did you know about it?" Gina asked.

"I've been stung myself before. Somebody told me about it. Now I tell you. Word of mouth."

"Well, we're very grateful. We're getting married here on the island and I didn't want anything to mess this time up for us," Derek said.

I raised my glass in a toast. "Congratulations to you. This is a lovely place to get married. When is the ceremony?" I asked, sipping my drink.

"Tomorrow," Gina said, running her arm through Derek's. "I'm so excited."

I nearly drowned her in rerouted rum punch but managed to turn away and choke myself instead. I pounded my chest and waved off any assistance.

"Are you okay?" Derek asked.

"Yes, yes, I'm fine," I said as I got myself under control. Tomorrow? How the hell could it be tomorrow? "Sorry. I was trying to talk when I was drinking. Just doesn't work that way."

Derek asked if he could buy me another drink and I let him take my glass to the bar.

"I read the tourist brochure about getting married on the island. How long does it take for them to approve an application? They only said that you have to be on the island for two days before you can submit an application."

Gina leaned forward and touched my knee. "It usually takes two or three days, but Derek found a way to hurry things up. He sent the papers down early to the manager here and he agreed to file them for us as if we were on the island. It'll be ready tomorrow morning and we'll get married right after noon."

"That's wonderful. Where will the ceremony be?" My head was spinning.

"Here at the hotel. Down on the beach. They provide a cake, champagne, photographs, flowers. Would you join us afterward to celebrate?"

"Thank you, that's very kind. I'm not sure that I'll still be here, though. My plane leaves in the afternoon, and you know with that ride back to the airport, I might be gone. If I'm still here, I'd be delighted."

Derek returned with drinks and sat close to Gina and looped an arm around her.

"Honey, I hope you don't mind, but I invited Mr. Haggerty to join us after the ceremony." She smiled anxiously.

"No, that sounds great, love to have you. By the way, it sounded like you've been to the islands before. This is our first time. Have you ever gone scuba diving?" Derek was all graciousness.

"Yeah, are you thinking of trying it?"

"Maybe, they have a course for beginners tomorrow. We were talking about taking the course and seeing if we liked it," he said.

"I'm a little scared. Is it really dangerous?" Gina asked.

Absolutely lethal. Russian roulette with one empty chamber. Don't do it. Wouldn't recommend it to my worst enemy.

"No, not really. There are dangers if you're careless, and they're pretty serious ones. The sea is not very forgiving of our mistakes. But if you're well trained and maintain some respect for what you're doing, it's not all that dangerous."

"I don't know. Maybe I'll just watch you do it, Derek."

"Come on, honey. You really liked snorkeling. Can you imagine how much fun it would be if you didn't have to worry about coming up for air all the time?" Derek gave Gina a squeeze. "And besides, I love the way you look in that new suit."

I saw others heading to the dining room and began to clean up the tiles from the board.

"Mr. Haggerty, would you—" Gina began.

"I'm sure we'll see Mr. Haggerty again, Gina. Thanks for your help this afternoon," Derek said, and led her to the dining room.

I finished my drink and took myself to dinner. After that, I sat and watched them dance to the *shak-shak* band. She put her head on his shoulder and molded her body to his. They swayed together in the perfect harmony only lovers and mothers and babies have.

They left that way, her head on his shoulder, a peaceful smile on her lips. I could not drink enough to cut the ache I felt and went to bed when I gave up trying.

Del was in when I called and gave me the brief bad news.

"The mailman was a dead end. I went over to the school library and talked to teachers and students. So far, nobody's had anything useful to tell us. I've got a class list and we're working our way through it. Walt did get a lead on him, though. He's a junior partner in a small law firm, a 'boutique' he called it."

"What kind of law?" Come on, say tax and estate.

"Immigration and naturalization."

"Shit. Anything else?"

"Yeah, he's new there. Still don't know where he came from. We'll try to get some information from the partners first thing in the morning."

"It better be first thing. Our timetable just went out the window. They're getting married tomorrow at noon."

"Jesus Christ, that puts the screws to us. We'll only have a couple of hours to work with."

"Don't remind me. Is that it?"

"For right now. Clancy is hitting bars looking for people that play this 'Ultimate Frisbee' thing. He's got a sketch with him. Hasn't called in yet."

"Well, if he finds anything, call me no matter what time it is. I'll be around all morning tomorrow. If you don't get me direct, have me paged, as an emergency. Right now we don't have shit."

"Hey, boss, we just ran out of time. I'm sure in a couple of days we'd have turned something up."

"Maybe so, Del, but tomorrow around noon somebody's gonna look out over their heads and ask if anybody has anything to say or forever hold your peace. I don't see myself raising my hand and asking for a couple of more days, 'cause we're bound to turn something up."

"We did our best. We just weren't holding very good cards is all."

"Del, we were holding shit." I should have folded when Scolari dealt them.

I hung up and readied my bedroom to repel all boarders. Under the netting, I sat and mulled over my options. I had no reason to stick my nose into Gina's life. No reason at all to think that Derek was anything but the man she'd waited her whole life for. Her happiness was real, though. She was blossoming under his touch. I had seen it. And happiness is a fragile thing. Who was I to cast a shadow on hers? And without any reason. Tomorrow was a special day for her. How would she remember it? How would I?

I woke early from a restless night and called the office. Nothing new. I tried Scolari's number and spoke briefly to him. I told him we were out of time and had nothing of substance. I asked him a couple of questions and he gave me some good news and some bad. There was nothing else to do, so I went down to see the betrothed.

They were in the dining room holding hands and finishing their coffee. I approached and asked if I could join them.

"Good morning, Mr. Haggerty. Lovely day, isn't it?" Gina said, her face aglow.

I settled into the chair and decided to smack them in the face with it. "Before you proceed with your wedding, I have some news for you."

They sat upright and took their hands, still joined, off the table.

"Gina's uncle, Enzo Scolari, wishes me to inform you that he has had his attorneys activate the trustee's discretionary powers over Miss Dalesandro's portion of the estate so that she cannot take possession of the money or use it in any fashion without his consent. He regrets having to take this action, but your insistence on this marriage leaves him no choice."

"You son of a bitch. You've been spying on us for that bastard," Derek shouted, and threw his glass of water at me. I sat there dripping while I counted to ten. Gina had gone pale and was on the verge of tears. Marshall stood up. "Come on, Gina, let's go. I don't want this man anywhere near me." He leaned forward and stabbed a finger at me. "I intend to call your employer, Mr. Scolari, and let him know what a despicable piece of shit I think he is, and that goes double for you." He turned away. "Gina, are you coming?"

"Just a second, honey," she whispered. "I'll be along in just a second." Marshall crashed out of the room, assaulting chairs and tables that got in his way.

"Why did you do this to me? I've waited my whole life for this day. To find someone who loves me and wants to live with me and to celebrate that. We came here to get away from my uncle and his obsessions. You know what hurts the most? You reminded me that my uncle doesn't believe that anyone could love me for myself. It has to be my money. What's so wrong with *me*? Can you tell me that?" She was starting to cry and wiped at her tears with her palms. "Hell of a question to be asking on your wedding day, huh? You do good work, Mr. Haggerty. I hope you're proud of yourself."

I'd rather Marshall had thrown acid in my face than the words she hurled at me. "Think about one thing, Miss Dalesandro. This way you can't lose. If he doesn't marry you now, you've avoided a lot of heartache and maybe worse. If he does, knowing this, then you can relax knowing it's you and not your money. The way I see it, either way you can't lose. But I'm sorry. If there had been any other way, I'd have done it."

"Yes, well, I have to go, Mr. Haggerty." She rose, dropped her napkin on the table, and walked slowly through the room, using every bit of dignity she could muster.

I spent the rest of the morning in the bar waiting for the last act to unfold.

At noon, Gina appeared in a long white dress. She had a bouquet of flowers in her hands and was trying hard to smile. I sipped some anesthetic and looked away. No need to make it any harder now. I wasn't sure whether I wanted Marshall to show up or not.

Derek appeared at her side in khaki slacks and an embroidered white shirt. What will be, will be. They moved slowly down the stairs. I went to my room, packed, and checked out. By three o'clock I was off the island and on my way home.

It was almost a year later when Kelly buzzed me on the intercom to say that a Mr. Derek Marshall was here to see me.

"Show him in."

He hadn't changed a bit. Neither one of us moved to shake hands. When I didn't invite him to sit down, he did anyway.

"What do you want, Marshall?"

"You know, I'll never forget that moment when you told me that Scolari had altered the trust. Right there in public. I was so angry that you'd try to make me look bad like that in front of Gina and everyone else. It really has stayed with me. And here I am, leaving the area. I thought I'd come by and return the favor before I left."

"How's Gina?" I asked with a veneer of nonchalance over trepidation.

"Funny you should ask. I'm a widower, you know. She had a terrible accident about six months ago. We were scuba diving. It was her first time. I'd already had some courses. I guess she misunderstood what I'd told her and she held her breath coming up. Ruptured a lung. She was dead before I could get her to shore."

I almost bit through my pipe stem. "You're a real piece of work, aren't you? Pretty slick, death by misinformation. Got away with it, didn't you?"

"The official verdict was accidental death. Scolari was beside himself, as you can imagine. There I was, sole inheritor of Gina's estate, and according to the terms of the trust her half of the grandfather's money was mine. It was all in Scolari stock, so I made a deal with the old man. He got rid of me and I got paid fifty percent more than the shares were worth."

"You should be careful, Derek, that old man hasn't got long to live. He might decide to take you with him."

"That thought has crossed my mind. So I'm going to take my money and put some space between him and me."

Marshall stood up to leave. "By the way, your bluff wasn't half-bad. It actually threw me there for a second. That's why I tossed the water on you. I had to get away and do some thinking, make sure I hadn't overlooked anything. But I hadn't."

"How did you know it was a bluff?" You cocky little shit.

Marshall pondered that a moment. "It doesn't matter. You'll never be able to prove this. It's not on paper anywhere. While I was in law school I worked one year as an unpaid intern at the law firm handling the estate of old man Scolari, the grandfather. This was when Gina's mother died. I did a turn in lots of different departments. I read the documents when I was xeroxing them. That's how I knew the setup. Her mother's share went to Gina. Anything happens to her and the estate is transferred according to the terms of Gina's will. An orphan, with no siblings. That made me sole inheritor, even if she died intestate. Scolari couldn't change the trust or its terms. Your little stunt actually convinced Gina of my sincerity. I wasn't in any hurry to get her to write a will and she absolutely refused to do it when Scolari pushed her on it.

"Like I said, for a bluff it wasn't half-bad. Gina believed you, but I think she was the only one who didn't know anything about her money. Well, I've got to be going, got a plane to catch." He smiled at me like he was a dog and I was his favorite tree.

It was hard to resist the impulse to threaten him, but a threat is also a warning and I had no intention of playing fair. I consoled myself with the fact that last time I only had two days to work with. Now I had a lifetime. When I heard the outer door close, I buzzed Kelly on the intercom.

"Yes, Mr. Haggerty?"

"Reopen the file on Derek Marshall."

ACKNOWLEDGMENTS

I'd like to thank the following people for their contributions to this story: Joyce Huxley of Scuba St. Lucia for her information on hyperbaric accidents; Michael and Alison Weber of Charlottesville for the title and good company, and John Cort and Rebecca Barbetti for including us in their wedding celebration and tales of "the spork" among other things.

· LAWRENCE BLOCK ·

The Merciful Angel of Death

This was Lawrence Block's second Shamus for short story. The first was for a story published in 1984 and this one was for 1993. Nine years apart and still winning awards. This gives you some idea of the quality of the man's work. In 1993 he also hit the quinella by winning the best novel award for The Devil Knows You're Dead.

"PEOPLE COME HERE TO DIE, MR. SCUDDER. THEY CHECK OUT of hospitals, give up their apartments, and come to Caritas. Because they know we'll keep them comfortable here. And they know we'll let them die."

Carl Orcott was long and lean, with a long sharp nose and a matching chin. Some gray showed in his fair hair and his strawberry blond mustache. His facial skin was stretched tight over his skull, and there were hollows in his cheeks. He might have been naturally spare of flesh, or worn down by the demands of his job. Because he was a gay man in the last decade of a terrible century, another possibility suggested itself. That he was HIV-positive. That his immune system was compromised. That the virus that would one day kill him was already within him, waiting.

"Since an easy death is our whole reason for being," he was saying, "it seems a bit much to complain when it occurs. Death is not the enemy here. Death is a friend. Our people are in very bad shape by the time they come to us. You don't run to a hospice when you get the initial results from a blood test, or when the first purple K-S lesions show up. First you try everything, including denial, and everything works for a while, and finally nothing works, not the AZT, not the pentamidine, not the Louise Hay tapes, not the crystal healing. Not even the denial. When you're ready for it to be over, you come here and we see you out." He smiled thinly. "We hold the door for you. We don't boot you through it."

"But now you think—"

"I don't know what I think." He selected a briar pipe from a walnut stand that held eight of them, examined it, sniffed its bowl. "Grayson Lewes shouldn't have died," he said. "Not when he did. He was doing very well, relatively speaking. He was in agony, he had a CMV infection that was blinding him, but he was still strong. Of course he was dying, they're all dying, everybody's dying, but death certainly didn't appear to be imminent."

"What happened?"

"He died."

"What killed him?"

"I don't know." He breathed in the smell of the unlit pipe. "Someone went in and found him dead. There was no autopsy. There generally isn't. What would be the point? Doctors would just as soon not cut up AIDS patients anyway, not wanting the added risk of infection. Of course most of our general staff are seropositive, but even so you try to avoid unnecessary additional exposure. Quantity could make a difference, and there could be multiple strains. The virus mutates, you see." He shook his head. "There's such a great deal we still don't know."

"There was no autopsy."

"No. I thought about ordering one."

"What stopped you?"

"The same thing that keeps people from getting the antibody test. Fear of what I might find."

"You think someone killed Lewes."

"I think it's possible."

"Because he died abruptly. But people do that, don't they? Even if they're not sick to begin with. They have strokes or heart attacks."

"That's true."

"This happened before, didn't it? Lewes wasn't the first."

He smiled ruefully. "You're good at this."

"It's what I do."

"Yes." His fingers were busy with the pipe. "There have been a few unexpected deaths. But there would be, as you've said. So there was no real cause for suspicion. There still isn't."

"But you're suspicious."

"Am I? I guess I am."

"Tell me the rest of it, Carl."

"I'm sorry," he said. "I'm making you drag it out of me, aren't I? Grayson Lewes had a visitor. She was in his room for twenty minutes, perhaps half an hour. She was the last person to see him alive. She may have been the first person to see him dead."

"Who is she?"

"I don't know. She's been coming here for months. She always brings flowers, something cheerful. She brought yellow freesias the last time. Nothing fancy, just a five-dollar bunch from the Korean on the corner, but they do brighten a room."

"Had she visited Lewes before?"

He shook his head. "Other people. Every week or so she would turn up, always asking for one of our residents by name. It's often the sickest of the sick that she comes to see."

"And then they die?"

"Not always. But often enough so that it's been remarked upon. Still, I never let myself think that she played a causative role. I thought she had some instinct that drew her to your side when you were circling the drain." He looked off to the side. "When she visited Lewes, someone joked that we'd probably have his room available soon. When you're on staff here, you become quite irreverent in private. Otherwise you'd go crazy."

"It was the same way on the police force."

"I'm not surprised. When one of us would cough or sneeze, another might say, 'Uh-oh, you might be in line for a visit from Mercy.'"

"Is that her name?"

"Nobody knows her name. It's what we call her among ourselves. The Merciful Angel of Death. Mercy, for short."

A man named Bobby sat up in bed in his fourth-floor room. He had short gray hair and a gray brush mustache and a gray complexion bruised purple here and there by Kaposi's sarcoma. For all the ravages of the disease, he had a heartbreakingly youthful face. He was a ruined cherub, the oldest boy in the world.

"She was here yesterday," he said.

"She visited you twice," Carl said.

"Twice?"

"Once last week and once three or four days ago."

"I thought it was one time. And I thought it was yesterday." He frowned. "It all seems like yesterday."

"What does, Bobby?"

"Everything. Camp Arrowhead. 'I Love Lucy.' The moon shot. One enormous yesterday with everything crammed into it, like his closet. I don't remember his name but he was famous for his closet."

"Fibber McGee," Carl said.

"I don't know why I can't remember his name," Bobby said languidly. "It'll come to me. I'll think of it yesterday."

I said, "When she came to see you—"

"She was beautiful. Tall, slim, gorgeous eyes. A flowing dove-gray robe, a bloodred scarf at her throat. I wasn't sure if she was real or not. I thought she might be a vision."

"Did she tell you her name?"

"I don't remember. She said she was there to be with me. And mostly she just sat there, where Carl's sitting. She held my hand."

"What else did she say?"

"That I was safe. That no one could hurt me anymore. She said—"

"Yes?"

"That I was innocent," he said, and he sobbed and let his tears flow.

He wept freely for a few moments, then reached for a Kleenex. When he spoke again his voice was matter-of-fact, even detached. "She *was* here twice," he said. "I remember now. The second time I got snotty, I really had the rag on, and I told her she didn't have to hang around if she didn't want to. And she said *I* didn't have to hang around if *I* didn't want to.

"And I said, right, I can go tap-dancing down Broadway with a rose in my teeth. And she said, no, all I have to do is let go and my spirit will soar free. And I looked at her, and I knew what she meant."

"And?"

"She told me to let go, to give it all up, to just let go and go to the light. And I said—this is strange, you know?"

"What did you say, Bobby?"

"I said I couldn't see the light and I wasn't ready to go to it. And she said that was all right, that when I was ready the light would be there to guide me. She said I would know how to do it when the time came. And she talked about how to do it."

"How?"

"By letting go. By going to the light. I don't remember everything she said. I don't even know for sure if all of it happened, or if I dreamed part of it. I never know anymore. Sometimes I have dreams and later they feel like part of my personal history. And sometimes I look back at my life and most of it has a veil over it, as if I never lived it at all, as if it were nothing but a dream."

Back in his office Carl picked up another pipe and brought its blackened bowl to his nose. He said, "You asked why I called you instead of the police. Can you imagine putting Bobby through an official interrogation?"

"He seems to go in and out of lucidity."

He nodded. "The virus penetrates the blood-brain barrier. If you survive the K-S and the opportunistic infections, the reward is dementia. Bobby is mostly clear, but some of his mental circuits are beginning to burn out. Or rust out, or clog up, whatever it is that they do."

"There are cops who know how to take testimony from people like that."

"Even so. Can you see the tabloid headlines? MERCY STRIKES AIDS HOSPICE. We have a hard enough time getting blood as it is. You know, whenever the press happens to mention how many dogs and cats the SPCA puts to sleep, donations drop to a trickle. Imagine what would happen to us."

"Some people would give you more."

He laughed. " 'Here's a thousand dollars—kill ten of 'em for me.' You could be right."

He sniffed at the pipe again. I said, "You know, as far as I'm concerned you can go ahead and smoke that thing."

He stared at me, then at the pipe, as if surprised to find it in his hand. "There's no smoking anywhere in the building," he said. "Anyway, I don't smoke."

"The pipes came with the office?"

He colored. "They were John's," he said. "We lived together. He died . . . God, it'll be two years in November. It doesn't seem that long."

"I'm sorry, Carl."

"I used to smoke cigarettes, Marlboros, but I quit ages ago. But I never minded his pipe smoke, though. I always liked the aroma. And now I'd rather smell one of his pipes than the AIDS smell. Do you know the smell I mean?"

"Yes."

"Not everyone with AIDS has it but a lot of them do, and most sickrooms reek of it. You must have smelled it in Bobby's room. It's an unholy musty smell, a smell like rotted leather. I can't stand the smell of leather anymore. I used to love leather, but now I can't help associating it with the stink of gay men wasting away in fetid airless rooms.

"And this whole building smells that way to me. There's the stench of disinfectant over everything. We use tons of it, spray and liquid. The virus is surprisingly frail, it doesn't last long outside the body, but we leave as little as possible to chance, and so the rooms and halls all smell of disinfectant. But underneath it, always, there's the smell of the disease itself."

He turned the pipe over in his hands. "His clothes were full of the smell. John's. I gave everything away. But his pipes held a scent I had always associated with him, and a pipe is such a personal thing, isn't it, with the smoker's toothmarks in the stem." He looked at me. His eyes were dry, his voice strong and steady. There was no grief in his tone, only in the words themselves. "Two years in November, though I swear it doesn't seem that long, and I use one smell to keep another at bay. And, I suppose, to bridge the gap of years, to keep him a little closer to me." He put the pipe down. "Back to cases. Will you take a careful but unofficial look at our Angel of Death?"

I said I would. He said I'd want a retainer, and opened the top drawer of his desk. I told him it wouldn't be necessary.

"But isn't that standard for private detectives?"

"I'm not one, not officially. I don't have a license."

"So you told me, but even so—"

"I'm not a lawyer, either," I went on, "but there's no reason why I can't do a little pro bono work once in a while. If it takes too much of my time I'll let you know, but for now let's call it a donation."

The hospice was in the Village, on Hudson Street. Rachel Bookspan lived five miles north in an Italianate brownstone on Claremont Avenue. Her husband, Paul, walked to work at Columbia University, where he was an associate professor of political science. Rachel was a freelance copy editor, hired by several publishers to prepare manuscripts for publication. Her specialties were history and biography.

She told me all this over coffee in her book-lined living room. She talked about a manuscript she was working on, the biography of a woman who had founded a religious sect in the late nineteenth century. She talked about her children, two boys, who would be home from school in an hour or so. Finally she ran out of steam and I brought the conversation back to her brother, Arthur Fineberg, who had lived on Morton Street and worked downtown as a librarian for an investment firm. And who had died two weeks ago at the Caritas Hospice.

"How we cling to life," she said. "Even when it's awful. Even when we yearn for death."

"Did your brother want to die?"

"He prayed for it. Every day the disease took a little more from him, gnawing at him like a mouse, and after months and months and months of hell it finally took his will to live. He couldn't fight anymore. He had nothing to fight with, nothing to fight *for*. But he went on living all the same."

She looked at me, then looked away. "He begged me to kill him," she said.

I didn't say anything.

"How could I refuse him? But how could I help him? First I thought it wasn't right but then I decided it was his life, and who had a better right to end it if he wanted to? But how could I do it? How?

"I thought of pills. We don't have anything in the house except Midol for cramps. I went to my doctor and said I had trouble sleeping. Well, that was true enough. He gave me a prescription for a dozen Valium. I didn't even bother getting it filled. I didn't want to give Artie a handful of tranquilizers. I wanted to give him one of those cyanide capsules the spies always had in World War Two movies. You bite down and you're gone. But where do you go to get something like that?"

She sat forward in her chair. "Do you remember that man in the Midwest who unhooked his kid from a respirator? The doctors wouldn't let the boy die and the father went into the hospital with a gun and held everybody at bay until his son was dead. I think that man was a hero."

"A lot of people thought so."

"God, I wanted to be a hero! I had fantasies. There's a Robinson Jeffers poem about a crippled hawk and the narrator puts it out of its misery. 'I gave him the lead gift,' he says. Meaning a bullet, a gift of lead. I wanted to give my brother that gift. I don't have a gun. I don't even believe in guns. At least I never did. I don't know what I believe in anymore.

"If I'd had a gun, could I have gone in there and shot him? I don't see how. I have a knife, I have a kitchen full of knives, and believe me, I thought of going in there with a knife in my purse and waiting until he dozed off and then slipping the knife between his ribs and into his heart. I visualized it, I went over every aspect of it, but I didn't do it. My God, I never even left the house with a knife in my bag."

She asked if I wanted more coffee. I said I didn't. I asked her if her brother had had other visitors, and if he might have made the same request of one of them.

"He had dozens of friends, men and women who loved him. And yes, he would have asked them. He told everybody he wanted to die. As hard as he fought to live, for all those months, that's how determined he became to die. Do you think someone helped him?"

"I think it's possible."

"God, I hope so," she said. "I just wish it had been me."

"I haven't had the test," Aldo said. "I'm a forty-four-year-old gay man who led an active sex life since I was fifteen. I don't *have* to take the test, Matthew. I assume I'm seropositive. I assume everybody is."

He was a plump teddy bear of a man, with black curly hair and a face as permanently buoyant as a smile button. We were sharing a small table at a coffeehouse on Bleecker, just two doors from the shop where he sold comic books and baseball cards to collectors.

"I may not develop the disease," he said. "I may die a perfectly respectable death due to overindulgence in food and drink. I may get hit by a bus or struck down by a mugger. If I do get sick I'll wait until it gets really bad, because I love this life, Matthew, I really do. But when the time comes I don't want to make local stops. I'm gonna catch an express train out of here."

"You sound like a man with his bags packed."

"No luggage. Travelin' light. You remember the song?"

"Of course."

He hummed a few bars of it, his foot tapping out the rhythm, our little marble-topped table shaking with the motion. He said, "I have pills enough to do the job. I also have a loaded handgun. And I think I have the nerve to do what I have to do, when I have to do it." He frowned, an uncharacteristic expression for him. "The danger lies in waiting too long. Winding up in a hospital bed too weak to do anything, too addled by brain fever to remember what it was you were supposed to do. Wanting to die but unable to manage it."

"I've heard there are people who'll help."

"You've heard that, have you?"

"One woman in particular."

"What are you after, Matthew?"

"You were a friend of Grayson Lewes. And of Arthur Fineberg. There's a woman who helps people who want to die. She may have helped them."

"And?"

"And you know how to get in touch with her."

"Who says?"

"I forget, Aldo."

The smile was back. "You're discreet, huh?"

"Very."

"I don't want to make trouble for her."

"Neither do I."

"Then why not leave her alone?"

"There's a hospice administrator who's afraid she's murdering people. He called me in rather than start an official police inquiry. But if I don't get anywhere—"

"He calls the cops." He found his address book, copied out a number for me. "Please don't make trouble for her," he said. "I might need her myself."

I called her that evening, met her the following afternoon at a cocktail lounge just off Washington Square. She was as described, even to the gray cape over a long gray dress. Her scarf today was canary yellow. She was drinking Perrier, and I ordered the same.

She said, "Tell me about your friend. You say he's very ill."

"He wants to die. He's been begging me to kill him but I can't do it."

"No, of course not."

"I was hoping you might be able to visit him."

"If you think it might help. Tell me something about him, why don't you."

I don't suppose she was more than forty-five, if that, but there was something ancient about her face. You didn't need much of a commitment to reincarnation to believe she had lived before. Her facial features were pronounced, her eyes a graying blue. Her voice was pitched low, and along with her height it raised doubts about her sexuality. She might have been a sex change, or a drag queen. But I didn't think so. There was an Eternal Female quality to her that didn't feel like parody.

I said, "I can't."

"Because there's no such person."

"I'm afraid there are plenty of them, but I don't have one in mind." I told her in a couple of sentences why I was there. When I'd finished she let the silence stretch, then asked me if I thought she could kill anyone. I told her it was hard to know what anyone could do.

She said, "I think you should see for yourself what it is that I do."

She stood up. I put some money on the table and followed her out to the street.

We took a cab to a four-story brick building on Twenty-second Street west of Ninth. We climbed two flights of stairs, and the door opened when she knocked on it. I could smell the disease before I was across the threshold. The young black man who opened the door was glad to see her and unsurprised by my presence. He didn't ask my name or tell me his.

"Kevin's so tired," he told us both. "It breaks my heart."

We walked through a neat, sparsely furnished living room and down a short hallway to a bedroom, where the smell was stronger. Kevin lay in a bed with its head cranked up. He looked like a famine victim, or someone liberated from Dachau. Terror filled his eyes.

She pulled a chair up to the side of his bed and sat in it. She took his hand in hers and used her free hand to stroke his forehead. You're safe now, she told him. You're safe, you don't have to hurt anymore, you did all the things you had to do. You can relax now, you can let go now, you can go to the light.

"You can do it," she told him. "Close your eyes, Kevin, and go inside yourself and find the part that's holding on. Somewhere within you there's a part of you that's like a clenched fist, and I want you to find that part and be with that part. And let go. Let the fist open its fingers. It's as if the fist is holding a little bird, and if you open up the hand the bird can fly free. Just let it happen, Kevin. Just let go."

He was straining to talk, but the best he could do was make a sort of cawing sound. She turned to the black man, who was standing in the doorway. "David," she said, "his parents aren't living, are they?"

"I believe they're both gone."

"Which one was he closest to?"

"I don't know. I believe they're both gone a long time now."

"Did he have a lover? Before you, I mean."

"Kevin and I were never lovers. I don't even know him that well. I'm here 'cause he hasn't got anybody else. He had a lover."

"Did his lover die? What was his name?"

"Martin."

"Kevin," she said, "you're going to be all right now. All you have to do is go to the light. Do you see the light? Your mother's there, Kevin, and your father, and Martin—"

"Mark!" David cried. "Oh, God, I'm sorry, I'm so stupid, it wasn't Martin, it was Mark, Mark, that was his name."

"That's all right, David."

"I'm so damn stupid—"

"Look into the light, Kevin," she said. "Mark is there, and your parents, and everyone who ever loved you. Matthew, take his other hand. Kevin, you don't have to stay here anymore, darling. You did everything you came here to do. You don't have to stay. You don't have to hold on. You can let go, Kevin. You can go to the light. Let go and reach out to the light—"

I don't know how long she talked to him. Fifteen, twenty minutes, I suppose. Several times he made the cawing sound, but for the most part he was silent. Nothing seemed to be happening, and then I realized that his terror was no longer a presence. She seemed to have talked it away. She went on talking to him, stroking his brow and holding his hand, and I held his other hand. I was no longer listening to what she was saying, just letting the words wash over me while my mind played with some tangled thought like a kitten with yarn.

Then something happened. The energy in the room shifted and I looked up, knowing that he was gone.

"Yes," she murmured. "Yes, Kevin. God bless you, go on, you rest. Yes."

"Sometimes they're stuck," she said. "They want to go but they can't. They've been hanging on so long, you see, that they don't know how to stop."

"So you help them."

"If I can."

"What if you can't? Suppose you talk and talk and they still hold on?"

"Then they're not ready. They'll be ready another time. Sooner or later everybody lets go, everybody dies. With or without my help."

"And when they're not ready—"

"Sometimes I come back another time. And sometimes they're ready then."

"What about the ones who beg for help? The ones like Arthur Fineberg, who plead for death but aren't physically close enough to it to let go?"

"What do you want me to say?"

"The thing you want to say. The thing that's stuck in your throat, the way his own unwanted life was stuck in Kevin's throat. You're holding on to it."

"Just let it go, eh?"

"If you want."

We were walking somewhere in Chelsea, and we walked a full block now without either of us saying a word. Then she said, "I think there's a world of difference between assisting someone verbally and doing anything physical to hasten death."

"So do I."

"And that's where I draw the line. But sometimes, having drawn that line—"

"You step over it."

"Yes. The first time I swear I acted without conscious intent. I used a pillow, I held it over his face and—" She breathed deeply. "I swore it would never happen again. But then there was someone else, and he just needed help, you know, and—"

"And you helped him."

"Yes. Was I wrong?"

"I don't know what's right or wrong."

"Suffering is wrong," she said, "unless it's part of His plan, and how can I presume to decide if it is or not? Maybe people can't let go because there's one more lesson they have to learn before they move on. Who the hell am I to decide it's time for somebody's life to end? How dare I interfere?"

"And yet you do."

"Just once in a while, when I just don't see a way around it. Then I do what I have to do. I'm sure I must have a choice in the matter, but I swear it doesn't feel that way. It doesn't feel as though I have any choice at all." She stopped walking, turned to look at me. She said, "Now what happens?"

"Well, she's the Merciful Angel of Death," I told Carl Orcott. "She visits the sick and dying, almost always at somebody's invitation. A friend contacts her, or a relative."

"Do they pay her?"

"Sometimes they try to. She won't take any money. She even pays for the flowers herself." She'd taken Dutch iris to Kevin's apartment on Twenty-second Street. Blue, with yellow centers that matched her scarf.

"She does it pro bono," he said.

"And she talks to them. You heard what Bobby said. I got to see her in action. She talked the poor son of a bitch straight out of this world and into the next one. I suppose you could argue that what she does comes perilously close to hypnosis, that she hypnotizes people and convinces them to kill themselves psychically, but I can't imagine anybody trying to sell that to a jury."

"She just talks to them."

"Uh-huh. 'Let go, go to the light.' "

" 'And have a nice day.' "

"That's the idea."

"She's not killing people?"

"Nope. Just letting them die."

He picked up a pipe. "Well, hell," he said, "that's what we do. Maybe I ought to put her on staff." He sniffed the pipe bowl. "You have my thanks, Matthew. Are you sure you don't want some of our money to go with it? Just because Mercy works pro bono doesn't mean you should have to."

"That's all right."

"You're certain?"

I said, "You asked me the first day if I knew what AIDS smelled like."

"And you said you'd smelled it before. Oh."

I nodded. "I've lost friends to it. I'll lose more before it's over. In the meantime I'm grateful when I get the chance to do you a favor. Because I'm glad this place is here, so people have a place to come to."

Even as I was glad she was around, the woman in gray, the Merciful Angel of Death. To hold the door for them, and show them the light on the other side. And, if they really needed it, to give them the least little push through it.

· A NOTE ON THE TYPE ·

The typeface used in this book is a version of Weiss (also known as Weiss Antiqua), designed in 1926 by Professor Emil Rudolf Weiss (1875–1943) for the Bauer type foundry in Frankfurt, Germany. Weiss, a distinguished graphic artist, was commissioned by Bauer as part of its aggressive program in the 1920s and '30s to encourage new type designs. (Bauer's efforts during this period were paralleled, though on a smaller scale, by English Monotype's under Stanley Morison.) Weiss worked very slowly, but the care he lavished on his design may account for its continuing popularity because it has some quirks that might have prevented its success. Its "upside-down" S has often been noted, an illusion caused by the equal size of the two curves—in contrast to the S of most typefaces, whose upper curve is somewhat smaller; another peculiarity is a marked widening toward the top of the vertical stroke of lowercase letters like *l*.